ON SOVEREIGN GROUND

By

BRENT MELTON

ISBN:
ISBN-13:978-0-692-78800-4

ACKNOWLEDGMENTS

Thank you to Sergeant First Class Scott Hebert for all of his help and insight in writing this book.

Contents

CHAPTER 1
Al-Dana, Syria

The afternoon heat rising up from the road forced Sargent Sebastian Gray to turn his head away as he stepped out of the Command Center and onto the main street of the Al-Dana Forward Operating Base. Located at the Southeast edge of Al-Dana, Camp Gladiator was a twenty-five acre, L-shaped complex. Main Street was bustling with soldiers moving from one place to another as they carried out their duties. Passing the mess hall, Sebastian spied a group of soldiers playing soccer on the basketball courts with members of the Free Syrian Army (FSA) who occupied the base with the Army.

To Sebastian, Syria was no different from Afghanistan or Iraq where he had spent his first four tours. He had spent his entire adult life fighting for his country, enlisting in the Army immediately after high school. Upon graduation from his Advanced Individual Training at Fort Leonard Wood, he was shipped off to Afghanistan. After two tours in Kabul he was stationed in Iraq for two more. Now he was protecting his country by fighting in Syria, seemingly against the wishes of the President who had sent him here. The first attempt by United States President Barrett Adama to combat the Islamic State in the Levant, also known as ISIL, had failed miserably. The plan had been to provide the FSA with weapons and drone support in order to keep U.S. troops out of the area. That plan made no sense to Sebastian. The FSA didn't have the manpower or training to combat both ISIL and the Syrian Army, which was controlled by President Bashar al-Assad. The President's poor choice in military strategy had allowed ISIL to take control of the eastern portion of the country. Eastern Syria made up one-third of Syria's land mass and was mostly desert. The desert contained almost all of Syria's oil and gas production and refineries, which, under ISIL control, allowed the terrorists to take in around two million dollars a day in black market oil sales. Sebastian couldn't believe that the United States had allowed ISIL to become the wealthiest terrorist organization in the world. ISIL had used their wealth to establish their own government, known as a Caliphate, and court system ruled by Sharia law. The terrorists had even built hospitals and schools, which gained them the support of the people in the region.

President Adama had not run his campaign on the War on Terror and his view on the subject was apparent to Sebastian and the rest of the world. If you ignore the terrorists, then they do not exist. The President's reluctance to fight in Syria had given ISIL two years to establish themselves. Finally the President gave into the demands of Saudi Arabia and other allies in the region. He committed to sending troops into Syria to help the FSA combat ISIL. Camp Gladiator had been the first US base to be established. It didn't matter to Sebastian where he was stationed. If it kept terrorists from attacking back at home, he would gladly fight anywhere.

Dressed in his Scorpion Operational Camouflage Pattern Army Combat Uniform (ACU), which was standard dress on the base, Sebastian smiled as he moved across the street toward the CHU's, or Contained Housing Units, which served as the barracks for his men. His patrol team was sitting outside. He twisted the top off a bottle of water and took a long drink. The Syrian heat reminded him of home, except for the lack of humidity. Not too many places could compare to a hot Texas summer. Sebastian's confident, carefree attitude complimented his athletic build and made him the type of man that his squad would follow anywhere and do anything for. His gait was quick and steady, which told his men that they were about to go back out into the city. His men could always tell when Sebastian was serious, because his slow, easy gait became more upright, his pace quickened and he walked with purpose.

"What's up, Sarge?" asked a lanky, dark headed young man with a Cajun accent. He was incredibly athletic, which was surprising considering his thin, lanky frame. "You got that look on your face like either you're constipated or we just got volunteered for some shit detail, like go hold the FSA's hand again."

"Every time I have to carry you with me it's a shit detail, Coop," replied Sebastian, revealing his bright white teeth and dimples. "Command has it on good intel that a significant sized ISIL force has made its way back to Al-Dana and is planning an attack. Y'all know the drill. We'll be doing door-to-doors over a four block grid, with the FSA working the parallel streets."

"Not again. Except for the officers, those guys don't know shit. You would think the Syrian Army would've trained them better before they defected to other side."

"Yes again. You guys head over to the armory and gear up. Full battle rattle." Battle rattle was a term that meant full gear, which included a Kevlar helmet, body armor, ammunition, weapons and other basic military equipment. In total, it added up to about fifty pounds of gear which made a definite rattle when the soldiers walked. "We head out at fourteen hundred."

"Damn, Sarge, we did pull a shit detail," chimed in Eduardo Cortez. "Are you sure we have to take the FSA with us? Those guys are tools. They fight more like gang bangers than soldiers. My parents didn't immigrate to the States just so I can get popped by friendly fire from the FSA."

"You got that right, Eddie. Door-to-door with the FSA? We might as well have my little sister covering our asses," quipped Doc.

"Hey, Doc, I would rather have your sister cover my ass anyway," laughed Michael "Elroy" Donaldson "Not only is she better looking, but I got money that says she don't death blossom when the shit goes down. Every time they hear a gunshot, those FSA guys start shooting in all directions. They don't even try to figure out where the gunfire comes from."

"Yeah, I know they suck," interjected Sebastian. "But they're what we have to work with at the moment. This is the war we were given. President Assad controls the South and the West."

"*And* he's an asshole that deserves to have his ass kicked," chimed in Coop.

"Roger that. We've got ISIL in the East," continued Sebastian, "and the Kurds have their little piece of the pie in the Northeast. I guess we could side with them, except for the fact that they are just relocated Iranians and all Iranians hate us."

"It's a lose –lose situation, Sarge," said Doc.

"Exactly. But that leaves us with the FSA. Unless you guys want to fight this war all alone."

Elroy skipped a rock off the road and stood up. "It still sucks."

"So embrace the suck and go get your ass ready to earn your paycheck," said Sebastian.

Tony "Hollywood" Banks was sitting on the ground, his back resting against the wall of sandbags that protected the entrance to their barracks. He put his hand over his eyes to block out the sun as he looked up at Sebastian. "Well, Sarge, if you ask me this whole soup sandwich is like one big gang war, and everybody's fighting over turf. FSA, Kurds, ISIL... Crips, Bloods, Latin Kings... they're all the same. At least the Crips are honest enough to say they fight for money and power and don't hide behind religion."

"It's more like the Cartels down in Mexico, Hollywood," said Darnell "Boom" Henderson, looking at Banks. "The Cartels and ISIL are both trying to overthrow the government and replace 'em with themselves. Them dudes know what they're doin'. The Cartels understand that you ain't gotta run from the POPO when you *run* the POPO. Besides, the Crips and Bloods ain't organized enough to run a government, but the Cartels and ISIL... they be some organized MOFOs. A helluva lot more organized than the FSA."

"Hooah!" replied Hollywood, slamming his knuckles into Boom's massive fist.

Bravo Team rendezvoused with the FSA at the main gate. After doing a weapons and coms check, they moved through the main gate passing by the giant guard towers located on both sides, leaving the security of the eight-foot blast walls which surrounded Camp Gladiator. The team advanced twelve blocks on foot to their designated section of the city. The team cleared the first block of buildings on K-Street in one hour, without incident. The military had renamed all the streets in Al-Dana with letters, as the Arabic pronunciation of the streets was difficult for Westerners. K Street was four blocks long and ended in a T-intersection. There was a bullet-riddled adobe wall lining the far side of the cross street. The street narrowed, making it appear as though K Street ran straight into the wall.

K-Street had buildings lining both sides. The first block contained all one-story buildings, which had been easy to clear. The second block was guarded on the east by a group of one and two-story buildings which were connected to each other. To the west stood a four story skeleton of a building whose outer walls had been blown away during the shelling of the city by the Assad regime in 2011. Between the revolution which had begun as a part of the Arab Spring, and the continuous battles for control of the city between the FSA and ISIL, the city had become a ghost town, uninhabited by civilians.

The team cleared the first building on the second block in ten minutes. When they reached the second building, a two story dwelling with a balcony, Sebastian said, "Coop, you, me and Wiz stay outside and cover the street. Everybody else get inside and let's get this done. I don't like being exposed like this."

"That's what she said," quipped Eddie as he opened the door.

Boom entered the building first, moving to the left side of the room. Elroy slid past him to the right. Doc, Banks and Eddie followed, each with their rifles readied and pointed in front of them. Doc and Elroy cleared the adjoining room while Eddie and Hollywood moved up the stairs with their rifles trained on the opening at the top. The top of the stairs opened into a dark room with a single window for light. Eddie heard Doc and Elroy call out "clear" from down below. Before his eyes could focus to the dark, he heard someone cry out.

"*Allahu Akbar!*"

Then, too late, he heard the *brat-at-at-at* of an AK-47. Eddie saw the flash of the muzzle one second before he felt the bullets ripping through his body.

"Oh shit," said Hollywood. "Contact second floor! Eddie's down!"

He managed to fire off three rounds before a bullet pierced his skull, causing the world to disappear in a bright white flash.

Boom fired at the top of the stairs as Elroy unleashed his M249 SAW (Squad Automatic Weapon) directly into the ceiling, spraying mortar and dust throughout the room and causing a wave of screams to erupt from the second floor. Doc dove to his right toward the stairs, rolling as he landed and popping up like a shortstop who had just made a diving stop.

"Frag out!" he cried as he pulled the pin out of a grenade and hurled it up the stairs to the second floor. The grenade let out a deafening boom, sending up a wall of smoke and shards of stone and steel hurtling in all directions.

Doc hurriedly yet cautiously climbed the stairs. He moved his right hand to Hollywood's neck to check for a pulse, but Hollywood was gone. At the top of the stairs, Doc saw eight bodies sprawled out across the room. Each one was littered with bullet holes from Elroy's SAW and fragments from the grenade. None of them were still breathing.

"Clear!" he exclaimed.

As Boom and Elroy reached the second floor, the window exploded from the force of the high-powered bullet which pierced through it and grazed Doc's helmet. The men instantly dropped to the floor as they heard the thunderous sound of bullets crackling through the air on the street below.

Where the hell did that shot come from? thought Sebastian. He had heard the shot ring out from across the street, but he could not see which floor.

"Sniper to the west!" he cried, firing at the building. Coop and Wiz began firing in the sniper's direction, each one covering a different floor. When they stopped firing, Sebastian heard the thunder of a

Kalashnikov PK machine gun and the street filled with 54mm bullets, screaming towards the trio like a swarm of killer bees.

"Contact to the north!" screamed Sebastian as he turned to his right. "Find some cover!"

The men dove back onto the front porch as the PK was joined by numerous assault rifles, probably AK-47s, FN FALs or Steyr Augs, all of which were readily available, cheaply purchased and common favorites among Al-Qaeda and ISIL. The small adobe porch wall in front of them shook as it took the punishment. Coop looked at Sebastian. "Where the hell all these Muji's come from, Sarge? I didn't see a soul to the north." The debris flying from the wall caused Coop to bury his face between his bicep and forearm.

"They're hiding behind that wall at the end of the street," replied Sebastian, raising his open hand in front of his face to protect himself from the stone fragments flying about.

"I guess they never heard of coming out and fighting like a man," said Coop.

"Nah, not enough John Wayne growing up," said Sebastian. "Government controlled TV."

"So dat's what wrong with these guys? They pissed 'cause they can't watch the Duke. Man, I would've wanted to kick Assad's ass too, if I was deprived of my most essential and basic freedom in life. You gotta have the Duke. How else are you gonna learn how to kick ass and sound tough doing it?" Coop said as he threw a grenade over the wall.

"Yep. It's just a lack of good role models. Probably never saw Clint Eastwood either," said Sebastian as he squeezed off another salvo of shots.

"I say we call Direct TV and get them a subscription to the Western channel," Coop snorted with a big grin on his face as he ducked behind the porch wall. A bullet cut through his right sleeve as it zipped passed him

"Ya think that will get them to quit hiding behind that damn wall?" asked Sebastian, spinning back onto the porch. He spit out the dust that had filled his mouth as a barrage of bullets hit the adobe building.

Doc, Boom and Elroy came rushing out of the front door.

"Looks like you boys have stirred up a hornets' nest out here," Boom said.

"Where are Hollywood and Eddy?" inquired Sebastian. Boom shook his head and Sebastian knew what he meant. "Somebody get eyes on that sniper and take him out."

"Roger dat," replied Coop.

"Boom, on my mark I want you to put a 40 millimeter grenade right in the middle of that damn wall and take out that fuckin' PK," ordered Sebastian. "Wiz, you get on coms and let HQ know that we have encountered heavy opposition forces. We are moving our position. Doc, you and Elroy provide covering fire on that wall and we will move back down K Street and then east at the cross street. Ready... three... two... one... mark."

Boom whirled around the corner of the porch and fired his M203 grenade launcher. The wall at the end of the street collapsed into rubble when the M433 grenade exploded.

"Popping smoke!" Sebastian cried out, throwing a smoke grenade into the street to cover their retreat. At the same time, Coop fired a single shot at the third floor of the building to the west, exploding the back of the sniper's head.

"Nighty-night, pilgrim," Coop said in his best John Wayne voice.

"Let's move," Sebastian ordered his men. Coop led the way, staying close to the building, followed by Boom, Wiz and Sebastian. Doc and Elroy walked backwards while firing at the wall to the north.

As Coop neared the intersection, he spied a group of twenty nasty looking terrorists coming down the cross street armed with AK-47s. One was carrying a Rocket-Propelled Grenade Launcher. He turned his head back, saying, "Contact right."

Doc aimed the sights of his rifle at the terrorist carrying the RPG and squeezed the trigger in twice. Both bullets struck the terrorist in the chest, sending him catapulting backwards into the man behind him.

Sebastian leveled his sights on the terrorist closest to him. He fired off two quick shots, the first striking the man in the left shoulder, spinning him inward. The second struck the terrorist under his left eye, spraying blood and gray matter outward and covering the men closest to him. Wiz and Doc joined in the fray, taking out two more of the terrorists. It took a moment for the band of terrorists to realize their dire situation. By the time they realized their luck had run out, the terrorists had already lost six of their men.

"*Allahu Akbar!*" A thin terrorist with a long beard screamed as the group began searching for cover, but they were in the middle of the street in a ghost town and there was none to be found.

From behind him, Sebastian heard the familiar *ka-thunk* of Boom's M203 grenade launcher sending out another high explosive round. The grenade, which had a five-meter kill radius, landed in the center of the scattering terrorists. The explosion sent rubble, smoke and bodies flying into the air with such force that the skeletal wall of the building shook violently as it stopped their lifeless corpses. It appeared to Sebastian as though the grenade had taken out all the terrorists, but he wasn't sticking around to find out.

"Smoke out," exclaimed Elroy, tossing a smoke grenade toward the fallen terrorists to cover their movement. With his rifle trained straight ahead and ready, Coop turned to his left and headed east down the left side of the road. His eyes were alert for any sign of more terrorists. Coop could hear the sounds of automatic weapon fire and explosions behind them, indicating that a large scale battle was being fought.

"When we get to J Street up there, Coop, you and Elroy cover the south. Boom, you and Doc cover the north and if anything peeps from that damn wall, you level it," ordered Sebastian in a calm tone that sounded more like a quarterback leading his team than a man in the middle of a firefight.

"Hooah, Sarge," replied the team in unison.

"Wiz, get HQ on the line and tell them we are in the middle of the shit and headed east. We are requesting immediate exfil," said Sebastian, asking for an immediate extraction.

Upon reaching J Street, the men moved into position.

"Covering right," said Elroy, turning to the south to cover the street with his SAW.

"Covering left," said Doc as he moved around the corner facing the north end of the street. He bent down on one knee and braced himself against the wall.

Boom swung around the corner, standing over Doc. "Clear left," he said.

"Covering right," said Coop. "All clear." *We must have gotten ahead of the terrorists*, he thought. With all the noise coming from the west, it sounded like ISIL had its hands full fighting with the FSA.

Sebastian moved out into the dusty street and surveyed the situation. He looked back toward Bravo Team. "We're going across the street and then down that alley." He pointed toward the narrow alleyway across the street. Sebastian moved to the far side of J Street and aimed his rifle toward the adobe wall at the end of the street. Did Boom's 40mm take them all out? Something about that wall bothered him. Elroy and Coop crossed over next and set up their positions at the alley opening to cover the south end of J Street. Wiz darted across the street with his rifle up and ready, moving down the alley to cover their movement to the east. Boom reached down with his hand and tapped Doc on his shoulder, indicating that Doc was next to move. Doc stood up and bolted across the street. He was three feet from the sidewalk when Sebastian heard the unmistakable *ku-tah* of the Dragunov sniper rifle.

The bullet struck Doc in the temple, snapping his head hard to the right. Doc's body went limp and dropped to the ground with a thud. Sebastian could not help but think to himself that it looked like Doc had been hit by a right cross from Chuck Liddell.

"Sniper at the wall!" Sebastian cried out as he opened fire on the wall.

Boom saw Doc go down and mumbled under his breath, "Oh no you didn't." He launched a grenade and began firing his M16 before the grenade had time to reach the wall. The explosion tore through the wall, sending up a volcano of rubble, flames and smoke. "Yippee ki- yay, Mother Fucker," Boom smiled to himself and then fired another twelve rounds into the wall.

After the wall exploded, Sebastian and Elroy kept firing at the wall until their clips were empty. Reloading their weapons, they waited and watched until the smoke cleared. Sebastian wiped the sweat from his forehead with his left hand as he kept his scope pointed at the wall.

"What do you think, Boom? Did we get him?"

"I don't know how he could have survived that," replied Boom. "Ain't but one way to find out, Sarge." Boom took three deep breaths to calm himself before bolting out into the road. It took him less than two seconds to make it to Doc's body. That was when he heard the *ku-tah* come from his left.

"Damn" he said. And then everything went black.

Sebastian watched Boom collapse onto the ground next to Doc. His face turned red hot as his anger swelled. Sebastian fired his M16 wildly at the wall, not caring if he hit man or stone. His men were dying and, by God, he wasn't going to lose another one. He continued to fire until he heard the click of his empty rifle. He wasn't sure how long he had been firing at the wall, but he could hear Coop and Elroy yelling at him.

"Sarge… Sarge… we've gotta move."

"I'm good," Sebastian said, dropping the empty clip from his M16 and replacing it with a fresh one from his vest. "Let's move. Wiz, you're on point."

He followed his men down the alleyway, which was darkened by shadows. The pathway was narrow, barely three feet wide. If they were spotted, it would be like shooting fish in a barrel. Fortunately for Bravo Team, the alleyway turned at the end of the second building. A sharp right turn, followed by a left and the team came upon another dusty road which was spotted with one-story houses, unlike the multi-story buildings they had been clearing on K Street a mere seven minutes prior.

Coop was covering the north while Elroy guarded the south. Sebastian surveyed the street and noticed a gate to the northeast of the alley which opened into the courtyard of a large house. Since the residents of Al-Dana had long since left the war zone for the more peaceful farmlands surrounding it, odds were real good that no one would be home.

"Over there," he said pointing to the gate. "That looks like a good place to hold up and regroup."

The team moved in formation across the road and through the gate. Elroy pulled a large wooden board down into place to barricade the gate and turned around.

"Holy Crap, Sarge, would you look at the size of this place? This would be a mansion even back in the States. There had to be a real important asshole that lived here, considering every other house in Syria is a shit-hole." The two story home was between five thousand and six thousand square feet, complete with a swimming pool and what appeared to be a seventy-two-inch television located in the main living area, which was visible through the wall of windows and glass doors that allowed access from the courtyard into the house. "I wonder why nobody's snagged that TV yet."

"Wiz, what's the status on that exfil?" Sebastian asked calmly. "Elroy, you keep your eyes on the road. I want to know the second you see any movement. And everybody, do an ammo check. This could turn out to be a very long day."
Sebastian leaned his back against the wall and slid down until he was sitting on the ground. It felt good to rest, even if it was only for a few seconds.

"Sarge, HQ says that exfil is en route. They've encountered heavy resistance and are having difficulties getting through to our position," said Wiz.

"Well, I feel better now," quipped Sebastian. "I thought it was just us having a bad day." Wiz, Coop and Elroy laughed a little at his joke. Sebastian smiled and closed his eyes.

Inside the house, Khalid Muhammad al-Jabiri was speaking fluent Spanish into the phone. "I understand your anger, Juan Carlos." He brushed his medium cut black hair away from eyes as he listened to the man on the other end of the phone rant about his situation. Khalid was from a well-to-do Syrian family and his father had been a classmate of President Assad's at the University. Khalid himself had studied psychology at the University of Oxford. He was wearing a solid white Didashah, the traditional one-piece robe worn by Syrian men. "I am sure I can make them available for you. It should not be a problem."

An athletically built Syrian man wearing a black suit entered the room. "Sir, four armed American soldiers are in the courtyard. I believe that we should leave."

"Juan Carlos, a pressing matter has just been brought to my attention. Unfortunately I must take care of it immediately. Rest assured, I will make this deal work. I will call you tomorrow and we can work out the details. Adios, my friend." Khalid ended the call and turned to the man in black. "Now tell me about these soldiers, Sharif. What exactly are they doing?"

"They are on the far side of the courtyard by the gate leading out to the road. They are just sitting there."

"Do they know that we are inside the house?" inquired Khalid.

"It does not appear so. It looks like they are waiting on someone or something."

"Very well. Tell Omar to ready the car. I believe that it is time for us to take our leave. I will be down in a moment," said Khalid calmly as he walked over to a large office desk which contained a computer, four large monitors, a laptop and tablet. As Sharif exited the room, Khalid picked up a satchel from the marble floor next to the desk and placed the laptop and tablet into it. He pressed a small black button located underneath the desk and gracefully walked toward the door. The thermite charge was on a delay and did not ignite for thirty seconds. Once ignited the incendiary device sent the desk and everything on it up in a ball of flames.

Burning at four thousand degrees Fahrenheit, the flames quickly spread throughout the room filling the entire second floor with billowing smoke.

"Hey, Sarge, did you see dat?" asked Coop, pointing up to the second floor of the mansion. "That whole freaking room just went up in flames."

"Huh? How does a room just go up in flames?" asked Sebastian.

"I dunno," said Coop. "Spontaneous combustion."

"How about the Human Torch doing that flame on thing?" chimed in Elroy.

"Pet dragon," stated Wiz. "Yeah, I'm definitely going with the dragon thing. Look at that, the windows are melting. If it is a dragon, then we should get a picture. We'll be rich."

Sebastian laughed. "Well then, let's go get us a pet dragon." He stood up, pulled his M16 tight against his shoulder and aimed it at the house. "Let's move."

He walked towards the back door of the house. Wiz and Elroy moved around to the right of the large swimming pool, while Sebastian and Coop circled to the left. As they reached the large glass doors located in the center of the window wall, Sebastian remarked, "And if you guys see a dragon, remember to shoot it first and then take the picture."

Elroy grinned and opened the door. The men entered the colossal living area, which contained two L shaped leather sofas which formed a large U in the middle of the room. Elroy and Wiz moved hurriedly toward the hallway on the right. Weapons ready and eyes alert, Sebastian and Coop moved across the marble floor towards the large open doorway that led to the kitchen. Sebastian entered first, moving to his left to allow room for Coop to slide in beside him.

Sebastian spotted Khalid, who was reaching for the handle of the rear door. With his olive skin and dark brown eyes, he reminded Sebastian of Enrique Iglesias, the Latin pop star.

"Hands... Hands! Let me see your fucking hands!" exclaimed Sebastian. He had had enough of being shot at today and was not taking any more chances. The island in the middle of the kitchen prevented him from seeing if anything was in the man's right hand. "Stop reaching for that door and get your hands up right now."

"What is the meaning of this?" asked Khalid in a smooth, British-sounding accent. "Why have you broken into my home?"
"We firemen. Saw the fire upstairs and came in to help out," stated Coop sarcastically. "This whole town is a ghost town. What are you doing here?"
The sound of a Brügger and Thomet MP9 machine pistol echoed from the hallway that Elroy and Wiz had taken. The noise caused Sebastian and Coop to turn their heads toward the hallway. Seizing his opportunity, Khalid fired three rounds from his FN57 pistol and escaped through the rear door.

Out of the corner of his eye, Sebastian saw the muzzle flash coming from Khalid's pistol. A searing pain shot through him as the SS190bullet struck Sebastian above his body armor. The bullet ripped through him, shattering his collarbone and sternum before piercing his lung. The next two bullets hit the center of his chest plate with such impact that he was lifted off his feet. He fell helplessly towards the floor. His gaze fell toward Coop, who was firing at the Syrian coming through the doorway. Sebastian watched as the Syrian's head rocked backward and muttered, "Good shot, Coop."

Then the world faded away.

CHAPTER 2
Piedra Negras, Mexico 24 hours ago

"What is this?" Hector Gonzales, an Inspector in the Policia Federal's Division Antidrogas or Anti-Drug Division, asked, pointing toward the bald American who stood in the middle of the squad room addressing Hector's squad of *Federales*, who were dressed in their usual dark gray combat fatigues. "Did I miss a consultation memo?"

The American was an athletically built man, dressed in black combat gear. His green eyes provided an appealing contrast to his tanned, olive skin. He walked over to Hector and offered his right hand.

"I'm sure there was a memo, Inspector, but this is not a consultation," said the man with a distinctive Texas drawl. "I'm Special Agent in Charge Sean Ray, United States Drug Enforcement Agency."

He spoke in a tone that let everyone in the room know he was in charge. Ray's team was one of five of the U.S. Drug Enforcement Agency's Foreign-deployed Advisory and Support Teams. The FAST teams were the enforcement arm of the DEA's Drug Flow Attack Strategy. The official mission of the FAST teams was to conduct special enforcement operations, train and mentor foreign narcotics law enforcement units and to collect and assess intelligence in support of U.S. and bilateral investigations. Ray and his team had been deployed to Afghanistan on multiple occasions for the purpose of disrupting the opium trade. However, this was the first time that his FAST team had been deployed to Mexico.

"I'm here to intercept drugs coming into the United States from Piedra Negras, by way of the La Familia Cartel."

Hector shook Ray's hand, taking notice of the American's overly firm grip. "Well, Special Agent Ray, of the *United States* DEA, One... you have no jurisdiction here in Mexico. Two... if La Familia had a drug shipment coming out of Piedra Negras today, I am sure that I would know about it. And three... you have absolutely no authority to address my men without my knowledge or consent," he said, holding up a finger on his left hand each time he counted. "So why don't you take your FAST team and head back across the border? You Americans have some nerve. You think that you own the world and can do whatever you want, whenever you want."

Ray's square jaw started to tense. He could feel his anger begin to sweep over his entire face. He did not like being talked down to, especially by a potentially corrupt Federale. And Mexico was full of corrupt *Federales* eager to line their pockets with cartel drug money. He took a breath to calm himself and then politely stated, "Inspector, I apologize. I should not have briefed your men without your knowledge. However, I am here because there *is* a shipment coming out of Piedra Negras today. Furthermore, I'm here on the orders of the President of the United States and upon the request of the President of Mexico, Vincente Mota himself. It was my understanding that you had been apprised of the situation and informed of our presence. My orders are to work in conjunction with the Policia Federal. We are to take the lead on the operation and you are to receive all of the credit. Now this is a time sensitive operation and we need to get moving. So, if you don't have any more objections, I need to finish my Operation Briefing so that we can get rolling. Are we good?"

"*Señor*, I have no knowledge of any authority granting you the right to be here. But if time is of the essence, then I will allow you to continue to brief my men while I go back to my office and verify your story. If you check out, then I will ride with you and you can brief me on the way."

"I'm good with that. Thank you, Inspector." Sean's lips formed a slight grin as he turned around and strode back toward the front of the room.

Hector had lied. He had been notified weeks ago of the DEA's upcoming operations in Mexico. However, he had not been told that they would be here today, nor that they were targeting the La Familia Cartel. As he entered the stairwell leading up to his second floor office, Hector reached into his tactical vest and pulled out his cell phone, hurriedly dialing the number.

Santiago Ortiz was singing along to the music which blared through the speakers of his truck as he turned the corner and sped casually towards his uncle's concrete plant. Santiago was a handsome young man with a contagious, youthful exuberance. Although he was only nineteen years old, he possessed a wisdom and maturity that was well beyond his years, traits that he had developed as a result of the many years spent working for his uncle, Juan Carlos

Real. Santiago had begun working for his uncle when he was nine years old. His mother, Juan Carlos' sister, had been a professor at the prestigious St. Edwards University in Austin, Texas, as had his father. After his parents' tragic deaths in an automobile accident, Santiago had been sent to Mexico to live with his uncle. His first job had been running messages from his uncle to the cartel lieutenants and now he was himself a lieutenant: the man in charge of transporting all of his uncle's products out of Mexico and into the United States.

His cell phone rang and Santiago pressed the button on the steering wheel to answer the call.

"Bueno, Hector. How is my favorite Federale today?"

"Santiago, I don't have much time. You need to cancel the shipment and get the hell away from the concrete plant," said Hector hurriedly and in a hushed voice. In addition to being on the payroll of Juan Carlos Real, the head of the La Familia Cartel, Hector and Juan Carlos were close friends and had been since they were small children growing up in Piedra Negras. "They are about to raid it."

"Take it easy, Hector. I will give them some of the product like always and send them on their way." Santiago replied, easily noticing the worrisome tone in his friend's voice. "There is nothing to worry about."

"No, *mi sobrino,* you don't understand. It is not us who are doing the raid. It's the Americans - the *pincha* DEA. They just showed up today and informed me of their plan to raid the plant. I knew that they were coming, but not *who* they were coming for. I was led to believe that they were going after the Gulf Cartel. I just this second got a chance to steal away and let you know what's happening."

"Okay, *Tio,* when will they get here? I will tell the men to get everything out of the plant." Santiago often called Hector *Tio*, which was Spanish for uncle, as a sign of affection and respect.

"I will hold them off as long as possible, but they are ready to move out now. I would guess that you have maybe twenty minutes. Now get the hell out of there before they find out who you are. Oh, and Santiago, please be careful. These Americans are real cowboys. They don't play around."

"Adios," said Santiago as he pressed the button to end the call. He pushed the voice button on the steering wheel. "Call the plant."

He turned the wheel to the right and started down the side street to make his escape.

"Hello?" answered a voice on the other end of the line.

"Ramon, listen very closely. The American DEA is about to raid the plant. Has the shipment arrived yet?"

"No, Santiago. They are not here," replied Ramon. "They should be here any minute."

"Okay. When they get there..."

"Shouldn't we tell them not to come here if the Americans are about to raid us?" asked Ramon, cutting off Santiago in mid-sentence.

Santiago could hear the panic in Ramon's voice. "No. If they know when and where we are moving the product, then they also know how we are moving it," he replied very calmly to make Ramon feel more at ease. He could not afford to have Ramon lose his head. His plan needed to move quickly and there was no time for panic. "Now, when it gets there, I need you to make sure that it goes directly to the truck barn. Do you any concrete mixers ready to go out?"

"*Si*, I have six that need to leave now for El Moral. We loaded the concrete in them twenty minutes ago."

"*Perfecto.* When the product gets there, put all of it in the back of one mixer."

"Inside the concrete?"

"Yes. Inside of the concrete. Then I want you to send out four mixers. One north to the El Centinela, one to the east to the border, one south toward Los Monteras and the one with the package to the north to Ciudad Acuna. Wait two minutes and then send the van back out. Wait one minute and send out every gravel truck we have in every possible direction. Do you *sabe*?"

Santiago wanted to make sure that Ramon understood the plan. Ramon was very loyal and trustworthy, but sometimes he wasn't all that intelligent.

"*Si*, Santiago. Put the package in the mixer. Send a mixer in all four directions. Wait two minutes and send out the van. Wait one minute and send out all of the gravel trucks. I got it, Santiago."

"Good. As soon as you send out the last truck, I want you to *vamonos* out of there and call me to let me know what happens."

"You got it, *Jefe. Adios*."

"*Adios*," Santiago pressed down the phone button on his steering wheel to end the call.

SAIC Sean Ray stuck his head into Hector Gonzales' office.

"You ready, Inspector?" he asked.

"*Si*," replied Hector as he slid his Beretta 92M pistol into the holster attached to his right leg. "Let's go get these guys, Special Agent Ray. And you can call me Hector."

The two men entered the stairwell and quickly descended the stairs toward the parking garage.

As he climbed up into the bulletproof Chevy Suburban, Hector spoke. "So Special Agent Ray, can you get me up to speed before we get there?"

"Please, Hector, call me Sean," replied Ray as he turned the ignition on the vehicle. "We know that the shipment is heroin. We know that it is coming into Piedra Negras by cargo van, which should be arriving at the Real Concrete Plant at thirteen hundred hours today. We also know that it will be shipped out of the plant and across the border in the back of one of their eighteen-wheeler gravel trucks within an hour of arriving at the plant."

Special Agent Ray pulled the Suburban out onto the street and turned left toward the Real Concrete Plant.

"With all of that *knowing,* why is it that you have waited this long to come after the La Familia Cartel? It has been my experience that if you know that much about an operation, you either have a man inside or a very reliable rat."

"Hector, we have very reliable Intel on just about every Cartel down here in Mexico. For the most part we let you guys do your thing down here and we take care of our side of the border." Ray turned his head toward Hector. His jade eyes locked onto Hector's in an earnest stare as he continued. "Believe it or not, we really don't like stepping on y'all's toes. You *Federales* do a damn fine job considering what y'all are up against down here."

"Well, if you truly believe that, then maybe you could share some of the Intel that you have on the Gulf Cartel. They are much more of a problem down here than La Familia. The G.C. are many times larger than La Familia. They are responsible for much more drugs going into the United States and…" Hector paused and a sad yet angry look came over his face. "They also smuggle people. Not migrant workers looking for jobs, but women and little girls. Sex slaves who they send all over the world." The anger took over his face. His eyes squinted and narrowed to small slits. His forehead wrinkled inward and his teeth clenched. "*Puto madre!*" Hector slammed his fist down onto the dashboard of the Suburban. "That's who we need to be going after. Compared to them, La Familia is small time."

Hector truly did hate the Gulf Cartel. He had no tolerance for human trafficking. There was no honor in it.

SAIC Ray turned left and sped down the Fausto Martinez Freeway. The four Federale SUVs followed close behind him. "To tell you the truth, Hector, La Familia brought this upon themselves. My team and the other four FAST teams have all spent a considerable amount of time in Afghanistan burning hash and poppy fields and training the locals. We spend almost all of our time working with Homeland Security. We have never come into Mexico out of respect for you guys and the work that you do. Like I said before, we don't like to step on toes. When La Familia was just sending weed and coke over to the States, Homeland couldn't give two cents about them. But when they got into the heroin business, they got into bed with Al-Qaeda. That got Homeland's attention. In my opinion, Homeland's view is that the good people of the U.S. can smoke and snort whatever they want so long as their fun doesn't fund the terrorists with whom the government is fighting a war. That's why we are using our Intel against them and not the Gulf Cartel. The G.C. doesn't do business with Al-Qaeda. That being said, I don't see why we can't participate in a little inter-agency cooperation. You know, to facilitate a little international brotherhood." Sean gave a Hector a sly look and winked.

As Ray turned right on Netzahualcoyotl Street and sped toward the front gate of the Real Concrete Plant, he noticed the men on the street talking on cell phones. He depressed the button and spoke into the microphone attached to his left shoulder. "Okay, everybody, look sharp. We are almost there."

When they were two blocks away from the plant, Ray noticed the concrete mixers racing out of the entrance.

"Team Two, do you see what I see?" Ray asked into the microphone as he pushed down on the gas pedal to catch the speeding mixers.

"Roger that," came the reply over the speaker. "Now why are those guys moving so fast? You think they know we're coming, Boss?"

"They most likely had spotters all along our route," Hector explained to Ray. "Definitely once we turned onto Netzahualcoyotl."

"Inspector Gonzales is certain they have spotters down here and I think we've been made," said Ray into the mike. "They are splitting up. Two, you and me have the two headed north. Three, you take the one headed south and Four, you take the guy headed east. Five, you've got the front entrance."

Ray hit the lights and sirens and flew down the street toward the fleeing Concrete mixers. The two trucks heading north split up and took separate roads. He slammed the brakes and took a hard left onto Vasquez Narro Avenue, while Teams Two, Four and Five sped by him. The tires of the Suburban spit gravel and the vehicle leapt into action as he accelerated towards the concrete mixer. It only took eight seconds for Ray to speed in front of the big truck. He slammed on the emergency brakes and turned the wheel hard to the right, sliding the SUV to a complete stop and blocking the road in front of the truck. Immediately, Sean, Hector and the two *Federales* riding with them bounded from the vehicle with their weapons drawn and aimed at the driver of the rig.

"*Manos Arriba!* Hands up where I can see them," screamed Hector to the driver. The two *Federales* immediately started searching the vehicle. A young thin *Federale* went to the cabin of the truck while the second Federale hopped up on the rear to check the mixer.

"It's full of concrete, Inspector," the Federale called out to Hector.

"There's nothing in the cab either," explained the thin Federale.

"Where are you heading to in such a hurry?" Hector quizzed the driver.

"El Centinela," explained the driver "They are running low on concrete and need another truckload in a hurry or they will have to start the job all over."

Ray's Communications speaker came to life. "One... this is Five. We've got a cargo van headed our way in a hurry. It looks like he is wanting out of the plant in a bad way. How do you want me to proceed?"

"Intercept and detain that vehicle," ordered Ray into his microphone. He pressed on the mike again and said "Two, Three and Four, have you intercepted the vehicles?"

"One, this is Three. Affirmative and there is no cargo on board. Driver says he's going to Los Monteras. Special order of concrete or some crap like that."

"This is Two. I've got the same story here, Boss."

"Okay everybody, let's load up and head back to the plant. Let the drivers go on their way. It looks like these guys are decoys," Ray said into the transmitter. Hector and the officers finished with the driver and headed back toward the SUV when the call came over the speaker.

"One, this is Five. The van is empty. They must have already made the switch."

"Roger that, Five. We are loading up and headed back to your location. ETA one minute. Detain all employees and do not let anyone out of the plant. We will have to do this the hard way and search every inch of the plant." Ray turned his head toward Hector. "Inspector, we are going to need a few more men."

"I can arrange that," replied Hector.

"Holy shit! One, this is Five. Our situation is all FUBAR over here!" Ray could hear the automatic gunfire in the background as the DEA agent's voice came screaming over the speaker. FUBAR was military and law enforcement slang for a really messed up situation. "They came out of nowhere... I just looked up and there they were."

"There who were, Five?" asked Ray into his mic.

"Gravel trucks, Boss. They just came busting through the gate. Took out our SUV and split off in all directions."

Ray stared ahead as he neared the intersection. An eighteen-wheeled gravel truck was speeding down the street and heading straight for them. "How many trucks, Five? I have eyes on one now."

He spun the SUV to a halt, blocking the road and sending his passengers flying against the doors. Once again the smell of brakes and burning rubber filled the air inside the Suburban.

"All of them, boss. The whole damn fleet. And they aren't stopping for nobody," came the reply.

"*Dios mio*, they are going to ram us!" screamed the young Federale from the rear of the SUV. He opened the door and dove from the vehicle. Ray, Hector and the remaining Federale followed suit.

The asphalt street scraped flesh from the side of Ray's face as he rolled to a stop against the concrete building. He watched helplessly as the semi smashed through the roadblock that he had created with the SUV, sending sparks and metal hurling through the air as it collided with the SUV and flung it to the side of the road in a crumpled mass of metal and smoke. Ray ducked and covered his head as the shards of white hot metal and glass filled the air around him.

"This is One, my vehicle is down. All teams give me a situation report," Ray called into his microphone.

"This is Two. We are at the east end of the plant. Our vehicle is also out of commission but all personnel are okay," came the call on the radio.

"Three here, Boss. We are on Garcia Avenue. Damn big rig ran us into a building. Except for a few bumps and bruises, we are five by five. But our SUV is toast."

"Four checking in. We are on the west corner of the plant. One of the *Federales* - Rodriguez, I think - broke his arm in the crash when we slammed into the wall. Our SUV is wasted as well. That was one hell of a Fast and Furious they pulled. Looks like we're walking home with our tail tucked between our legs."

"Roger that. All teams rendezvous with Five at the entrance. We'll have Inspector Gonzales call for a ride and extra men to help search the plant," ordered Ray, his eyes darting toward Gonzales. Frustrated, he threw a lug nut in the direction of the SUV and shattered what was left of the windshield of the Suburban. "Dammit, Hector! They knew we were coming! That wasn't just spotters along the road. That was a well thought out plan. You've got a leak somewhere over here on your side. One that almost got all of us killed."

Inspector Gonzales was screaming into his handheld radio. "*Necsito todas las unidades disponibles para detener todos los camiones Real Concreto.*"

He turned toward Special Agent Ray. "I have just dispatched all available units in Piedra Negras to apprehend those trucks. I believe that you are correct, but don't you worry, Sean, I will track down the rat and make him pay."

Santiago was talking into the speaker of his truck as he pulled into the long drive leading up to his Uncle Juan Carlos Real's villa. The Villa was located on one hundred and twenty sprawling acres just outside of Jiménez, Coahuila, Mexico.

"You are certain that they have no idea where it is, Ramon?"

"I am positive, Santiago," replied Ramon. "We left all of them stranded on the side of the road. All of their SUVs were totaled. Plus, they wouldn't know which truck to follow. I sent at least one truck to every city and town in Coahuila. You should have confirmation from Acuna in about two hours."

"Bueno, Ramon. You did well. I will talk to you soon," said Santiago as he ended the call.

He let out a sigh of relief and exited the pickup and walked up the steps to the front door of the villa. He liked it when a good plan came together. Now he just had to tell his uncle the good news.

The clopping of his wood-soled boots echoed through the villa as Santiago walked swiftly toward Juan Carlos Real's office. His uncle was seated behind a large oak desk and speaking on the phone as Santiago entered. The room had huge bay windows that overlooked the Olympic-sized swimming pool and manicured back lawn of the estate.

"I am telling you Khalid, my good friend, it was the fucking Americans. Can you believe that? On Mexican soil. Those *culeros* have some nerve. After everything I do for them. I don't smuggle just anyone across the border, only hard working Coahuilans. No trouble makers or *terroristas,* no offense, like the other Cartels. It is our unspoken deal. They leave me alone to conduct my business and I protect their border. But no longer." He paused as the man on the other end of the line spoke. "What I need, my friend, is weapons. Not shotguns and hunting rifles. I mean AK-47s, Uzis and RPGs. If the Americans want a war, I will give them one, but I need the weapons to do it." Juan Carlos paused again. "Very good, my friend. I knew that I could count on you. Whatever you want I will gladly pay." He paused again and then said, "I understand. You are a busy man. I will talk to you soon."

Juan Carlos hung up the phone and then sprang up from his desk and rushed over to his nephew.

"Are you alright?" he asked Santiago.

"Yes, uncle. Hector reached me before I even reached the plant."

"I assume that the shipment was destroyed before the Americans could take it?"

"Well, yes and no." Santiago smiled and told Juan Carlos about his plan and how the heroin had been moved inside of the concrete mixer and sent over to the Acuna plant. "We should be able to salvage the whole thing with a few jack hammers. I have already called the police and reported that while our plant was closed today, hijackers broke in and stole all of our trucks."

"That is fucking genius, Santiago. And you thought of all of this in less than a minute? That, my nephew, is why you are in charge of transportation. Anybody else would worry about saving their own ass and not the product. You are the only one smart enough to do both. Now we must talk about what we are going to do with these fucking Americans who do not know how to stay on their side of the river."

It had been two hours since the fiasco at the concrete plant and Special Agent Sean Ray had not yet calmed down. They had arrived back at federal Police Headquarters in Piedra Negras, courtesy of Inspector Gonzales, less than ten minutes ago and his boss was already on the phone.

"No sir, it was by the book. I personally briefed the *Federales* and we immediately hit the streets." There was a brief pause. "No, sir, the only personnel present were the personnel who accompanied us." His jaw and lips tightened as he listened to his superior. "Dammit, Warren, I know." Ray slammed his palm down on the desk, sending papers shooting up into the air and swirling across the room. "But I'm telling you that they knew we were coming. They were too well organized. This wasn't a case of a kid on the corner hearing a whistle and running. It was a coordinated effort by a fleet of fifty or so trucks. They knew exactly how many trucks to send out in the initial diversion and then they attacked us while the rest of the trucks got away. There is no way it was improvised. Besides that, the asshole had already called all the trucks in as stolen before we even got back to police headquarters."

Ray pulled the phone down, held it against his chest, counted to five and then lifted it back up. "Yes, sir. I will, sir. Oh, and Warren? We're gonna get this guy. La Familia is going down." After a short pause, he said, "Corpus Christi. Really? How did you make that happen? Okay, I will see you there."

Hector walked over to Special Agent Ray and handed him a cup of coffee. "That did not sound very pleasing. How did he like the part about the trucks being called in stolen before we even searched the plant?"

Ray removed his combat vest and his sweat-soaked black T-shirt outlined his muscular frame. He took a long drink of coffee. "What he said shouldn't ever have to be repeated. Hector, I apologize for the fiasco and the miscommunication, but I promise you that we will get La Familia. Right now I have to collect my team and head back across the border."

"Back to Arlington? I hear Virginia is very nice this time of year," Hector remarked.

"No. The DEA has an office in Corpus Christi, Texas, and the boss wants us there for now."

Hector extended his hand to Special Agent Ray. "It was nice to meet you, Sean. Maybe next time it will be under better circumstances."

Ray shook his hand. "I hope so, Hector. *Adios.*"

CHAPTER 3
Abu Kamal, Syria

Abu Kamal was a medium sized town of about forty thousand people located in eastern Syria on the Euphrates River, near the Iraq border. It was a lush farming community rich with life - a stark contrast to its neighboring region, the Syrian Desert.

At one of these farms, Khalid Muhammed al-Jabiri was sitting at a small yet exquisite dining table drinking his tea. He sat deep in thought, his left hand holding his tea while his right hand rhythmically tapped his pursed lips with a small teaspoon. His brows were slightly turned down as he gazed out of the window at the cattle grazing in the countryside meadow, awaiting the arrival of his close friend and mentor Abdul Aleem bin Faisal.

Abdul was the Saudi leader of a small, secretive group of Al-Qaeda upper echelon, called the Al-Yad, who secretly controlled and coordinated all Al-Qaeda activities. The ultimate goal of the Al-Yad was the creation of a worldwide Caliphate. A Caliphate whose establishment hinged on the ultimate defeat of the West, especially the United States. Bin Faisal had been a confidant to Osama bin Laden and was one of only a handful of people that Osama confided in about the 911 strikes. The Al-Yad was only a whisper in Intelligence circles. No one in the CIA, Mossad, MI6 or Mabahith had been able to discover the identity of even one of its members.

Al-Yad was not an individual terrorist organization, but rather the oligarchy which controlled all Al-Qaeda organizations, coordinating strikes in Afghanistan, Egypt, Syria, and Turkey as well as France and other western nations. The Al-Yad was the mastermind behind all Al-Qaeda core organizations and affiliates. It was responsible securing funds and purchasing weapons for all Al-Qaeda groups. More importantly, the Al-Yad was force behind the development and establishment of the new governments and policies in the conquered lands in Syria, Iraq and Afghanistan. Whether it was the Taliban in Pakistan and Afghanistan, or any of the many Al-Qaeda terrorist groups in the region, if they were fighting in the jihad to defend Islam, they were controlled by the Al-Yad. By allowing each Al-Qaeda affiliate to have its own publicly recognized leader, the Al-Yad had insured their anonymity and thus allowed themselves the ability to operate freely and undetected, especially by the United States.

Abdul Aleem bin Faisal entered the room from the living area. Abdul was a man in his early forties, with dark hair that was beginning to show signs of gray around the sides. His round glasses and slight build made him look more like a college professor than a ruthless sociopath. His outstretched arms and broad smile were a welcome sight for Khalid. As they embraced, Khalid realized how much he had missed his mentor. Abdul and Khalid had served together on Bin Laden's Shura Council, advising him on all matters concerning Al-Qaeda. Abdul, being at least a decade older than Khalid, had taken the younger man under his wing. He nurtured Khalid's fighting skills and fostered his hatred of everything not Muslim.

"*As-salaam alaykum,*" said Abdul.

"*Wa-alaykum as-salaam*," replied Khalid.

"Khalid, my old friend, it is so very good to see you. Especially still in one piece. I am sorry about Sharif - he was a good man. May Allah accept him and reunite us in the highest paradise. Tell me what happened in Al-Dana? How did the Americans find you?"

"By sheer luck, I believe," replied Khalid. "The Americans had intelligence about our increased forces inside the city and sent out patrols with the FSA. One of the patrols discovered some of our men in one of the buildings, which caused the assault to begin early. I believe that the circumstances of the battle caused the American patrol to run from our main forces and they happened upon my safe house by accident. There is no reason to believe that they knew my identity. They were not a Delta strike team, merely ordinary soldiers."

"Very good," said Abdul. "How about our Mexican associates? Can we expect our income from heroin to continue to increase?"

"Our relationship with the La Familia Cartel is very good," explained Khalid. "As you know, I first thought of them as mindless infidel thugs, who were merely a source for selling our heroin and a means of getting it into the United States so that the infidels can destroy themselves with it. But after many dealings and conversations with the leader, Juan Carlos Real, I have come to admire and respect him. In many ways, La Familia is similar to us."

Abdul's eyed widened, showing signs of intrigue. "How so?"

"Despite being a devout Catholic and not a Muslim, his faith is every bit as strong as ours. His fight is not that dissimilar from our own. His desire is to make a prosperous home for his people, the people of Coahuila. He wishes to overthrow the corrupt government that chooses to line its own pockets with no thought of the welfare of *his* people. Unfortunately, he has the Great Satan, the United States, for a neighbor. Therefore it is impossible for him to overthrow the entire government, or even a portion of the government, through warfare as we have done in Afghanistan, Iraq and here in Syria. The United States would most surely step in and put an end to any revolution that would threaten the Mexican government." Khalid raised his teacup to his lips and sipped the hot oolong. "It was my conversations with Juan Carlos that gave me the idea to follow his blueprint. He builds schools and hospitals and churches in Coahuila. He provides his citizens with jobs in his businesses, both legitimate and illegal. He polices and controls the entire State. There is no crime committed that is not carried out or sanctioned by his Cartel. The people come to him to solve their issues, they no longer go through the Mexican Courts. He is effectively the *real* government of Coahuila. By providing for the people of Coahuila, he has won their hearts and minds. This has allowed him to have his people elected to positions of power within the government. He has people in both chambers of the Mexican Congress and his own sister is now the Governor of Coahuila, despite the best efforts of President Mota to insert his own candidate to the position."

Abdul nodded in approval and sat back in his chair. "So this is why you told me to build mosques and hospitals in the lands that we have taken under our control? To make the people faithful to us?"

"Certainly. Our ultimate goal is a worldwide Caliphate, or sovereign nation, by joining the government nations that we have set up using our different Al-Qaeda groups throughout the Levant. Juan Carlos has shown me a proven method of setting up new governments more easily and efficiently. More importantly, of gaining the approval of the people. According to him, the people will support the rule of any new government so long as it supports their most basic needs. Especially when their government has betrayed and murdered them, as in Syria. The Caliphate has to be better for them than the previous government, or we will not only be fighting wars with our Shiite enemies but with the Sunni people of our newly conquered lands as well."

Abdul placed his teacup onto the saucer. "I believe that you have a good understanding of La Familia and this Juan Carlos. It seems that he is indeed a valuable source of information. I never realized how much the current plight of the Mexican people resembled that of the Sunni. Except maybe for our mutual hatred of the United States. Can we depend on him to continue to buy the heroin? Even with the acquisition of the Syrian oil fields, we still depend heavily upon heroin as our primary source of revenue."

Khalid smiled and leaned in towards his mentor. "As a matter of fact, in addition to the regular shipment of heroin, the Cartel has requested that we secure Russian-made automatic weapons and RPGs. The United States attacked Juan Carlos' facility in Piedra Negras. This has him out for blood and ready to wage war against them and the Mexican National Police."

"Very good," said Abdul, his smile widening to show his pearly white teeth. "Every ally gained in the fight against the United States brings us one step closer to defeating the Great Satan. Get me the specifics and I will speak with Mahmoud to secure weapons and arrange transport."

"Excellent. I will let Juan Carlos know that we will deliver what he needs." Khalid placed his elbows on the table and brought his hands together like a steeple close to his mouth. His thumbs rested under his chin. "Have you heard the latest of the American President's Executive Orders?"

"Something about amnesty for children, I believe," replied Abdul. "Is there something special about it? Can we use the Mexican children?"

Abdul knew that Khalid was smart. He had always exhibited an intelligence far above most others, but of what use could uneducated, Catholic children be to the Al-Yad?

Khalid smiled from behind the steeple of his hands. His eyes appeared to be nothing more than mere slits. "No, my friend. We cannot use the children. They are also devout Catholic and are not sympathetic to our cause. I have tried recruiting in Mexico and South America, but to no avail. Their devotion to their religion always gets in the way."

"That is a shame. One day, after we have defeated the United States, we will have to remove the infidels south of their border as well."

"This is true, my brother," agreed Khalid. "But for now we have use for them in our war with the United States. The American President's Executive Order not only allows for the immediate issuing of resident status to children who have travelled illegally into his country, but *also* to anyone who has entered illegally and has been living inside the United States for at least five years."

A puzzled look came over Abdul's face. "I am sorry, Khalid. I still do not see how this Executive Order can be of use to us. We do not have anyone currently living illegally in the United States. Even if we were to sneak some in, we have no way of proving that they have been there for five years. This order appears useless to me."

Khalid placed his arms flat the table and leaned in toward his friend. "We have La Familia. Juan Carlos has been smuggling his people from Coahuila into the United States for decades. He can not only smuggle our operatives into the United States, but he can also equip them with identities that prove they have been there for at least five years. Thus, once we have our operatives inside the United States, they will also have legal resident status."

"Will they not be Mexican identities that he has secured?" Asked Abdul. "The people of the Levant are not remotely Mexican."

"Yes, they will be Mexican identities," replied Khalid. "However, my men have been training for years for this operation, knowing that one day the opportunity would arise in which we would be able to strike the Great Satan down with one blow from Muhammad's Sword. They have mastered not only the language of the Mexican people, but their regional accent as well. They have all met the height requirements. The Mexican people are not a tall people, and Syrians and Saudis can pass for Mexican. Our hair, eyes and skin tone match perfectly. Besides, the white Americans always say that all Hispanics look the same, whether they are from Venezuela, Mexico, Guatemala, or Brazil. Not because they *do* look alike, but because the whites do not actually pay attention. I promise you that Muhammad's Sword will work."

Abdul leaned forward and placed his hand on his friend's knee. "Muhammad's Sword requires great coordination. How is it that we may achieve that from here? What is your time line?"

"I will need to see how easily we can smuggle our people into the United States and how many identities La Familia can provide. Once I have gotten into the United States with the first group, I will have a better understanding of La Familia's capability. Then I will have a detailed timeline for you."

"Once *you* enter the United States?" Abdul questioned.

Khalid placed both of his hands on top of his friend's. "Yes, Abdul. Certainly you would not expect me to allow a mission such as this to proceed without my direct supervision? As you said yourself, we cannot possibly coordinate Muhammad's Sword from here. Besides, think of what all I can accomplish once I am inside the belly of the beast."

"You are correct. I would expect nothing less of you." Abdul smiled even wider and reached over to the table for his teacup. "How is your other recruitment going?"

In addition to being the primary broker for Al-Qaeda's heroin trade, Khalid was also in charge of North American recruitment for the organization. He oversaw a network of bloggers whose job was to promote their cause and recruit Westerners, primarily in the United States and Canada. His bloggers used a combination of websites: YouTube, Facebook and other social media mediums.

"Recruitment is going very well. We have had great success with over one thousand brothers from North America joining in our fight against the Great Satan. We have had our best recruitment in what the Americans call the 'Blue States', especially in the larger cities such as Denver, Los Angeles and New York. Our best results have come from Detroit and Chicago. It is no secret that both cities have rapidly declining economies. Their city governments are in alarming states of debt and both have rapidly increasing crime rates. These circumstances make for optimal recruitment. Oddly, we seem to have great success in recruiting rap musicians. There is some correlation between that brand of music and the jihad that I have not been able to comprehend completely," replied Khalid.

Abdul took a drink and set his teacup back onto its saucer. "If there is a connection, I trust that you will find it, Khalid. Gather the men that you need and travel to Mexico. Be sure that you keep me informed of your progress. Although I need not say it, please be careful. You are far more valuable to me than one thousand mujahideen."

Khalid rose from his chair and embraced his mentor. "*Ma'a as-salaama,* Goodbye, Abdul."

"*Rihla muwaffaqah*, successful journey, my friend."

CHAPTER 4

Aleppo, Syria

Sebastian opened his eyes and the darkness gave way to a bright white light. He winced and quickly turned his head to the right while his left hand shot upward to block out the blinding light.

"Owwww!" he exclaimed as he tucked his chin into his chest, trying to see where the source of the horrific pain was coming from. His eyes fixed on the white mass of bandages extending from his chest to his chin. "What the hell?"

It was like there was a giant cloud in his mind that was keeping him from remembering what had happened and why the bandages were there.

"Well, look who's back from the dead," said Coop. "It's damn good to see ya, Sarge. You had me scared there for a little while. I thought you were just going to sleep away the rest of the war."

Will Cooper slid his hands forward quickly and sent the front wheels of his wheelchair shooting upwards toward the sky. He rode the wheelie across the room toward Sebastian.

"Will, what happened?" Sebastian asked eying the wheelchair.

"Will? Since when do you call me Will?" asked Coop.

"Since you're in a freaking wheelchair, that's when!"

"Oh, this? I pick this up at the front door every time I come to see you. There's a ton of them up there and the nurses dig it. I've gotten three dates with this thing," said Coop, smiling from ear to ear.

"You mook! You scared the shit out of me."

"I think that's what the catheter is for, Sarge," quipped Copper.

The fog in Sebastian's head was beginning to clear and he started to remember the house. "What about Wiz and Elroy?"

A somber look came over Coop and he shook his head from side to side. "They didn't make it, Sarge. It's just you and me. For a while it looked like it was just going to be me. The doc said that if the bullet had hit you a half inch lower it would've got your heart and a half inch higher? It would have taken out your carotid artery. They didn't know if you were gonna make it for a long time. I told them that you didn't have a heart, so you would pull through."

"How long have I been out?"

"Too long. Six days."

"Oh man. Coop, I'm sorry," said Sebastian. He could feel a lump starting to swell in his throat as he tried to fight off the wave of emotion that was surging over his body.

"Sorry for what?"

"I got everyone killed. Eddie, Hollywood, Doc, Boom, Wiz, and Elroy. It's all my fault. If I had just..."

"Hey, Sarge!" said Coop as he wheeled over to the bed. He locked eyes with Sebastian. "You didn't do anything wrong. That wasn't a patrol that we ran into. That was an ISIL surge. They were trying to take the city. That's why it took so long to get our extraction. Army Intelligence said that there were over a hundred Muji's in our grid alone. They wiped out all the FSA troops to our west. We... *You* did exactly what we needed you to do. It was just bad luck. Our guys died because it's war. And we all knew what could happen going in. The way I see it, you saved my life and you never have to apologize for that."

"Thanks," said Sebastian, the emotion still trying to consume him, "But I know that there was something that I should have done better. Something that would have kept them alive."

"Yeah, well, you're high on morphine. Now quit feeling sorry for yourself. Once you get up and about, I'll get you one of these," Coop said, pointing down at his wheelchair, "and we can go score some nurses."

 Sebastian laughed and then said, "Don't make me laugh. It hurts."

"Roger that, Sarge. No jokes... no nurses... no fun," said Coop as he wheeled towards the door.

"Hey Coop," Sebastian said. "What were those guys doing in that house? There are no residents left in Al-Dana and they were definitely not ISIL foot soldiers."

Cooper whirled his wheelchair around. "Don't know, Sarge. All I know is that they were in a hurry to get out of there when they saw us and they didn't want anyone to know what was upstairs because they burned down the whole house. And that only one of them got out of there alive." Coop grinned again.

"Hooah," said Sebastian, smiling back at his friend. As Sebastian watched Coop wheel himself through the doorway, he closed his eyes and let himself slip away into the darkness.

Sebastian awoke to the most beautiful face that he had ever seen. The young woman staring back at him had perfect crystal blue eyes and her dark hair was pulled back.

"I must have died," he said, unable to turn his gaze from the beautiful woman staring down at him. "You're an angel, right?"

The nurse finished adjusting his blanket and smiled back at him. "No, honey, I'm no angel."

"Well, you look like an angel to me. What's your name?" inquired Sebastian.

She gave him a look that said *stop being naughty*. "I believe that is the morphine talking. My name is Claire. I'm your nurse, not your next date."

"Well, since I'm not dead, why not both?" Sebastian winked.

"Let me answer that for you, nurse."

Sebastian tried to sit up in order to see who the other voice belonged to. A sharp pain shot through his entire body and settled at a point that consumed the entire left side of his chest.

"Damn, that hurts," said Sebastian as he collapsed back into his pillows.

"Now don't go messing up all of my good work, Sergeant. That's an order. I'm Doctor Sanchez. Glad to see you finally up and awake. You were beginning to worry me. The reason that this beautiful young lady cannot be both your nurse and your date is because you are not strong enough for dating yet. The bullet that struck you pierced your left lung, causing it to collapse. Fortunately for you, it did not strike your aorta or carotid artery. I had to remove a portion of the upper lobe of your lung, but it should heal just fine. The pressure that you are feeling is from the chest tube that we have inserted into your chest cavity. It suctions out the air and fluids in your chest cavity which helps us keep your lung inflated."

"I won't have to keep this thing forever, will I, Doc?"

Doctor Sanchez gave Sebastian a comforting smile. "No. Once your lung heals and is healthy enough to remain inflated on its own, we will remove the tube."

"Cool," said Sebastian. "So Claire, it looks like we may have to wait a couple of days."

"Weeks," interjected the doctor.

"Weeks," corrected Sebastian. "Before we can have that date."

"My, you are a persistent one, aren't you, Sergeant?" Claire replied with a little laugh.

Sebastian gave her his biggest 'aw shucks' country boy smile. "Yes, ma'am. I am nothing if not persistent. Except maybe ruggedly handsome... and smart... funny... charming..."

"Slightly overconfident," Claire said smiling as she checked the tubes going to his IV. "I tell you what. If you're still alive in a few weeks, then maybe I will let you ask me out for coffee. But only then."

Doctor Sanchez shook his head and smiled at the couple. "If you two are done, then I would like to finish as well."

"Go right ahead, Doc. You have the floor," said Sebastian.

"Once the tube is removed, you will start respiratory therapy. We will start with deep breathing exercises and then walking and strength building exercises. If everything goes well, you will be back to full speed in about three to four months."

"So let me see if I've got this straight. In three to four months, Claire and I will line dancing at the rec center. Hell, I got that. If I am anything, it's persistent."

"Well you're close, Sergeant. In three to four months you can be line dancing, but probably not with Claire. Once you are able to be transported, you will be sent back to the States. You're going home."

Sebastian looked at Doctor Sanchez like he had just been punched in the nose. "You kinda buried the lead there, Doc." He looked over at

Claire. "We don't have much time, angel. Doc, do you think we can hold off on that transfer paperwork until after the first date?"

CHAPTER 5
Detroit, Michigan

Dennis Johnson sat nervously in the Defendant's chair, contemplating his future. His attorney, Chet Davis, was a court appointed defender. Chet was a decent guy, he guessed, but he knew that Chet would end up trying to make him take a plea bargain just like all the other court appointed defenders had done in the past. Dennis had just had his eighteenth birthday and this time it was different. He was an adult now. He would have to do real time.

If only he had stayed home that day. When Deonte and Terry had showed up in that stolen Escalade, he should have just stayed home. But did he? No. He'd hopped right in and gone along for the ride. He hadn't even gone into the store with them. He'd stayed out in the parking lot, smoking his Cool menthol and minding his own business. Next thing he'd known, the cops had been sweeping into the parking lot. He hadn't even had a chance to run. He hadn't known Terry and Deonte were going to rob the store, but he had been there. Now he was going to jail for a long time.

Judge Simons walked into the courtroom and the bailiff told the court to rise and then to be seated. Dennis sat nervously, rubbing his hands together under the table, and looked at his attorney. "Chet, man, I can't do no hard time. You can't plea this thing out. I didn't do nuthin." The bailiff announced his case as the People versus Dennis Johnson. "This time," he added.

Chet did not have a chance to reply before Judge Simons began to speak. "Before we get started, I would like to see both attorneys in my chambers."

Dennis placed his elbows on the table and rested his forehead on his hands. Looking down at the table, he let out a sigh and closed his eyes. He knew that this could not be a good sign. "Chet, don't leave me hangin', man."

"Don't worry, Dennis, I have this. I will take care of you," Chet replied as he headed toward the oak door behind the judge's bench.

Judge Simons sat down in the plush leather chair behind his large office desk. As he leaned back in his chair, he placed his hands on the back of his head with his elbows outward.

"Gentlemen, the way I see it, this kid was in the wrong place at the wrong time. It appears to me that, while his friends were intent on committing a crime, he had no idea what they were doing."

"Your Honor," interjected Assistant District Attorney Henry Sikes. "The Defendant has a long juvenile history of burglary, theft, assault and various other misdemeanors. It is more likely that he was the lookout for his conspirators than he was in the wrong place at the wrong time. Furthermore,…"

"Mister Sikes, when I want you to speak I will let you know," said the judge, cutting him off in mid-sentence. "Chet, was he apprehended in the parking lot, smoking a cigarette with headphones on?"

"Yes, Judge, he was."

"That's not much of a lookout. He was raised in Osborn and gets caught smoking a cigarette. C'mon, Henry, every seven-year-old in Osborn knows how to be a lookout. Especially if his friends are robbing the damn store. You are going to have to do a lot better than that. Plus, I have seen his jacket. There was nothing serious in it. No more than you had in yours when you were his age. You grew up here and look how you turned out."

"I went to college when I was his age, Judge." Sikes felt Judge Simon's menacing look burn through him. "I apologize, Your Honor. I thought that was meant for my response."

"I am well aware of your history, Henry. I wrote the letter of recommendation that got you into law school. You had the benefit of basketball to get you out of Detroit. If not for your scholarship to Oklahoma State, you might have been the lookout. This kid, Dennis, he doesn't have a scholarship. He doesn't even have a manufacturing job to look forward to anymore because ninety percent of those have been shipped out of state due to the unions just about bankrupting the auto makers. All he has is a bleak future and no path available to him that could take him to Oklahoma State, or even State College for that matter. He has six point five miles of the deadliest zip code in Detroit. There were thirty-eight shootings in Osborn last month and that was a slow month. There are no jobs available to speak of and all of his friends are either dead, in jail or headed to jail. He has grown up knowing that he will get none of the opportunities that will allow him to get out of here and yet, at the age of eighteen, he still hasn't joined a gang or committed a serious felony. I am tired of sending decent kids to jail just to have them come out as trained, hardened criminals."

Henry Sikes raised his right hand like a student in class. "Your Honor, you don't mean to tell me that you want to set this kid free?" He could feel the heat emanating from the judge's stare.

"Don't be absurd, Henry. If I let him go without any punishment, he will just end up back here in a few months having committed a more serious crime. Have you not been listening? There have been more murders committed in the 48205 zip code than any other zip code in the nation. The problem isn't the kids. It's the city. Detroit is a war zone that has become as bad as Kabul, Fallujah or Al-Dana."

Chet raised his hand as if to ask for permission to speak. "Judge, in Dennis' defense. He is a good kid. He joined a church this last year and goes faithfully. He hasn't been in any trouble since he was fourteen. He really was in the wrong place at the wrong time."

Judge Simons shot Chet a glare that made him feel extremely uncomfortable. "You two really need to learn not to interrupt me when I am speaking."

"Yes, Judge," they replied in unison.

"Now where was I? Oh yeah, the problem is the city. And the fact that there are no opportunities for these kids. And the fact that there is no way for them to get out of the city in order find an opportunity. Now obviously I cannot allow this young man to go back out on the streets unpunished. The Grand Jury has deemed this a worthy case to be tried. Chet, you can take your chances with a jury, if you so choose, but I would like to offer a suggestion as to a plea deal. One that will give your client a chance for a real life. I propose a Deferred Adjudication that will allow Mr. Johnson to enlist in the U.S. Military. Upon the honorary discharge from the branch of his choice, all charges against him will be dismissed. If for some reason he fails to enlist, or receives a dishonorable discharge, he will be charged and convicted of armed robbery. A felony which carries a sentence of two years to life."

Henry Sikes stood up from his chair. "So Judge, you're telling me to offer everybody that comes before the court the opportunity to join the army? That's absurd!"

"No, Henry. I'm telling you to offer *this* kid, this one good kid who was in the wrong place at the wrong time, an opportunity to get the hell out of this diseased city and make something useful out of his life. Consider it his Oklahoma State basketball scholarship." Judge Simons stood up and casually started to walk around his desk toward the door leading back into the courtroom. "So what do you say, boys? Is this deal acceptable?"

"Yes, Judge. I can make this work," replied Sikes.

"I will have to ask Mr. Johnson, Your Honor, but I am sure that he will take it over the alternative," said Chet.

"Alright then. Let's get back to work," said Judge Simons as he motioned toward the door.

Chet walked back quickly to the Defendant's table. "Dennis, I have a plea deal for you that will not require you to do any time in jail."

Dennis listened intently as Chet described the details of the plea deal and quickly agreed to the terms.

Judge Simons slammed his gavel. "I understand that there is a plea deal in this case. Do both parties agree to the deal?"

Henry Sikes nodded approval and responded, "Yes, Your Honor, the State agrees to the deal."

"Yes, I agree, Your Honor," affirmed Dennis.

"Good. Mr. Johnson, you have been given an opportunity that most young men in your position are rarely given. You have an opportunity to completely escape the life path that you are obviously headed down. I suggest that you use your opportunity to escape this city and never come back. If I ever see you back in this courtroom, I will levy against you the heaviest penalty afforded to me by the laws of the State of Michigan. Do I make myself perfectly clear?"

Dennis' face almost glowed with delight as he shifted his weight back and forth between his two feet. "Yes, sir, Your Honor, sir. I won't disappoint you, sir," replied Dennis excitedly. "I will never be in here again, sir."

Forty minutes later, Dennis stepped off the bus and turned right on Dorothy Street. He had joined the mosque during his senior year of high school. It had given him a refuge from the harshness of the streets. Osborn, Michigan, was not that bad during the daytime, but at night all hell would break loose. Tiki, Dennis' mother, worked two jobs trying to make ends meet and was hardly ever at home. Dennis was the third of four children. His older brother, Darrell, was serving two years at the Baraga Correctional Facility for dealing heroin. Danecia, his older sister had moved to Dearborn and his baby sister had been killed four years ago in a drive-by shooting. Having never known who his father was, Dennis had been alone for most of his life.

In contrast to the harsh and unforgiving world of Osborn, the mosque had given him a refuge. A safe place where he could study and discuss the Quran. He fit in easily with the mostly Yemeni population that lived in and around the neighborhood surrounding the mosque. Imam Suhaib Abdullah had taken him under his wing and taught him the wisdom of the Prophet Muhammad. Suhaib taught Dennis how Islam took care of all who believe. He also enlightened Dennis to all of the ways that the government of the United States failed its citizens. However, Dennis did not need much more exposure to the failings of the government than the experiences he had from his own life. Sharia law, as it was applied in the neighborhoods around the mosque, had brought peace and prosperity to a section of

Detroit known to be one of the most violent and desolate in the entire city. Islam had made an oasis in a desert of hopelessness.

Dennis pushed open the door to the mosque and quickly walked inside. As he entered the great room, he weaved in and out of the tables that had been set up. It was Tuesday and the *masjid* hosted a dinner for the worshippers just after *Maghrib* and *Isha,* which were the last two prayers of the day. He swiftly navigated the tables and dashed through the rear door which led to a hallway where Imam Suhaib Abdullah's office was located. He bolted through the door and found the Imam sitting behind his desk.

"Imam Suhaib, you won't believe it, man, I'm not going to jail. I got this sweet deal and not a single day of jail time."

Suhaib stood up and began to walk around the desk. "That is wonderful news. Dennis. Please sit down and tell me how this has come to be."

"All praise is to Allah. Cuz I just knew I was goin' to jail, even though I didn't do nuthin' but ride with those two jokers. With my history and the fact that them fools was usin' guns, shoot, I knew I was a goner. But as soon as my case was called, the judge called back both attorneys to his chambers. I was thinkin' like, oh shit... I'm sorry about that. I mean, oh crap, this can't be good. So anyway, they stay back there a long time and I'm thinking theys gonna throw the book at me. Well, they come out and BAM! Chet, my attorney, he tells me how they done made this kickin' deal. I don't do a day of jail time. All I gotta do is enlist and do three years in any branch that I want and when I get out all the charges is dropped."

"That is definitely good news, Dennis. Allah works in mysterious ways. I believe that military service will have its benefits for you. It will train you and give you skills that you can use after you return. Maybe you can become a mechanic and work on cars."

"Or maybe I become a kick ass soldier and I can go to Raqqa and fight against the oppressive government of Syria. Aww, man," said Dennis as his cheeks started to feel hot. "I cursed again. I'm real sorry about that, Suhaib. I'm workin' on it."

"It is quite alright, Dennis. I was once young myself." Suhaib was stroking his long, salt and pepper beard. "Believe it or not, I was a lot like you in my youth. I am very happy for this fortunate turn of events. Our talks had begun to prepare you for life in prison. I am afraid I have not prepared you for life in military service. They will try to brainwash you and trick you into thinking that the military and the government of the United States is the only important thing in the world. Do not let them. Remember that there is no God but Allah and Muhammad is his messenger. Your faith is the most important thing."

"Man, don't you worry about that. I know that the only reason I ain't in prison is cuz Allah saved me."

Suhaib started writing something on the notepad located on his desk. Once finished, he tore the paper from the pad and handed it to Dennis.

"Dennis, this is the e-mail address of a dear friend of mine. His name is Khalid. He is a great man and a true believer. He will be able to help you with your transition into the military. I want you to contact him as soon as you get home after prayer tonight. I am thrilled to hear of this great news." Suhaib stood up and opened his arms wide. He embraced Dennis, giving him a strong hug. "*Allahu Akbar.* God is the greatest."

CHAPTER 6
Chicago, Illinois

"You want some of me? Alright then, get you some of this."

Malik Faraj was playing basketball in his driveway with his best friend, Dominique. Malik had lived in South Shore his entire life. South Shore was once an exceptional Chicago community. When Malik's parents first moved to South Shore, it was a haven for predominantly middle class Afro-American families. Over the last decade, the average family income had been on the decline. More families like Dominique's had moved into South Shore as they became capable of escaping from the public housing deeper inside the city. Although crime was on the rise, South Shore was still a decent place to live. Dominique had moved next door five years ago and the two had been inseparable ever since.

Dominique slid left and put his hand down low to steal the ball from Malik.

"What you got sucker? You don't want none of this." He shifted his weight to the right and turned as Malik crossed the ball over to his left hand and darted toward the basket. "Damn!" he said as Malik jammed the ball through the basket. "I can't believe you're leaving me, man. That's just not right. We had a plan, remember?"

Dominique dribbled the ball to his right. Malik slid to his left and placed his hand on Dominique's back.

"I know man, but things change." He stepped back toward the basket as Dominique drove him backwards with a post-up move.

"Like what changed?" asked Dominique spinning to his left.

"Like you getting a football scholarship to Florida." Malik moved left to block him.

"You could come too," said Dominique spinning back to his right.

"Yeah, right. Like my parents can afford to send me to college in Florida." Malik moved right and raised both hands up in the air. "I'm a city college guy at best."

Dominique took one step backwards and leaped into the air, shooting the ball with a flick of his wrist.

"Swoosh. Nothing but net. That's game, homey." Dominique followed Malik to the garage and the two took a seat on the ground. "Okay, maybe. But did you have to join the army? I figured you growing up going to that Muslim school you would be anti-army everything."

Malik had gone to the Muhammed University of Islam his entire life. He was third generation Muslim. His grandparents had studied under Elijah Mohammed and his parents had studied under Louis Farrakhan at the Mosque Maryam located next door to his school. When he was younger, his grandparents had repeatedly told him the story of how Elijah Muhammad had placed an MUI next to every mosque during his creation of the Nation of Islam.

"Well I'm not. Being Muslim doesn't make you un-American. Or a punk for that matter. Muhammed Ali was Muslim."

"Yeah, but he wouldn't go fight in the Army. Killing is supposed to be against your religion," said Dominique.

"Don't worry about me. I don't have any plans on fighting. I was thinking about becoming an MP. That way I can become a cop when I get out." Malik sucked down half of his bottle of Gatorade.

"Or you can be my bodyguard when I go pro." Dominique smiled and slid up off of the ground. "I just wish you weren't leaving so soon. You realize that we only got one week left to hang out? That sucks."

"I wish we had more time too. But you leave for Florida in two weeks anyway." Malik finished off the Gatorade that was left in his bottle and replaced the lid.

Dominique began walking down the driveway. "I gotta jet before my mom starts hollering that it's dinner time. I'll catch you tomorrow."

"You got it. I'll see you tomorrow." Malik turned and walked inside his house.

He tossed the empty Gatorade bottle into the trash can on his way through the kitchen and climbed the stairs leading up to his bedroom. Malik closed his bedroom door and reached over to turn on his television and Xbox. He shuffled backward until he reached the beanbag chair sitting in front of his bed and plopped down into it. Grabbing the controller, he navigated the menu to his messages. His heart skipped a beat when he saw that he had a new message from VitalManiac2183.

"Man, I been waiting for you to get back with me," he said as he clicked the message to open it.

Malik, I am most excited about your choice in joining the army, he read. *I am pleased to see that you followed my advice. I have done the research for you and you will want to request that your Military Occupational Specialty be with the Military Police. I am organizing a private Xbox party for all of our loyal servants who are joining the military. Look for your invitation soon. May God keep you safe. Your friend, Khalid.*

An Xbox party was an event that could be set up from anyone's Xbox. They could invite their friends to play a game or enjoy a group chat. It was completely private and left no traces, like internet chat rooms did. Nobody other than the participants would be able to see or hear what they were saying.

"This is awesome," thought Malik. "*Allahu Akbar.*"

CHAPTER 7
Jiménez, Coahuila, Mexico

Khalid was seated in a lavish leather chair, staring out of the large bay window located in the great room of Juan Carlos Real's Hacienda. He carefully studied all twenty of his men who were lounging around the Olympic-sized pool. Some were enjoying the company of the many females staying at the Hacienda, courtesy of Juan Carlos. He was an excellent host who knew how to treat his guests properly. The women also provided an opportunity for Khalid's men to practice their Spanish. Khalid had forbidden the men from speaking anything else since leaving Syria.

The cool blue water looked inviting. He was weary from his journey and the pool reminded him of his own back in Al-Dana. How he missed his morning swims. It had taken eight days to reach

Mexico, a trek which took them from Syria through Saudi Arabia, Yemen and Egypt, collecting new members at each stop.

From Egypt they had flown to Cuba. Khalid hated Cuba. After the Death of Fidel Castro, the dictator's brother, Raul, had taken over. As it was with the death of any dictator, the successor was not as strong as the former. Cuba was already beginning to fall apart. If not for its proximity to Mexico, which made it a valuable waypoint in transporting their heroin, it would have no value whatsoever.

Unlike his brother, Fidel, Raul Castro had no apprehension about illegal narcotics. The new dictator relished the money that he received from the Al-Yad. Castro also gave the Al-Yad a strategic position from which they could operate under the nose of the Great Satan. From Cuba they had sailed into Tampico, Mexico and on to Jiménez.

As Khalid reached for his teacup, Juan Carlos came rushing into the room.

"Khalid, my good friend. How are you doing? I apologize for my tardiness. I was at the opening of one of my new hospitals and the ceremony ran long. You know how it goes with bureaucrats."

Khalid rose out of his chair to greet Juan Carlos. "Think nothing of it, my friend. Your hospitality has been most gracious." He spoke in perfect Spanish.

Juan Carlos placed his hands on Khalid's shoulders. "Let me look at you. You are as handsome as ever." Juan Carlos was a passionate man whose charisma was contagious. "Did you know that without your beard you look like Enrique Iglesias? And your Spanish is perfect. You have even managed a good Coahuilan accent. Maybe you want to come live here with me? No?"

Khalid gazed at Juan Carlos, whose brown eyes were smiling back at him. "Juan Carlos, I have never known a time when you did not greet me with a sincere compliment. It is no wonder that you are so loved by your people. It is truly an honor to know such a great man."

"Now it is you who flatters me. My home is at your disposal, for you and your men. However, I did not expect you to have such a large entourage. When you asked me to get you across the border, I did not expect so many people."

"Will this be too difficult for you to accomplish, Juan Carlos?" Khalid returned to the lounge chair. "You had given me assurances that you would be able to accommodate as many people as I needed. That is how I was able to provide you with your weapons. The Al-Yad absorbed the price of the weapons in exchange for passage and documentation."

Juan Carlos sat down on the matching leather sofa and turned to face Khalid. "This is no problem, my friend. Twenty people is no problem. I will have everything you need waiting for you when you arrive in the United States. Hell, fifty people is no problem. It is just that I did not have the maids prepare so many rooms. They are almost done now. The problem with such a large house is that you rarely use all of the bedrooms."

As I told you though, it will be a few more days until our tunnel is finished. We are not like the Sinaloa Cartel. We do not have one hundred miles of open border land that we just let people run across. We have the Rio Bravo or, as the Americans call it, the Rio Grande River, which separates us from the United States. The cliffs on either side of the river are hundreds of feet high and there are fences guarding the cliffs on both sides. Crossing into the United States is not as easy as just swimming across the river. In the past we have had to use Coyotes, or smugglers, who could escort our honest working Coahuilans over the border in New Mexico through Sinaloa territory. But once we have our tunnel finished, you and your men will be the first ones to pass. It will be a wonderful day."

Khalid sipped his tea and held the cup in both hands just above his lap. "It will be a most wondrous day indeed, Juan Carlos. I presume that this tunnel is safe. If the river stands between Mexico and the United States, I am a bit perplexed as to how you built a tunnel."

"It is perfectly safe, Khalid. It is an ingenious creation that I owe all to my nephew Santiago. He is a smart one, that Santiago. Thanks to him we were able to build the tunnel underneath the river. Like that tunnel in New York City that goes under the Hudson River. It is amazing to see. Tomorrow we will go to my plant and you can see for yourself. Now about my weapons - when can I expect them to arrive?"

"I look forward to seeing this astounding tunnel. As for your weapons, they will be here within two weeks. We had a shipment en route to Nigeria which we redirected to you. Thus there has been a slight delay due to the change in course. Now, if you do not mind, Juan Carlos, I am weary from my journey and would like to rest before dinner."

"Why certainly, Khalid, I will show you to your room," said Juan Carlos as he rose from the leather sofa.

The men walked toward the hallway, allowing Khalid to take in the beauty of the Hacienda. The white stone walls stood in contrast with the dark tile floor and wooden ceilings.

"Juan Carlos, I could not help but notice these exquisite sculptures."

"Yes, my friend. They were made by the famous Mexican artist Leonora Carrington just for me as a housewarming gift. She was a good friend of mine, God bless her soul."

As they walked down the wide hall, Khalid inquired again: "And these sketches and paintings lining the hallway, are they originals also?"

"Yes, the paintings on the right are by the Spanish painter Francisco José de Goya and the paintings on the left are by Diego

Velázquez. Each of the bedrooms has their own artist from Coahuila, like Xavier Guerrero, who was from San Pedro, Rodolfo Escalera from Torreon and Diego Rivera from Ciudad Acuna. It makes me happy that you would notice such things, my friend. You have a definite eye for the small details."

"That reminds me, were you able to acquire the items that I requested?"

The men approached the immense bedroom that Juan Carlos had designated for Khalid and he motioned towards the seventy-inch high definition television mounted on the wall. "I have everything that you requested. Although I must be honest with you, I did not take you for a video gamer. I purchased for you the newest Xbox One. I did not know what games you preferred, so I bought one of each."

"Thank you, Juan Carlos. That is most excellent. I will see you at dinner, my good friend."

Khalid closed the door and turned toward the bed. He found the remote control lying on the luxurious, handcrafted king-sized bed and let down the wooden window blinds to block out the light of the southern sun. He lay down upon the black sheets. The custom made one-thousand thread count sheets were compromised of one-hundred percent pure Egyptian cotton and had fourteen carat gold woven directly into the fabric. He would indeed rest well. Maybe after dinner he would partake in the comforts of the swimming pool. He released an uncontrollable yawn and his thoughts swiftly left as he allowed himself to collapse into a deep sleep.

CHAPTER 8
Jiménez, Coahuila, Mexico

Santiago strode into the dining room.

"*Buenos días,* uncle, how are you today?" He set his cup of coffee on the table as he took his seat next to Juan Carlos. "I've asked Tito to ready the vehicles for our trip to the plant. Do you know how many will be joining us? It appears that our guest has brought quite an entourage." The cook arrived, placing a full plate in front of Santiago. "Thank you, Alma. It looks delicious."

Juan Carlos finished chewing his *huevos rancheros*, a traditional Mexican breakfast meal consisting of fried eggs served atop of lightly fried corn tortillas and topped with chili sauce.

"I am not sure how many will be coming with us this morning. Khalid did not make it to dinner last night. He must have been *muy cansado.*"

"I was very tired, Juan Carlos," explained Khalid as he walked toward the table. He was dressed in black jeans, a white T-shirt and wore a blue scarf wrapped around his neck. "And the accommodations that you have provided me were so luxurious that I slept completely through the night. That is something that I have not done in a number of years. I am in your debt for giving me such a rare pleasure." Khalid placed his left hand on his chest as a sign of his sincerity. "You must be the infamous Santiago that Juan Carlos has been telling me about."

Santiago arose from his chair and turned to face Khalid. As he extended his right hand, he thought to himself that his uncle was right: with his high cheekbones and medium cut black hair, Khalid really did look like Enrique Iglesias. "Well, I don't know about infamous, but I am Santiago. You must be Khalid. It is my honor to meet such a great man."

Khalid smiled and turned to Juan Carlos. "He certainly has your charm."

Juan Carlos leaned back in his chair. "He has my charm, but his brains, those he got from his mother. My sister was always much smarter than me. That is why she became the University Professor and I became..." Juan Carlos paused. "I became what I became."

"I believe, Uncle, that you underestimate just how smart you really are. You had the intelligence to become the richest and most beloved in man in all of Coahuila. Most men from Piedra Negras never meet anyone who wasn't born and raised there. And here you are with an esteemed guest from the other side of the world. That cannot be discounted as pure luck." Santiago sat back down and dug his fork into his plate. "Now let's finish this fine meal, or Alma will have our heads."

"And he is a natural born politician to boot," laughed Juan Carlos.

"Indeed he is," laughed Khalid as he took his seat.

Alma, the cook, was a short woman standing about five foot two inches tall and was nearly as broad as she was tall. She served Khalid his plate of food.

"I hope you like it, *señor*."

"If it is one half as delicious as you are beautiful, Madame, I am sure that I will," replied Khalid as he positioned his napkin in his lap.

Alma slapped Khalid lightly on the shoulder. "*Señor*, stop, or you will make me blush," she said and headed toward the kitchen.

"Now who is the politician? You had better watch yourself, Khalid, I think she is in love with you," prodded Santiago.

"I have always been a firm believer in making sure that the cook is happy. You are much less likely to be poisoned that way." Khalid spoke with such a straight face that Juan Carlos and Santiago shared a long pause before all three men laughed in unison. "As to your other question, I will be the only one visiting the tunnel. My men have no reason to be there until it is time for them to use it."

The men finished their meals and walked down the long hallway toward the elevator which led down to the garage. The garage was a massive structure that contained over thirty vehicles. As the men walked to the armored Suburbans that would take them to their destination, Khalid noticed a nineteen sixty-four Corvette, a nineteen sixty-seven Pontiac GTO and a nineteen seventy Plymouth Barracuda mixed in along with a Ferrari, Porsche and various high end vehicles.

"You have a very nice collection of automobiles, Juan Carlos."

"Why thank you, Khalid. That yellow one over there," he said, pointing to his right, "is a Mastretta MXT made right here in Mexico. It is the first Mexican car made without any influence from foreign car makers. I own one half of the company, so naturally it is the first one ever produced." Juan Carlos opened the rear door of the pearl SUV for Khalid and Santiago. "After you, gentlemen."

Once the men were inside, Juan Carlos looked toward Khalid. "If you do not mind my asking, Khalid, why do you need IDs for you and your men? You are not the first member of Al-Qaeda, Hezbollah or Hamas to ask me to take them across the border. It seems to be a desirable vacation destination for people from your side of the world. Naturally I have refused in the past because the United States has always left me alone to conduct my business and I did not want to poke the bear. But none of them ever asked me to obtain identification papers for them."

"Juan Carlos, it would not be prudent, for either of us, to lay out my entire plan. If any of my men or I were to be captured, then the less you know the better off you will be. I will tell you that, unlike the others who have approached you, we plan on staying in the United States. Although I am not, some of my men are on the no fly list, therefore we must resort to asking you to help us across the border. I assure you that we do not plan to be suicide bombers. My plan is intricate and requires for us to be in the United States legally. Fortunately for me, President Adama has practically opened his southern border and invited us into the country. First, he sent his open invitation to every country south of the United States to send their children. Most recently he made an Executive Order offering resident status not only to the thousands of children who have flooded into his country, but also to any illegal immigrant who has been in the country for at least five years. Once he signed his Executive Order, it became time for us to enter the country."

"That is good enough for me, my friend. I have been providing papers for my Coahuilans for years. One day there is going to be a thousand or so people in America who get very large Social Security checks because we have used their Social Security numbers for millions of Mexicans who now reside illegally in the United States. Not that I would use this method for you. Your papers will be much easier. I will provide you a driver's license, paycheck stubs along with a letter from your employer, utility bills and whatever else is required. Like I said, I have tens of thousands of Coahuilans living in America, so I can easily provide you with IDs and work histories going back five or more years."

Khalid seemed surprised by Juan Carlos' statements. "The United States has never caught on to the fact that millions of people are using just a few Social Security numbers? That seems amazing to me."

"They are too big, my friend. The Social Security Administration and IRS just process numbers. Once they realize that they have made a mistake, it is too late. I have one address every year, which I move from state to state, where I have my Coahuilans' income tax checks mailed to. Even the ones who do not have papers and have not had taxes taken out of their checks. By time they get their earned child income credits, it adds up. Last year the IRS mailed me sixteen million dollars. They realized that they had sent sixteen million dollars to one address in August, but by then I had sold the house and the money was sitting comfortably in my bank account in the Cayman Islands. The Social Security Administration catches on to us a little better, but all they do is mail a notice to the employers that the Social Security numbers are no good. The employers tell my people. My people get new numbers and everybody is happy. The best thing is that it's not just me. All the cartels do it."

Khalid shook his head in disbelief. "That is simply amazing. It seems impossible to believe that a country which has the ability to mobilize five-hundred thousand troops and send them halfway around the world in less than five days can be so inept with its money."

Juan Carlos smirked at Khalid's comment. "It's the bureaucracy and the politicians. If they streamlined the government like a business, it would be more efficient. But the bureaucrats only want to keep their jobs. So one department watches another department who watches another department. But nobody watches the money. Which is good for me." His face took on a more somber expression. "The military, on the other hand. That's one thing that the Americans know how to do well. They are the big dog, like Cujo from the Stephen King movie - part dog, part bear and part lion all rolled into one. When they decide that they want to kick you in the *cajones,* you had best watch out. America has been the Cujo for a long time and they do it well."

"I have first-hand knowledge of their military prowess," said Khalid. "It is an awesome force. They are well trained. It is their politicians and politically correct citizens who think that war is wrong that will ultimately be their demise. They do not realize that war is the only way to accomplish the goal."

"Which goal would that be, Khalid?" Santiago asked.

"Control of the world, of course, Santiago. Is it not the ultimate goal of all nations to be supreme above all others? Would it not make sense for the entire world to come together under the banner of one Caliphate or government? Would it not prevent all the wars that are currently happening and have happened in the past?"

"I guess that would depend upon who was in control," replied Santiago. "But I do not think that it will ever happen. Even if it did, it would not last for long. Maybe a hundred years, maybe a hundred and fifty."

"How so?"

"If the ruling government and people were too civilized, then eventually the less civilized members of society would end up taking over through civil war. Like Rome falling to the barbarians - except the barbarians would actually be a part of Rome. It's kinda like you said. When they stop believing in the usefulness of war and violence, they set themselves up for defeat." Santiago leaned in toward Khalid.

"If the ruling government was too barbaric and ruled through fear, it too would eventually lead itself to civil war. Pick any country in Africa as an example. Either way, you will eventually have people who completely disagree with the government to the point of civil war. Not to mention that whether civilized or barbarian, you have a proximity problem. It will be virtually impossible to control an area the size of the world. With six continents and a metric ton of little islands, it's just too big. Every great Empire - Egyptian, Roman, Persian, and British - they all fell because they became too big. The United States can't even keep track of everybody and everything within its borders and it makes up only about half of one continent. So as appealing as control of the world sounds, I think it is virtually impossible to achieve. You might be able to do it for a few generations. But I believe that it would still end with civil war and dismantle itself. I think it would be best just to carve out your own little section of the world like my uncle has in Coahuila and take care of that. Let the rest of the world deal with its own crap. And if their crap spills over into your section of the world, then you take them out."

Khalid smiled at Santiago. "Your uncle was correct, Santiago. You are very intelligent. That was quite an astute argument for such a young man."

"Thank you, sir."

The SUV rounded the corner and proceeded toward the front gate of the concrete plant. Juan Carlos turned to the two men. "You two are like Socrates and Aristotle. As much as I hate to break up your philosophical debate, I must. We have arrived at our destination."

The Real Concrete Plant was located on Amistad Street in an industrial section of Ciudad Acuña. As the Suburban turned through the front gates of the plant, Khalid noticed that it was surrounded by eight-foot concrete barriers similar to the ones used by the United States in their Forward Operating Bases.

"What is this building to the right?" he asked, tapping the window toward the concrete building.

"That is the crew building. It is over one-thousand square feet and contains the manager's office, a dining hall, lounge, and locker room for the men. These are the silos where the concrete is mixed and loaded into the trucks," said Juan Carlos pointing to his left at the eight giant silos which separated the crew building from the enormous building on the other side. "And the building on the other side is the garage where we park our fleet. That is where we are going to now. I own the land all the way to the Rio Bravo. All totaled, it contains eleven hundred and twenty acres."

"I must admit this is quite impressive, Juan Carlos," remarked Khalid.

"This is my largest plant by far. It has been my pride and joy. From Acuna I provide service to both sides of the River. The concrete plants provide me with all of my money. The other businesses, they pay for the things that I do for Coahuila - the hospitals, the schools, the roads etcetera."

The SUV pulled into the massive garage which held the fleet of concrete and gravel trucks. The driver weaved his way through the giant trucks until they reached the southwest corner of the giant structure, where he stopped.

"Here comes the cool part," said Santiago with youthful exuberance. He pulled out a remote control from his pocket and pressed the button. Suddenly the ground underneath the SUV began to move downward. "We use an automobile lift to lower us down to the tunnel area," said Santiago as he opened the door and exited the vehicle. "C'mon, Khalid, step outside. You have to see this for yourself."

Khalid climbed out of the SUV and noticed that the platform they were on was large enough to carry at least one eighteen-wheeled dump truck.

"It is quite remarkable, Santiago. This platform is quite large."

"Look up," said Santiago, pointing toward the ceiling.

Khalid noticed that the ceiling was moving downward at the same pace as the lift. "Is the ceiling moving downward?"

"It certainly is," replied Santiago. "The upper platform lowers down to cover the hole in the floor. If for some reason the *Federales* were to raid us, they would not be able to find the tunnel."

"That is very impressive," remarked Khalid. The lift stopped and Khalid looked out into the massive cavern. It was as wide as two football fields and almost as deep. There was more than enough room for at least two dump trucks to maneuver easily inside the cave. At the northern end there was an opening leading into the tunnel. "And so is all of this," he said, opening his arms wide.

"This is nothing. Wait until you see the tunnel," said Juan Carlos as he walked off the platform and over to a small fleet of electric vehicles. He climbed into the driver's seat of one of the vehicles, with a GEM e4 decal, which looked like a Volkswagen Beetle except that it had no doors.

"Climb in. We will head to the other side."

Khalid climbed in next to Juan Carlos and Santiago seated himself in the rear seat.

"These things are awesome. You just plug them in and they charge on a regular outlet. It will go three miles before you have to charge it again and it goes 25 miles per hour. Best of all, it is as quiet as a church mouse. Unfortunately, our tunnel is two and a half miles long so we have to have more of them at the other end for the return trip. Those eL XDs over there," he said, pointing at the space-age looking trucks, also with no doors. "We will use them to transport the drugs. Each one can carry five-hundred kilos in the bed."

He pressed on the pedal and the car sped off toward the tunnel opening.

Once inside the tunnel, Khalid noticed that it was well lit with halogen lights. From inside the vehicle Khalid eyed the massive semi-circular tunnel cut into the earth. At eighteen feet wide and eighteen feet tall, at the highest point of the arc, the tunnel was as wide as a two lane road. The walls, ceiling and floor were lined with concrete.

"Juan Carlos, I believe that you misled me when you said that your tunnel was patterned after the tunnels leading from Palestine into Israel. I do not believe that Hamas has ever had anything like this."

"Believe it or not, this is all Santiago's doing," Juan Carlos said, nodding backwards toward his nephew. "He asked why we did not have tunnels like the Sinaloa Cartel. I told him that they did not have a river running along their border. So he asked me if he can figure out how to build under the river, can we build a tunnel? Well, me knowing him to be the smart kid he is, I say, sure we can. Two months later he comes back and tells me he has it all figured out. He read a story about how the Hamas had built tunnels and lined them with pre-fabricated concrete sections for support. He says to me that we have plenty of concrete at our disposal and handed me the specs for the pre-fabricated sections. Then he tells me to get started on those and he would order the equipment. And if everything went according to plan, he would have me a tunnel built in four months."

"All of this from one article?" Khalid shook his head. "Simply amazing."

He motioned toward a gray box about the size of circuit breaker box with a red button in the center and a clear Plexiglass cover over the front. "What are those?"

Santiago let a grin spread across his face. "Those are our insurance policy. There is a box every two-hundred yards. Each one is a detonator for C-4 plastic explosive charges which will collapse a section of the tunnel. In case we are discovered on the other side of the Rio Bravo, we can keep them from making it over to our side of the river."

"Also impressive. What about air? Is the tunnel open on the other side?" Khalid asked.

"No. The tunnel on the other side leads to a house in the Rancho Villa community development. The entire garage floor lowers down just like the one on our side," said Juan Carlos.

"Are you not worried about the neighbors getting suspicious or calling the police?" inquired Khalid.

"Not at all, my friend," replied Juan Carlos. "Fortunately for me, I own the company that is developing the community. Therefore I can also control how fast it is finished and I only allow my people to purchase the homes. Trust me, none of the neighbors will ever call the police because of suspicious activity."

Santiago leaned forward and put his hand on the back of Khalid's seat. "The air is another thing altogether. We have two buildings located at the back of the concrete plant with ten fans in each one. The fans pump air into the tunnel through vents located all along the tunnel and keep it circulating. There is plenty of breathable air. I patterned it after the Holland tunnel in New York City."

"Amazing," said Khalid. "And just how did you get the vents along the tunnel?"

"He used a horizontal drilling rig, like the ones they use for drilling for oil, and drilled each vent into the tunnel. Is that not super smart?" Juan Carlos boasted. "I'm telling you, that kid is a genius. Albert Einstein couldn't hold a candle to him."

"He is definitely a very intelligent boy," replied Khalid.

As they approached the end of the tunnel, Khalid noticed the dump truck first. It was being loaded with dirt and rubble by a conveyer belt which was attached to a futuristic looking machine. The machine had a base that sat upon a caterpillar track, like a tank, with a long boom. The boom was attached to a large, spiked metal ball. The ball was eating away at the rock. The rubble that fell was scooped up by a panel at the front of the giant machine and moved onto the conveyor belt leading to the dump truck.

"What in the world is that?"

"That," said Santiago, "is a roadheader. They are using them all over the world to dig subway tunnels. It can tunnel almost three hundred feet in a day. The telescopic boom allows it dig down at an angle. That's how we got the tunnel under the river from the cave. It also allowed us to keep the tunnel below forty feet, so that the Border Patrol's ground penetrating radar cannot detect the tunnel on the other side of the river."

"You developed all of this from one article about Hamas tunnels? That is most impressive, Santiago," stated Khalid.

"Thank you."

"I am hungry," said Juan Carlos. "How about we head back? I know this great little restaurant in town where the food is almost as fantastic as the women."

CHAPTER 9
Naval Air Station, Corpus Christi, Texas

Sean Ray propped his feet up on his metal office desk. He scanned the pages of his FAST team's recent action report, trying to understand exactly what went wrong. The ringing of the phone broke his concentration. He pulled the receiver up to his ear and said "DEA, FAST Team Four, Special Agent in Charge Sean Ray speaking."

"Sean, this is Inspector Gonzales. How are you today?"

"To tell you the truth, Hector, I am a little bored and a lot pissed off. I am going over the action report for Piedra Negras and I still can't for the life of me figure out how they found out we were coming. We have conducted missions in Afghanistan, Haiti and Honduras and not once encountered anything like this."

"Well, to be honest, Sean, the Taliban is not as sophisticated as the Cartels. And La Familia seems to know everything that goes on in

Coahuila. They have the best intelligence gathering out of all the Cartels. I have been conducting an internal investigation. However, I have not found the leak yet. But I do have something that might be of interest to you."

"Really? Whatcha got, Hector? I could be interested in just about anything right now."

"As you know, my division deals with all of the drug Cartels in Mexico, not just La Familia. I have just received word through a good source that the Gulf Cartel is about to move a large shipment of cocaine into the United States from Matamoros. I was wondering if you might be interested helping me stop them."

Special Agent Ray sat up in his chair, pulling his feet off his desk and onto the floor. "Well, hell yeah! You just tell me where and when and we'll be there, Hector."

"Our intel says that they are moving the drugs the day after tomorrow, by truck. It is coming up from Tampico into Matamoros. Am I correct in understanding that you have a predator drone at your headquarters there at the Navy Station? It would come in quite handy in trying to track down the truck."

Ray shook his head, even though he knew that Hector could not see him. "I'm sorry, Hector. That bad boy is on loan to the Border Patrol and they are very stingy with it. I might be able to get my hands on it if you want to wait until they cross the border to bust 'em. The Border Patrol will want to claim the credit for the bust if we use their toys. I do, however, have full time access to a badass satellite network - it's better than a drone any day of the week."

"Well then, by all means let's use the satellites. I don't want the Border Patrol to get any credit when it is us doing all of the work."

"Amen to that, Hector. We'll meet you first thing tomorrow morning in Matamoros."

CHAPTER 10
Jiménez, Coahuila, Mexico

Khalid was sitting cross-legged on the floor of the bedroom. He rubbed his eyes as he looked intently at the laptop in front of him, studying the itinerary of his fellow Al-Qaeda soldiers who were making their way into Mexico from the Middle East. He took a long drag of his cigarette as he listened to the young girl speaking through his headset. He was chatting with seven young American recruits who were eager to join the Navy. This was his third Xbox party of the evening and he was growing weary, as each one took about one hour. The girl's name was Maryam Saleh and she was from Aurora, Colorado. Maryam's parents were Yemeni immigrants who owned a motel. She had graduated in the top ten percent of her class at Aurora West College Preparatory Academy and she was very excited about joining the navy.

"I just can't believe that I have been given such a glorious opportunity," she said. "This is my chance to really make a difference in the world."

"Yeah. Me too," chimed in Quentin Morris. Quentin was from Cleveland, Ohio. A diehard Browns fan, he had always wanted to make a difference in the world like his hero Jim Brown. It was impossible to grow up in Cleveland without knowing of the legend of Jim Brown, the greatest football player to ever set foot on a football field, star in a movie, or walk on the planet Earth.

"It warms my heart that all of you are so devoted to Allah and the jihad," said Khalid, stroking his beardless chin. "I know that each of you will train very hard and become the finest of soldiers. The jihad can only be successful if we have the best soldiers. It is because of your devotion that I am certain of our imminent victory. The Caliphate would not be possible if Allah did not have loyal servants such as all of you."

Juan Carlos paced angrily back and forth in his office. The wooden soles of his boots made a harsh clopping sound with each step.

"What do you mean, you do not trust them, Santiago?" He asked. "The Al-Yad have been very trustworthy allies. Why now do you have your doubts?"

Santiago was sitting back in the hand-carved Don Shoemaker Descanso armchair, his right leg crossed over his left. "On the contrary, Uncle, the Al-Yad have been a good supplier of heroin. They have a product that they need to sell and we purchase that product. We have a good relationship with them because they need us, but that is as far as it goes. You heard what Khalid said, they want to take over the world and they only want Muslims in it. We are not Muslim and I, for one, will not become one. If by some chance they actually defeat the United States, how long do you think it will take them to start looking south toward us? They might spare us for as long as they need us. Long enough to defeat the Mexican Government and maybe Central America, but eventually they will turn on us."

"I think you are getting ahead of yourself, nephew. Even though they plan to attack the United States, it is hardly likely that they will be able to defeat them." Khalid had told Juan Carlos and Santiago about the Al-Yad's plan on the drive back to the Hacienda after lunch. His hopes were that he could persuade Juan Carlos to coordinate an attack upon the United States with the Al-Yad's attack.

"They will have a better chance if we attack at the same time. Which I strongly urge against. The Americans already know that we buy the heroin from Al-Qaeda. If they suspect that we have anything to do with an attack on American soil, they will come down here with their entire army, not just one DEA team, and they will kill us all - not put us in an American prison, but kill us, *finito*. Just like they did with Saddam Hussein and Osama bin Laden. Please remember Uncle that even though their President is a weak and cowardly man, the U.S. Military is the greatest army on the planet and they will not hesitate to eliminate every single person associated with an attack on their sovereign ground."

"If the Al-Yad's attack goes according to plan, then the Americans will have other things to worry about than us," replied Juan Carlos, still pacing on the hard wood floor.

Santiago leaned forward in his chair. "But why should we give them a reason to worry about us at all? If we do not attack as Khalid asks us to, then they will forget about us altogether. They will have to focus all of their attention on Al-Qaeda. Hector has already said that he can keep the DEA busy with the Gulf Cartel and take their focus off of La Familia. The Border Patrol do not know about the tunnel and will not find it, so we can continue to conduct business as usual while they fight the *Terroristas*. They will most likely send troops to the border to protect themselves from another attack, but they will not dare come across it for fear of the upsetting the Mexican Government. One thing is certain about the Americans, they don't want to piss anyone off, even if they are fighting a war. Besides, I don't think that the Al-Yad's plan will succeed to the extent that Khalid has led us to believe. I don't even think that he thinks it will. They might be able to hurt the United States, but they will not cripple it. And a wounded bear is more dangerous than a sleeping one."

Juan Carlos stopped pacing and smiled at his nephew. "Which is why we shouldn't go poking it. Okay, Santiago, I will take your advice and not attack the bear. Once again you have proven to me that you are wise beyond your years. But I must ask you to do something for me."

"Anything, Uncle."

"I want you to go with Khalid and aid him in his endeavor. Gain his trust. I need you to be my eyes and ears. If he plans on betraying me as you believe he will, then I want to know. I will tell him that we are not prepared to attack the Americans directly, but that we will provide him with the identities he needs to help him with his attack. You will go with him to make sure that he gets everything that he needs."

CHAPTER 11
Matamoros, Tamaulipas, Mexico

Sean Ray looked out at the horizon through the window of the Bell UH-1N Huey helicopter. His anticipation, clearly displayed in his emerald eyes, was shielded from his team by his wrap-around Oakley sunglasses. It always amazed him at how beautiful the world appeared from the sky. Flying at one hundred and twenty-five miles per hour caused the ground below blur into one smooth tract of land, making the world appear peaceful and uninhabited. The deafening noise of the engines made it impossible to carry on a conversation without the use of a headset, so Ray used the one-hour ride from Naval Air Station Corpus Christi to Matamoros to take in the beauty of the sky and to ponder his last mission in Mexico. He was still having difficulty coming to terms with the failure that he experienced in Piedra Negras.

As they approached the helipad located on the top of the Federal Police Headquarters, he let his thoughts return to the current mission. Matamoros was the base of operations for the Gulf Cartel and they were bringing a shipment of cocaine up from Tampico by truck. The mission of his FAST team, along with the *Policia Federal,* was to intercept the shipment of cocaine once it had made its way into Matamoros. That seemed simple enough, but so had Piedra Negras. He was going to make sure that they got it right this time.

The chopper set down on the enormous red H painted inside a giant yellow circle on the helipad. Inspector Hector Gonzales emerged to greet them from a metal door which led into the building. Dressed in their solid black urban assault uniforms, Ray and his team exited the door of the Huey. Ducking under the whirling blades, they headed toward the Inspector.

"It is good to see you again, Sean," Hector yelled over the noise of the helicopter. "Come inside and we can get you set up before the briefing."

As they entered the peace and quiet of the stairway, Ray removed his sunglasses and let them hang by the lanyard straps around his neck. He turned toward Hector. "Thank you again for inviting us along, Hector."

"Thank you for your assistance," replied Hector. "It is your satellites that will make us successful. The Gulf Cartel uses three different locations in Matamoros for their drug shipments and without the satellites it would be difficult to catch them, because it is impossible to be in three places at one time."

"Speaking of which," Ray nodded back toward DEA Agent Travers, who was carrying a large metal case in each hand. "Do you have a room for Jace to set up his satellite monitoring equipment?"

"Certainly, Sean. I have a room set aside for just for him." Hector led the team down the stairway to the third floor and into the room that he had prepared for the satellite equipment. It was a large, well lit, fifteen by twenty-foot room, with white portable tables nestled up against each wall and a large oak conference table surrounded by six leather chairs located in the center.

Travers' brown eyes lit up as he entered the room. Someone had finally gotten it right. Whether it was Afghanistan, Nigeria, Cape Town or Columbia, he was always getting stuck in a room the size of a broom closet with equipment that was known to raise the room temperature by ten degrees. Hector had actually given him a room big enough to work in.

"Now this is what I'm talking about! Hector, you're awesome. Swanny, you and Dave grab two of those tables and bring them over here," he said, pointing to a position located against the far wall underneath the air conditioning vent. "Inspector, I can have my monitors and equipment set up and ready for business in about twenty minutes."

Hector motioned toward a set of cables that were taped to the floor. "I had my guys run fiber optic cables in here for you, just in case you needed them."

"That was mighty thoughtful of you, Inspector, but not necessary. These bad boys work on a direct uplink to the satellites," said Jace as he opened the first of the massive cases. "It keeps the bad guys from being able to hack into them. I'm good if you guys want to head down to the briefing. I will just need the coordinates for the three locations and the one in Tampico. Then, once I get my equipment set up, I can start monitoring them and get us some intel."

"I will send someone up with the coordinates. Now gentlemen," said Hector, looking toward the rest of the FAST team. "If you will follow me, we will head down to the briefing room."

It took three minutes to travel down the stairwell and navigate the hallways of the building. The team entered the briefing room, which was full of *Federales* casually talking to one another, and took their seats in the back of the room. Sean and Inspector Gonzales walked to the front of the room and turned to face their men. Hector moved to the center of the room and the men quickly quieted. This was a room full of professionals who knew exactly when to speak and when to listen.

Hector looked at the men solemnly. "Okay, men, as you know our target today is a cocaine shipment out of Tampico. It is being transported by truck into Matamoros. We believe it is going to one of the Gulf Cartel's three known delivery locations. SAIC Ray and his team are here to help us." Hector nodded toward Ray as he pointed to the FAST team. "They will be using their satellites to track the truck from Tampico to Matamoros and through the city in order for us to move in once the truck reaches its destination."

Hector turned down the lights and flipped on the projector, which shot a full size map of the city onto the wall behind him. "The three locations are here at the Reyes' Bodyworks in Las Flores. Area call sign Indio," he said as his laser pointer targeted the location in the far south side of Matamoros where Highway 101 entered the city. "Number two is here at the steel manufacturing plant on *Unione* Avenue. Area call sign Sol." The pointer landed on a manufacturing plant in the extreme northwestern portion of the city. "And number three is here on *Prof. Miguel Rivas Badillo* in the far northeastern section of the city. Area call sign Montejo. As you can see, the three locations are at such far extremes of the city that it would be impossible for us to move from one location to the other if we were to guess the location and be wrong. There are also many routes that the cartel can take, which will make it difficult for us strike until the last possible moment. SAIC Ray will have his man monitor the truck and all three locations. Once he determines the final location, we will move in. I want to place one sniper team immediately at all three locations. Arturo, you and Javier will take Indio. Antonio take Raul and go to Sol. Special Agent Swanson, you and your spotter will go to Montejo. The rest of us will hold our position here at the Station since it is central to all three locations. Once we determine the location of the meet, we will move out.

I want to remind you that Felix Torres, the Gulf Cartel's number two man, is going to be at this meet. He is our number one objective and code named *Borracho*. Once we capture him, we will have dealt a serious blow to the already delicate leadership of the Cartel. That being said, we want to make sure that we get the cocaine as well. Okay, you men know your assignments. Let's get ready to move. Jorge, go up to the second floor and give Special Agent Travers the coordinates for Sol, Indio and Montejo so that he can monitor the locations."

Special Agent Mike "Swanny" Swanson's lean and lanky frame allowed him to appear small and almost unidentifiable when he was in his nest. He was lying prone across an air conditioning unit on the rooftop opposite of Montejo with his black DEA hat turned backwards in order for him to see through the scope of his M110-SASS sniper rifle. It had taken him and Special Agent Dave Martin only eight minutes to reach the warehouse in normal driving conditions. Another four to reach the top of the building and set up the nest.

"Okay, Dave, I've got one building at twelve 'o'clock running east and west. Two floors with seven windows on the second floor, six on the first and a single door in the center. No visible tangos. One building at three o'clock running north and south. One story, with what appears to be two windows on either side of the door. Visibility is hindered on the south end by the front wall. One building at nine o'clock running north and south. No visible tangos. One story with two windows on either side of the central door. The visibility on the south end is also hindered by the front wall. No visible tangos. One brick wall approximately twelve feet tall. One red metal gate located directly in the center of the wall. No visible rollers, which rules out a slide gate, but I can't determine if it is a cantilever or swing gate. All visibility on the other side of the wall is obstructed for approximately eighteen to twenty feet. There are no visible tangos in the courtyard between the buildings. Do you confirm?"

DEA Agent Dave Martin was a hulking man. Standing at six feet two inches tall and two hundred fifty pounds, he was by far the largest man on FAST Team Four. Martin and Swanny had met at Army Ranger School where the two had been paired together as spotter and sniper. After their discharge from the Army, they joined the DEA together.

Dave was looking through the lens of his M151 long range spotting scope, verifying Swanny's calls as he made them. After three tours and thirty-five confirmed kills, Dave and Swanny had developed an uncanny ability to see the same things almost immediately.

"Roger that. I will call it in." He moved his left hand up to the throat microphone button attached to the collar of his black combat fatigues and quickly relayed the assessment of target area to Travers, who was call sign Maestro.

"Roger. Assessment received," replied Travers. "Now let's see what I can see."

He eyed the monitors directly in front of him, examining operation site Montejo. "No visible tangos in the courtyard. According to thermal imaging, you have four tangos in the building to the west, three tangos in the building to the east and four tangos in the building to the North. Thermal won't give me any info about weapons, so keep your eyes peeled. Over."

"Roger. Montejo One out," replied Martin.

Jace repeated the process with operation sites Sol and Indio. He allowed himself a little smile as he remarked that the three operation sites were named after Mexican beers. Travers looked at his monitors again to get a location on the cargo van, which was code named six-pack. It was right on schedule, driving at a steady pace and estimated to reach the outskirts of Matamoros in fifteen minutes.

When the van reached the General Servando Canales International Airport, it was joined by two identical vans. The first pulled out in front of the drug van and the second followed behind it. He called the information into Sean and Hector.

"Boss," said Travers over his microphone. "Six-pack is five minutes outside of the city and has just been joined by two identical vans. They could be decoys, or possibly armed escort. I will keep you advised."

"Roger," replied Sean as the message came through the speaker.

Hector Gonzales spoke into his throat mike. "All teams, we are mission ready. Six-pack is entering the city and has been joined by two more cargo vans. It is uncertain at this time whether they are decoys or reinforcements. Be ready for anything." He heard five affirmations almost in unison through his headset.

Jace Travers watched his monitors intently as the van and its escorts entered the city. He was also monitoring all three operation sites for any increased activity which would give him a clue as to which one was the actual target.

When the vans reached *Libramiento Emilio Portes Gil*, the beltway that ran around the outside of the city, one of the vans split off from the convoy and headed west. Travers grabbed his mike and quickly relayed the information to Special Agent Ray. "The first of the escorts has split off and headed west toward Sol. It looks like they are decoys. Six-pack and decoy two are moving north on Pedro Cárdenas toward Indio."

Movement on his monitor caused him to switch his attention to operation site Montejo. Three speed boats were speeding up the Rio Grande toward the warehouse. This struck Travers as odd because pleasure boats and civilian marine operations were not allowed on this section of the river. He zoomed the satellite in to see if he could identify Felix Torres. Unable to recognize Torres, he grabbed his microphone and relayed the information.

"Boss, I have three speed boats moving up the Rio Grande and headed straight toward Montejo. I have not been able to identify the occupants of the boats."

Sean reached up to his throat mike.

"Roger that." He locked eyes with Gonzales. "Three boats? Does Montejo have boat docks?"

"It does," replied Hector.

"If I was a betting man, I would say that that is our target. What do you think?"

"I would say that is safe bet, Sean." Hector pressed on his throat mike and asked, "Maestro, where is Six-pack now?"

"Coming up on Indio now," replied Jace. "Looks like decoy *numero dos* is pulling off and leaving Six-pack. All signs are pointing toward Montejo, but Six-pack could still head toward Sol if he turns west. He will pass right by you in about three minutes. I would suggest waiting until they turn on Lerma and then move in behind them."

The van moved north at a casual speed, driving directly in front of the *Policia Federale Station,* and turned east on Lerma, heading toward Montejo.

"Six-pack is headed east. It looks like we are a go for Montejo," said Travers. "Hector, you are now Montejo Actual and your teams are now Montejo Two and Three. You are clear to move out."

"Roger, that," replied Hector. "All teams proceed to Montejo."

Mike Swanson was watching the courtyard and surrounding buildings with even more concentration.

"Dave, are you catching all of this movement? I count five tangos in the courtyard, three from the west building and two from the east."

"Roger. All of them heavily armed. I see some M-4s and HK33 assault rifles and some FN-P90 and MP5 machine pistols. These guys aren't playing around. Maestro, are you seeing this?"

"Roger, Montejo One. Looks like our boaters have docked and are moving toward the courtyard. I count four tangos." He zoomed the satellites downward until he could clearly see the faces of all four men. The image was so clear that he could see a pimple starting to form on the nose of one of the criminals. "I count three MP5s, three FN Five-sevens and one big ass .45 revolver."

Felix Torres was known to carry his favorite pistol, which was a stainless steel Smith and Wesson Model 625, .45 caliber pistol with a black grip. It was an ominous and very recognizable weapon. He zoomed in to get a better look at the face of the weapon's owner. "Bingo! *Borracho* is in the building! I confirm *Borracho* is on site."

As he looked over at Sean, Hector could feel his heart beat faster in anticipation. They were following the cargo van, making sure to stay at least four cars back and hidden behind the large diesel trucks moving throughout the warehouse district. He reached up to his throat microphone.

"All units, we are a go. Remember that our primary objective is the capture of *Borracho*. Alive!" He placed emphasis on the final word.

Felix Torres was an evil man. In retaliation for the capture of one of his captains by the *Federales* in Monterrey, he kidnapped and cut off the heads of all twelve officers responsible for the man's incarceration. He then had each head delivered to the Police Station one day at a time for twelve consecutive days. Torres was never arrested because he could not be linked to the deaths of the officers. However, Hector's *Federales* knew that it had been Torres and he did not want them killing the man before he could be interrogated. He needed to get information on the Gulf Cartel first. After that, if Torres were to have some unfortunate accident while being transported to prison, then so be it.

As they neared the Montejo compound, Sean spoke into his microphone. "Montejo One, this is Montejo Actual. We are two blocks out. Do you have eyes on Six-pack?"

Dave Martin looked through his spotter's scope and located the van moving down the road toward the compound. "Roger. Montejo One has a visual on Six-pack. ETA to Montejo is one minute."

Sean knew that this was the critical moment of the operation. They needed to stay just far enough behind for the gates to open and let the van in, but they also needed to be close enough to bust through the gate before it closed. Speed was their ally because it gave them the element of surprise. With all the firepower inside the compound, they would need perfect timing to pull this off and get all of their men out alive.

"Do we have eyes on *Borracho*?"

"Roger, we have eyes on Borracho," replied Swanny as he kept his scope focused on the compound. "Torres has entered the courtyard and is standing outside the door leading to the north building. He's got two more tangos beside him. Be advised that we now have twelve tangos inside the courtyard, plus two inside the north building, for a total of fourteen tangos. Four of them are covered by the gate and I do not have a clear shot. They should be your primary tangos upon entry."

"Roger. Primary tangos are at the gate," replied Sean as he nodded in the direction of Hector.

The SUV neared the compound and Sean could see the rear of the van disappear as it entered the courtyard. He felt the driver hit the accelerator, and the vehicle sped toward the gate. He held onto the handle above his head as the driver turned the wheel hard to left and crashed the vehicle through the closing gate, slamming into the courtyard.

Sean quickly opened his door, spinning out and around. Bracing his back against the vehicle, he brought his LAR-15 up to his shoulder and zeroed in on the cartel member standing at the gate. "DEA! Drop your weapons and put your hands up!"

Out of the corner of his eye, he could see the second SUV barrel through the gate and come sliding to a stop on the far side of his SUV. As the *Federales* poured out of the vehicle, Sean felt the window behind him explode, sending broken glass hurling all around him. He ducked reflexively to protect his eyes from the flying debris that was embedding itself into his neck and shoulder.

"So much for the easy way," he said under his breath. He squeezed off two quick bursts from his rifle, which hit a portly cartel member with a thick mustache directly in the chest and sent him slumping to the ground against the corner of the building. Sean quickly turned to his right and fired three rapid shots at a pony-tailed drug dealer moving along the front gate. Pony-tail was firing his outstretched machine pistol wildly in Sean's direction. Two of Sean's bullets hit the man in the center of his chest, while the third travelled through the bridge of his nose, sending blood and brain matter spraying against the concrete wall. The dead man's finger was still squeezing the trigger, sending bullets spraying throughout the courtyard as he fell. Sean dove into the front seat of the vehicle, barely escaping the barrage of bullets zipping through the air from Pony-tail's weapon.

"Tango one down," said Swanny flatly as he readjusted the aim of his M110 semi-automatic sniper rifle toward the building to the north. He had ended the life of the muscle-bound cartel member standing outside the east building in one shot. The man had set his aim on Sean, but Swanny had taken him out before he managed get off a single round. Now Swanny trained his weapon on the short Mexican standing next to Torres and fired. The 51mm bullet rocketed through the man's chest, sending him flying backwards and through the window of the building.

"Tango two down." He readjusted his sights to the left of Torres and fired again, this time hitting a goateed outlaw just below the left ear, removing half of the man's face in a violent explosion of bone and flesh. "Tango three down. Dave, can you see that guy in the building? Never mind. I've got him," he said as coolly as if he was ordering lunch. He adjusted his aim toward the muzzle flash coming from the window of the north building and fired again.

Hector moved his head out from behind the door of the SUV and eyed the muscular man who had pinned him down with a salvo of bullets from his M4. The barrel-chested man dropped his empty clip and was inserting a new one when Hector fired his pistol, striking the man in the chest with two bullets in rapid succession. The impact spun the man around in a complete circle before he landed hard on the dirt floor of the courtyard. Hector fired four more rounds at a man who was running toward the van. The bullets struck the man in the head, stopping his momentum and sending him to the ground like a dying quail.

Sean spied Torres crawling towards the door of the north building. The sudden deaths of his two body guards had caused Torres to move toward shelter.

"Good job, Swanny," said Sean, sprinting across the courtyard toward Torres with his rifle raised. He fired a three-round burst into the van as he passed, hitting the driver directly in his right eye. Sean raced toward the open door and called out to Hector. "Torres is headed for the boats!"

With amazing speed, Sean crossed the remaining half of the courtyard and raced through the doorway. Instinctively he dove to his right, barely ducking the bullet whistling by his head and lodging itself into the brick wall of the building. He rolled and came up with his back pressed against the wooden packing crates, facing the front door.

"Shit! That was close," he said to himself. Four more bullets pummeled the side of the crate, sending splinters of wood flying around his face. "I've had just about enough of this crap," he said, wiping the splinters from his face. Switching hands, he moved his rifle around the corner of the crate and fired off five rounds. The crates in front of Torres took the full impact of the rounds, showering the man with wooden fragments.

"Damn, *Pelón,* that was close. I think you sent a splinter up my nose."

"Now Felix, I don't go making fun of your ugly mug. Why do you want to make fun of my shaved head?"

"No, *Cabrón*, you've got it all wrong. Most people can't pull that off. Their head isn't shaped right, or it's lumpy. But you pull it off well. Very handsome." Torres spotted Hector coming through the doorway. He aimed his pistol directly at Hector's head and squeezed the trigger.

Hector dove to his left barely escaping the projectiles.

"*Pendejo*," he muttered to himself, angry that he did not look closer before entering the building. He could see Sean, who was giving him a concerned look. Hector nodded to assure Sean that he was okay.

Sean released his magazine and replaced it with a new one.

"I tell you what, Felix. Since you were so complimentary, I'm gonna let you give yourself up right now and I promise that we won't shoot you."

"I don't think that I'm going to give up just yet," replied Torres with a chuckle as he fired off two more shots.

Sean squeezed off three rounds in Torres' direction as Hector moved up and across to the row of crates directly in front of Sean. As Hector fired two rounds into the crates above Torres' head, Sean moved up and over so that he was again positioned across from Hector.

"Are you sure about that? Because I gotta tell ya... I was going to shoot you, Felix. Without a doubt. Up until you said such nice things about me. I sure would hate for you to spoil this generosity that I'm feelin'. Besides that, you're out of bullets." Sean looked in Hector's direction, pointed at his chest and then toward the crates where Torres was located. Hector nodded, indicating that he understood Sean was about to move and that he was going to cover him. Sean held up three fingers and silently counted down three... two... one by removing his one finger on each count. When the count reached zero, Hector fired at the crates allowing Sean to move in - only to find an empty row.

"Shit! Where'd you go Felix?" he called out. Toward the back of the building, Sean heard the distinct sound of six metal jackets bouncing on the concrete floor of the warehouse and the cylinder of Torres' revolver clicking as it locked into place. Sean heard the sound of glass breaking. "Dammit! He's heading out the window. Hector, you go around after him. I'm going for the door. We can't let him get to those boats."

Hector navigated his way to the far end of the row and turned toward the rear of the building.

"Torres, I did not promise that I wouldn't shoot you. When I catch you, I am going to put a bullet in your ass." Hector rounded the corner just in time to see Torres leap through the broken window. He fired twice as he raced toward the opening.

Sean heard the shots as he burst through the rear door leading to the boat docks. He took the stairs four at a time, clearing them in a mere three paces. Felix Torres was thirty yards ahead of him and running fast. Sean knew he needed to cover the fifty yards to the boats before Torres reached them. He willed his legs to move even faster and closed the gap. When he was five yards away from Torres, he heard a gunshot ring out from behind them. Torres pulled up, holding his rear with his left hand.

Sean barreled into Torres, wrapping his arms around the outlaw with his head nestled up against the man's chest. He lifted Torres up and drove the man down hard onto the rocky turf. Holding Torres' right hand and pistol down firmly on the ground with his left hand, Sean let loose with three hard rights that landed squarely on the man's orbital bone. The blows opened a two-inch gash over the man's eye. Sean wrestled the revolver out of Torres' hand and tossed it into the river. Rolling him over, Sean zip-tied Torres' wrists with the handcuffs and pulled tight.

"Owww," said Torres.

"Quit your whining, Torres, you big baby. They aren't that tight," said Sean.

"*Chingate, pendejo.* Not the cuffs. That *Maricón* Gonzales shot me in my *culo.*"

Sean looked down and saw the blood coming out of a hole in the man's left butt cheek. "Heh-heh-heh. He sure did. Good shootin, Hector," he said winking at Hector who was approaching. "How far was that? Like thirty yards?"

"More like fifty. I was sitting in the window." Hector looked back toward the warehouse as if to gauge how far it was. "Now that I think about it, it looks more like seventy."

Sean shook his head in mock disbelief. "Damn, Hector. If I give you another minute or two, your story might be a hundred yards while he was swimming in the river."

"I like that story. Should we throw him in to make it believable?"

"Are you going in after him to pull him back out?"

"No, I hate the water. We will stick with seventy yards," said Hector with a chuckle.

"Either way that was a great shot from that distance with a pistol. What do you do? Sleep with that thing?"

"No, *Amigo*. I just aimed at his head," said Hector with a smile that went from ear to ear.

"Could you two stop flirting and get me to the doctor? I have a hole in my ass," complained Torres.

"Shut up, Felix," quipped Hector. "I told you I was going to shoot your ass, and that is exactly what I did. By the way, Sean, that was an amazing tackle. Where did you learn how to do that? DEA or perhaps when you trained with the Army Rangers?"

"Brownsboro High School 1997 Texas 2A State Champions."

"Torres is a championship prize himself. This should get the bad taste of Piedra Negras out of our mouths."

"It damn sure does, Hector. Like Coach always said, the best way to get over a loss is with a win."

CHAPTER 12
Aleppo, Syria

Sebastian slowed himself to a fast walk. He stopped the timer on his watch.

"Ten minutes twenty-eight seconds," he said to himself. It wasn't even close to his best time running a mile, but it was a start. It had been ten weeks since he was wounded in Al-Dana and this was the first time he had done any real exercise other than walking. Although his time was not great, his lung was holding up nicely. He had experienced no pain and he was not too winded from the run. No more winded than if he would have been had he taken two months off without having a bullet take out the top part of his lung. He wiped the sweat from his forehead and headed for his CHU. He had forty-five minutes to get ready for his coffee date with Claire.

Sebastian finished the bottle of water as he walked through the door of his CHU and tossed the empty bottle into the trash can in the corner. Out of the corner of his eye, he caught the figure of a man sitting in the dark.

"Is there something I can help you with?" he asked without missing a beat.

"You are Sebastian Gray?" The words came across as more of a statement than an actual question.

"Yes. But you already know that since you're in my CHU and sitting on my rack. Who the hell are you?" asked Sebastian turning on the lights to better see his uninvited guest. He studied the man closely. He was in his mid-forties with dark hair that was beginning to gray and a muscular physique. He was dressed in an Army uniform. By the way he sat upright on the bed, Sebastian figured that the man had been regular Army once, probably Delta or the Seals. He had the air of a warrior that Sebastian had sensed before when he had been around Delta guys. But the vibe that the man was giving off told Sebastian that this guy was some sort of spook, despite what the uniform said. It wouldn't be the first time that the CIA had posed as an officer on a military base.

"My name is Lt. Colonel Black. I would like some information about your last mission in Al-Dana."

"I've already been debriefed on that mission by both the regular Army and Army Intelligence, sir. What more could I possibly have to offer you and the…" Sebastian paused, hoping that the man in his room, whose name was obviously not Colonel Black, would give his organization's name. When the man did not offer the name, Sebastian continued. "CIA… NSA… Delta Force?"

"Who I work for is not important, Sergeant. What is important is the fact that you have information I believe is important."

"Yes, sir, Colonel. Anyway I can help, I will. But I kinda have an important meeting in a few minutes so can we get a move on?"

"Quick and to the point. I like that, Sergeant. I will be brief. I want to know everything you can tell me about the house you stumbled across and the men in it. Especially the man who shot you."

The man's question caught Sebastian off guard. All of his earlier debriefings had focused on the massive amount of ISIL forces he had encountered. This guy only wanted to know about the house. "Well, sir, there isn't much to tell about the house. What specifically would you like to know?"

"Everything," came Colonel Black's reply.

Sebastian moved his footlocker from the end of the bed and positioned it across from the Colonel. He took a seat on the footlocker and began to speak. "Okay. We were in the courtyard re-grouping, checking our exfil and doing an ammo check. We noticed that it was a large house, especially for Al-Dana. Coop - Private Cooper - noticed that a fire started on the second floor, so we headed toward the house to check it out."

"Do you normally run into burning buildings?"

"No, Colonel. But fires don't just suddenly start themselves and we were in the middle of one the biggest ISIL surges that I had ever seen. It was my opinion that whoever had started the fire was not a friendly and I ordered my men to move before we started taking fire. We were sitting ducks in that courtyard if anyone were to open fire from the house. We moved across the courtyard and entered the house through the rear door into a living area. It was a huge room with tile or marble floors, a leather sofa and a big ass TV hanging on the wall. Elroy and Wiz - Privates Donaldson and Campbell - moved down the hall to the right. Coop and I moved straight across the room to the kitchen. I entered first and that's when I saw Enrique."

"Enrique?" questioned Black.

"That's what I call him, sir. He looked like Enrique Iglesias. You know, the Latin pop singer."

Black tapped the pencil against his lips. "How did he remind you of this Enrique Iglesias? You didn't mention this in your previous debriefings."

"No, sir. It was apparent that both the Army and Army Intelligence were more concerned about the surge than the house. By the time we got to the part about the house, they were in a hurry to finish. They didn't seem to care about the people in the house, only the men that I lost. But I care."

"So do I, Sergeant. Please continue. He reminded you of Enrique Iglesias."

"Yeah. He was tall for a Syrian, about 5' 9". Olive colored skin. Late twenties to early thirties. Medium cut black hair with a thick full beard. His beard wasn't long though, like Osama." Sebastian was referring to Osama Bin Laden, the now deceased onetime leader of Al-Qaeda, who had worn a long beard which hung down well onto his chest. "He was thin, but muscular. He walked real graceful-like. You know, like a runner. He had high cheek bones, a square jaw and light brown eyes. If I had to guess, he was also well educated."

Black stopped writing on the notepad which he balanced on his right knee. "You would? What makes you think that?"

"When I told him to stop and put up his hands, he asked me what I was doing in his house."

"When he asked, what was his demeanor? Did he scream at you like you were most likely screaming at him?"

"No, Colonel, he was very calm. He spoke in a voice like you and I are talking right now. He also spoke in perfect English. His accent sounded more like a Brit, not like the uneducated Syrians who I have dealt with in the past. That's why I say I believe he was educated. Probably in England, if I was a betting man."

"That's an astute observation, Sergeant," said Black as he scribbled more notes into his notepad. He nodded at Sebastian to continue.

"Thanks. So I see Enrique and I tell him to stop moving toward the rear door and put his hands up where I can see them. He asks why we have broken into his home. By this time, Coop had moved into the room. Coop told him we were firemen and had come to put out the fire."

"That was an interesting response."

"Yeah, well, that's Coop - a real smartass. Actually, Colonel, we all are. Army MPs sort of have to have a little smartass in 'em over here. We get asked to kick down doors every day, not knowing whether there's a Muji on the other side who's going to shoot the second we walk in. The smartass attitude gets us in and out alive."

"Hooah, Sergeant."

"So, next thing I know I hear gunfire coming from the hallway where Elroy and Wiz were. But it wasn't their weapons, it was smaller like an MP9. The gunfire caused me to look toward the hallway. That's when Enrique shot me. Three times. The first one hit me here, just below the neck." Sebastian pointed to his wounded chest. "My chest plate caught the next two right here." Sebastian split his index and middle fingers about an inch apart and touched them to the center of his chest. "I've got to admit. I never saw a gun in his hand until he fired. He fired off three quick shots while drawing from a down position and put 'em into a tight grouping in the kill zone. Enrique has some marksman skills. Not too many people can do that, especially in that situation. Anyway, after he shot me everything went black and I woke up here in Aleppo, at the hospital."

"Thank you, Sergeant. You have been very helpful."

"You're welcome, Colonel. May I ask why you are just now coming to me? It's been almost three months since I was wounded."

"Your particular mission has just recently come to my attention."

"Can you tell me who Enrique really is?"

"No. I can't."

"You can't or you won't? Cuz if you can, I've got a bullet that would I love to return to him. Right in the center of his chest."

"I can't. I don't know the identity of the man who shot you. However, since he shot you, I will tell you this. But I have to warn you first that this is classified information and any disclosure by you to anyone will lead to a dishonorable discharge at best and incarceration as a traitor or death at worst. Do you understand?"

"I understand, sir. I won't tell a soul. This is just between you and me. One grunt to another."

"Good. I believe that the man you call Enrique is a member of an ultra-secret faction of Al-Qaeda which controls every move made by Al-Qaeda and its affiliates. This group is called the Al-Yad. The Al-Yad moves money to the many different factions and markets their assets, like the black market sales of ISIL oil from the Syrian oil fields. It also coordinates all of their troop movements and attacks. We believe that the surge you were in the middle of came from the direct orders of the Al-Yad, as did the recent attacks in Paris, Egypt, Lebanon and the United Kingdom. They are not only the bank but also the war generals for Al-Qaeda. We believe that they are also responsible for recruiting westerners for the war here in Syria, as well as Africa, Yemen and Lebanon."

"No offense, Colonel, but I have been in Syria for a while now and I have done two tours in Afghanistan and Iraq each. I have been hearing the Al-Yad rumors for years. The Al-Yad is a myth. It's a name that someone made up to get the CIA to stop waterboarding them. It's been perpetuated by the Administration and the media when they don't have any other terrorist organization to blame. If you don't want to tell me about Enrique, then don't tell me. But don't tell me that he's the boogey man, because the boogey man and the Al-Yad don't exist. Enrique does. I've got the scars to prove it."

"Sergeant, I assure you that the Al-Yad is very real. You're correct when you say that the Administration and the media blames them for attacks when no other group takes credit, but they do exist. They stay in the background, unseen, careful not to draw attention to themselves. They control everything. As a matter of fact, they do such a good job that they have most of the world believing ISIL and Al-Qaeda are two separate groups fighting for similar but separate ideals. And I believe that you are the only person who has ever laid eyes on a member. This Enrique, as you call him, is the key and I intend to find him."

Black stood up and headed toward the door. Sebastian noticed that he was a tall man, standing about six foot two inches with broad muscular shoulders. The outline of his bulging biceps could be seen against the sleeves of his jacket. His sheer physical stature and the manner in which he walked led Sebastian to believe that he was most likely once Special Forces and not always an intelligence officer. He was definitely not a pencil pusher.

"Thanks for the information, Colonel. What division did you say you were with again?"

"I didn't, Sergeant," said Black, smiling as he walked through the doorway and pulled his beret over his head. "And I was never here."

Sebastian smiled to himself and shook his head as he watched the mysterious Lt. Colonel Black disappear across the road and into the myriad of CHUs. He looked down at his watch and dashed toward the showers. He had ten minutes to get ready to meet Claire.

CHAPTER 13
Houston, Texas

Khalid Al-Jabiri was sitting on the custom Massoud leather sofa centered in the living room of his new apartment, which was located in Gulfton, a community in southwest Houston. He watched the television attentively while sipping his tea. He listened as the reporter for CNN described the ongoing war in Syria. The reporter was relating the recent surge by ISIL, which had taken the city of Homs, a moderate-sized city in western Syria about one hundred miles north of Damascus, the capital. Homs was a strategic location in ISIL's war with Al-Assad's forces in Damascus and the U.S. led forces in Aleppo and Al-Dana. The city, previously occupied by the FSA, had fallen after a week-long surge of over one thousand ISIL forces. According to the newswoman, it was the largest ISIL force seen to date. It was further evidence of the terror organization's ability to recruit soldiers from other countries, most notably Western countries such as France and Great Britain. The loss of the city was a devastating blow to the U.S. led Coalition Forces and now gave ISIL a foothold in the south, which would allow them to move their fighting forces closer to Damascus. It would also allow them to attack U.S. forces in the Aleppo region from two sides.

The reporter's assessment brought a smile to Khalid's face. Abdul bin Faisal had been brilliant when he suggested that the Al-Yad should make it appear as though Al-Qaeda had split ties with ISIL. Many of the Al-Yad had opposed his strategy. They argued that the appearance of a separation would make Al-Qaeda seem weak in the eyes of the West. Abdul assured them that it not only would make Al-Qaeda appear weak, but that the appearance of weakness was exactly what they wanted. He reminded them that, in order to establish a Caliphate in Syria and Iraq, it would be necessary to remove the United States military from the region. It was well known within the Al-Yad that the Iraqi military had been weakened when the Sunni Generals and soldiers defected to Al-Qaeda. And without the United States leadership, the Iraqi military would be like a feather on the wind, wandering aimlessly wherever the winds of conflict would take them. The Syrian Army was no better and they had never had the benefit of the Western military support.

Abdul had advised the Al-Yad that if Al-Qaeda appeared to be weakened by the split with ISIL, then President Adama, with all of his hubris, would declare his victory in the Middle East and pull the military out of Iraq. Although Khalid was the one with a Psychology degree, it was Abdul who understood the American President the best. Abdul had been correct on all accounts. The separation from ISIL caused the President to not only remove the U.S. Military from the region, but, in his arrogance, he also declared that Al-Qaeda had been defeated. It was not until ISIL had taken over all of the eastern and most of the northern regions in Syria and the western quarter of Iraq, including Mosul and Ramadi, that President Adama had committed U.S. soldiers to fight in Syria, all the while declaring that ISIL was the new terror threat and that Al-Qaeda was a struggling organization with no apparent leadership.

The reporter continued her report by stating that, along with the fighting in Syria, it appeared as though Al-Qaeda was gaining ground in Northern Africa and was beginning to once again grow in numbers. In closing, she commented that the worst-case scenario would be if ISIL and Al-Qaeda were to resolve their differences and come together against the United States. Khalid shook his head in disbelief. How blindly the people of the West believed everything they heard and read, and how easily they were led like sheep. The Al-Yad had been careful in how they distributed money and arms to the Al-Qaeda affiliates, making sure that the shell corporations and banks never intermingled between the two groups. However, with some good investigation and a little imagination, he was certain that someone could connect the two even if they could not prove it. But Western journalists were so eager to report a story and move on to the next one that they no longer researched what they were reporting before they reported it. Instead they relied on hearsay, conjecture and mostly fictional anonymous sources to get their story onto the television or in print. And the American people believed every word. They not only believed legitimate reporters, but they could also be motivated by bloggers, Facebook and Twitter.

As a matter of fact, it was Khalid's group of bloggers using social media that had helped incite anti-police riots in St. Louis and Cleveland. It took little for the infidels to turn against their own police force with nothing more than a few tweets and posts from about fifty of the over two thousand accounts that his bloggers controlled. It had taken days before tensions rose in St. Louis. By the time that the opportunity in Cleveland presented itself, his bloggers had learned from their first experience and had incited a riot in mere hours.

Not one single reporter, policeman, F.B.I. agent or member of any other intelligence agency bothered to investigate the tweets or posts to see if Al-Qaeda was involved. The sheep believed that it was solely an American problem, not the result of careful provocation by the Al-Yad. They believed that there was no way that Al-Qaeda could be involved with the riots because, not only was Al-Qaeda on the other side of the ocean, it had been defeated by President Adama.

Khalid's bloggers now scanned police reports in all major U.S. cities for their next opportunity to cause a riot and raise social tension and distrust of the American police.

Khalid was not fond of Houston. It was an enormous city, the fourth largest city in the United States by population, with over two million people. It had been quite easy to blend into the background. Due to his cover identity he was unable to attend *Salah* at one of the eighty Mosques in the city.

Phase One of Muhammad's Sword was progressing as planned. All of his operatives had made it through Mexico. Working briefly at Juan Carlos' concrete factory, before being smuggled through the tunnel, had helped them master their Mexican accents. All were currently in training and progressing nicely. Most were in the top of their respective classes, which would give them first choice for their Advanced Individual Training and would practically guarantee them the positions that they needed to carry out the plan to perfection.

The cover identities and credentials provided by Juan Carlos were more than sufficient for him and his men to secure their resident alien status. Juan Carlos had provided them with not only the proper documentation to prove five years of residence in the United States, but also with families women who posed as wives, and anchor babies, or children born in the United States, as our children. The children were the most necessary part of the cover identity, due to the fact that the Executive Order was very specific in that it would only provide amnesty for the parents of U.S. citizens or children born in the United States. The only concerning issue had been the mandate of finger prints. All of his men had been hand-picked and had no previous contact with the Americans. None were on any watch list, therefore they made it through with no issues. Khalid himself had used false fingerprints made from the man whose identity he was using. He did not want to have any link to his real identity, in order that he may return after the conclusion of the mission. The American's background checks were a joke. But even if they had been extensive, the identities provided by Juan Carlos were those belonging to citizens of Coahuila, who had never been in trouble with U.S. law enforcement.

Gaining entry into the military had been even easier. Ironically, the government workers who processed his men actually encouraged enlistment in the military as a way of expediting our citizenship. According to another Executive Order, any non-resident alien who enlists in the military and serves in active duty status during the period of the war against terrorists of global reach is granted expedited U.S. citizenship. What a paradox it was that the Executive Order used to recruit illegal aliens to fight terrorism was the same one that they were using to infiltrate the U.S. military.

Accomplishing Phase Two would not be an easy task. In order for them to move into Phase Three, Khalid needed to be successful at creating a series of events which will move the American's focus from the Levant and their southern border to within the heart of the United States. This was to be done through a series of lone-wolf attacks throughout the United States. The attacks, combined with the civil unrest that the Al-Yad had helped to create through the events in

Cleveland and St. Louis, would hopefully shift the Great Satan's focus to within its own borders.

Khalid's team had recruited many disenfranchised American citizens to join the jihad against the infidels, loyal mujahideen who are willing to give their own lives for the cause. He would use them for strategic strikes throughout the United States that have high visibility and large death tolls. The American media would latch on to the attacks and dictate that the politicians stop the attacks in any way possible. In America, it was the media who directed the politicians, not their own ideals and policies.

Khalid would use lone wolf recruits developed through their ISIL recruiting. The Americans were under the belief that only ISIL recruited inside the United States and the Al-Yad had been very successful in leading the infidels to believe that ISIL and Al-Qaeda were two separate entities. The recruits he used for Muhammad's Sword had never come under suspicion by the U.S. Government. They did not use any social media and had been tedious in their efforts to conceal all ties with Al-Qaeda. They were the most upstanding of citizens. His lone wolves would not be upstanding citizens. They would be similar to the recruits used in Dallas and Boston. People who had been under surveillance by the FBI, but taken off of the watch list. By using this type of lone wolf, Khalid would cause the American public to cry out for more police in order to keep suspects under surveillance. Americans are already so tired of the war abroad that they would gladly welcome more police at home to protect them from the ISIL threat. He was positive that some politician would even suggest that they should use their returning soldiers to replenish their depleted police force.

Khalid had been insistent, with Abdul, on his crusade to cause public outrage against the police in St. Louis and Cleveland. He knew that causing a divide between the citizens and local police forces would deplete the size of the police forces by apathy and attrition

The American people were narcissistic. When they went for any period of time without praise, or, more to the point, when they were being publicly shamed or defeated, they simply quit. By causing riots in just the two cities, St. Louis and Cleveland, the Al-Yad had caused a marked decline in the numbers of American police in other major cities such as Baltimore and Los Angeles. By the time Phase Two begins, he believed that the total number of American police would drop by at least another ten percent. If so, his campaign would have been successful in depleting the national police force to such an extent that when the lone wolf attacks begin, the American people would send out a public cry to replenish their ranks and restore order.

The lone wolf attacks in Dallas and Boston had been decoys, to make the Americans believe that they could easily catch his operatives. Khalid had used *mujahedeen* of relatively low intelligence, operating without a clear-cut plan. Their orders were to attack anything that they wanted to attack. The next wave of attacks would use the same profile of lone wolf recruits. However, these attacks would be aimed at high profile targets with high casualty rates, beginning on New Year's Eve. Khalid would use the lone wolf recruits to divert as much attention away from Muhammad's Sword as possible. His plan, however, would require ISIL to appear to retreat from certain strategic positions in Syria in order for the Americans to believe that they are winning their battle abroad and focus their attention back at home. Homs in particular. To get ISIL to relinquish Homs would be no easy task. ISIL believed that the city was not only key to taking control of Damascus, but also necessary for their continued control of Lebanon. Homs provided ISIL with a direct pipeline with which they can provide arms and soldiers to northern Lebanon. ISIL already believed that the Al-Yad were not being aggressive enough in their Syrian strategy. But ISIL was incapable of seeing the larger picture. Abdul would need to remind them that it was the Al-Yad who dictated the strategy of the jihad to ISIL and not ISIL to the Al-Yad. If that conversation did not work, it might be necessary to once again temporarily halt the sale of their black market oil to Turkey and Saudi Arabia to remind them that they did not exist without the Al-Yad. Khalid would prefer to convince them that a temporary retreat, to remove the American presence in Syria, would be more advantageous than to continue to fight and have the Americans reinforce their position with more military personnel. Once the Americans left, ISIL would easily take back Homs and continue the fight in both Syria and Lebanon. to help convince them, Khalid had recruited men skilled in the refining and production of oil. Men who would make their oilfields and refineries produce at maximum capacity. Between Saudi Arabia's increased production and the American President's policies against fossil fuels, hundreds of thousands of Americans working in the oil and natural gas industry had lost their jobs. These men, and many more to come, were willing to work in the Syrian oil fields and refineries. The funding from the increased production would compensate for the temporary retreat in Homs. All was going according to plan. Khalid allowed a smile to form on his lips as he raised his cup and took another sip of his tea.

CHAPTER 14
Fort Leonard Wood, Missouri

Dennis Johnson rushed to the building. Upon reaching it, he came to a stop and rested his back against the outer wall. Sweat formed on his forehead and his breath was heavy from the one hundred yards he had just sprinted across the open field from the helicopter. He was the first member of his team to reach the building, so he trained his M16A2 rifle toward the front of the building to protect them from any assailants who might come around the corner. He and his team were conducting their first training mission for Military Operations on Urban Terrain (MOUT).

The town, known as Stem Village, was a mock town with real buildings, designed by the Army to provide realistic training for multiple situations that real police officers face. The buildings were designed to be as realistic as possible, complete with windows and doors, post office boxes in the post office, as well as stuffed animals in the children's rooms inside the houses. Cars lined the streets and filled the driveways and garages of the houses. The village contained state of the art equipment which allowed operators in each of the buildings to control the lighting and inject the sounds of dogs barking and babies crying, as well as other real world sounds, such as traffic and church bells. The village buildings, which included residences, a fully stocked grocery store, a gas station, a church, and MP station among others, were all equipped with closed circuit video cameras. The cameras located both on the inside and outside allowed the instructors to monitor the trainees' movements. It also recorded them for review after the exercise.

As it was their first training exercise, Dennis' team was accompanied by their instructor, Sgt.1st Class Noah Spencer. Spencer was not a big man, standing only five feet six inches tall, but he possessed a strength that belied his small stature. Pound for pound, Spencer was the toughest dude that Dennis had ever seen. He had served three tours in Iraq as an MP, had been wounded twice, once in the leg and again in the shoulder, and he was as good as they come. With his walnut brown eyes and his raspy, Clint Eastwood voice, Spencer commanded a respect from Dennis and his entire team that bordered on fear. Although the screaming by the drill sergeants had pretty much ended after basic training, it was Sgt. Spencer's calm, raspy voice when he corrected them that made soldiers almost wish for the screaming to come back.

Once, when doing an active shooter response drill, one of Dennis' classmates had made the mistake of opening the door for the mock shooter, thinking the shooter was a victim. When Spencer replayed the video of the exercise, he stopped at the point where the classmate died. He looked directly at the recruit and in his calm, raspy voice said, "Well, class, due to a momentary lapse of good common sense, Private Sanchez is dead. Private Sanchez, if this had been a real-life event, that would be the last dumb thing you ever got to do in your short lifetime. I suggest that in the future when you are about to do something stupid, like get you and or your buddies killed, you refrain from such actions."

That was how Spencer was. He could make a man feel like crap and never even raise his voice. This being the first training exercise was nerve racking enough, but Sgt. Spencer being right there with them made Dennis more nervous.

Dennis felt the tap on his shoulder which was the signal that the team had formed up behind him. With his weapon tight against his shoulder and aimed toward the front of the building, he slowly moved forward. The exercise today was to take down drug dealers in a crack house two blocks from their current location. The drug dealer roles were being played by Marine Corps recruits. Unlike the Army, who did all of their training at the base, Marines went to basic training elsewhere and came to the Village to complete their training. All the weapons contained *simunition*, a non-lethal training ammunition that shot hot pink paint pellets that stung like hell when they hit. The lack of lethal ammunition, however, did not make Dennis any less nervous. Their mission was to successfully navigate the two blocks to the crack house undetected before they broke down the door and arrested the drug dealers. Dennis was on point, so it was his job to get them there without being detected.

As he reached the end of the building, he peered around the corner. No one was on the street. He turned back to his team and whispered "clear" to the next man who in turn whispered "clear" to the next man and so on it went to the last man.

"Moving," said Dennis as he turned the corner and headed out in front of the house. It took the team less than three minutes to navigate the distance to the crack house unnoticed. Dennis and three other recruits took their positions by the front door while the remaining three recruits moved to the rear of the house to cover the back door. The windows of the house were blacked out, making it impossible for Dennis to see inside and assess the situation. They were going into a situation where the number of people was completely unknown and with no way of knowing if the men inside were armed.

Dennis took his position to the left side of the door. Across from him was Private Baker, who was ready to slam open the door with a sledge hammer. Behind Baker was Estevez and directly behind Dennis was Torino. Dennis looked at Baker, held up three fingers and began counting down. When Dennis closed the last finger, Baker thrust the sledgehammer at the door knob, slamming the door wide open and allowing Dennis to throw a mock stun grenade through the doorway and into the room.

Without hesitation, Estevez entered the house and covered the left side of the room with his M16. Dennis waited two seconds, then moved into the doorway. Moving through the doorway and into the right side of the room, he shouted, "Military Police!"

He noticed a man sitting on a sofa in the center of the room who was holding his head to simulate the effects of the flash bang. Dennis ignored the man, knowing that Torino was moving in behind him to cover the center of the room. Dennis heard Estevez yell out, "Clear left!" as he moved closer to the kitchen.

Dennis entered the doorway and saw a man standing in the middle of the kitchen, wearing a black T-shirt and green shorts and holding a brown bag.

"Military Police! Get down on the ground right now," he shouted to the man, who turned and ran out of the rear of the kitchen. "Damn," said Dennis under his breath as he lowered his rifle and ran after the fugitive.

He burst through the door, which opened into a hallway. He detected a figure out of the corner of his right eye and instinctively dove to his left, turning his body as he flew through the air. He heard the unmistakable sound of a nine millimeter handgun being fired and managed to squeeze off a three-round burst before he hit the ground. Dennis landed on his back facing his target and could see that all three rounds had found their mark in the center of the man's chest. The marine smiled at him as he laid down on the ground to show he had been killed in the firefight.

Dennis noticed two more members of his team enter the hallway and look at the dead crack dealer.

"Rear is clear!" shouted McGee.

Dennis rolled over and climbed back to his feet. "I've got one suspect wearing a black shirt and green shorts. He headed down the hallway in this direction," he said, nodding ahead of him.

As he walked down the hallway, Dennis noticed the two bright pink paint spots on the door ahead of him. He smiled and thought to himself, "Man that was too close for comfort."

When they reached the doorway, Dennis moved to the right with McGee and Short on the left.

"Ready?" he asked.

"Ready," replied McGee and Short.

Dennis turned the handle on the door and kicked it hard with his left foot, sending it crashing into the wall inside of the room. Short threw in his mock flash-bang grenade. The men waited two seconds for the imaginary flash of light and bang caused by the fake grenade. McGee entered the room to the left to cover behind the door. He was followed by Short, who covered the right. Dennis entered the room straight ahead and saw the man in the black shirt laying on the bed, holding his eyes to simulate the effects of the one million candela produced by a real stun grenade. He quickly subdued the man as he had been taught and placed the zip tie handcuff restraints on him.

The team regrouped outside and Sgt. Spencer addressed his men with his calm and raspy voice. "All in all, you did okay for your first run. Except for a few mistakes that should have gotten you killed. Like you, Estevez, running into a room before the stun grenade even went off. You would have been deaf and blind and Baker would have had to cover your position. And you, Johnson, running after a suspect in close quarters. If you weren't so damn fast or lucky, I'm not sure which, you would have been dead and I would be stuck teaching a brand new recruit all the stuff that I've already taught you. Remember the name of this game is Surprise, Speed and Aggression. But not so much speed that you act before you think. Now, you men head back to the MP station and we will debrief there."

"Hooah," said the men as they turned and headed toward the MP station.

As he passed the house, Dennis saw Malik Faraj, the Marine he had shot in the house.

"You know it was luck that I didn't get you, right?" said Faraj.

"I would rather be lucky than dead any day of the week, homey."

Dennis and Malik had struck up a friendship over the last few weeks. Even though they were from different backgrounds and different branches of the military, they had hit it off immediately. Their good natured barbs at each other were just one indication of how close friends they had become. Dennis liked the military and the stability, discipline and camaraderie it gave him. He also knew the real reason why he was here. He was in training for the day that Allah would strike down the Great Satan. He hoped that Malik wasn't going to be stationed where he was on that day. He would hate to have to kill him for real.

CHAPTER 15
New York City, New York

Aziz Karimov could see the snow falling outside the front windows of the restaurant.

This will be a beautiful New Year's Eve, he thought to himself. Aziz was an immigrant from Uzbekistan. His parents had migrated to America when he was only three years old. He had grown up in Brooklyn, where he had regularly attended the mosque with his parents. His father was a taxi driver and his mother worked as a maid at the Roosevelt Hotel. After graduating from Abraham Lincoln High School he had come to the city to find work, just like hundreds of others each year. The allure of Manhattan had brought him here, the dream that he could make his mark on the world as a stockbroker, or television executive, or maybe even a newsroom anchorman.

Instead, he found that his calling was to be a waiter at T.G.I. Fridays. America didn't just hand out million-dollars-a-year jobs. The vast majority of the people living in Manhattan were just ordinary people struggling to survive. The American dream was just that, a dream. If you did not go to the right college or know the right people, then you were destined to a life of mediocrity and Aziz did not want to be mediocre. He wanted to be somebody memorable.

His recruitment by ISIL had been gradual. A friend had told him about a twitter account that was telling people how they could become heroes. How they could fight for a real cause. Aziz followed the twitter account for a while and bought into the propaganda. One day a tweet said to subscribe to *Inspire,* an online magazine published by ISIL, and that more information about how to become a soldier for Islam could be found there. Aziz was quickly seduced by the magazine, various YouTube channels and the message being delivered by ISIL. He could become a soldier for Islam. The magazine encouraged its readers to engage in lone wolf attacks. He had indoctrinated himself through the magazine and eventually made contact with ISIL. He was told to be patient and his time would come. Today was his time.

Aziz had worked in the restaurant for three years. Being a hard-working employee, he had managed to work his way up from busboy to waiter. He had been through the scrutiny of New Year's Eve in Times Square many times. The police officers conducting the security checks knew him. This year his security check had been even briefer than the last. The police always focused on the new employees. Those that they knew were given the gratuitous questioning, but no in-depth investigation, which is why the tenured employees always got to work New Year's Eve. This was a flaw in the system and one that, this year, would cause them to regret their arrogance.

Aziz's shift was almost over and he could see the people already crowding into Times Square. Some of them were even naked. He wondered what could possibly entice people to brave the cold of New York in the winter, naked. In a few hours, Times Square would be packed with thousands of people. They had been lining up for hours, waiting to pass through the security checkpoints, and were now making their way towards the stage that would later be filled with American pop stars like Taylor Swift and Justin Bieber. Aziz knew that he would be close to the stage at midnight when the ball would drop and all of America would be watching.

At the end of his shift, Aziz entered the break room where the employees stored their personal belongings. He said goodbye to his co-workers, who were also finishing their shift, and wished them a happy New Year. Once everyone had left, he closed the door and moved a chair to the rear of the room. Aziz climbed onto the chair and reached for the ceiling. He removed the ceiling tile and pulled down the vest which he had stored in the ceiling earlier in the week. The police had searched the building earlier in the day, but they had not brought explosives dogs in with them. They never did. Aziz knew this because he had been through the New Year's Eve security procedures for the prior two years. He knew that his vest would be safely hidden.

He pulled on the ball bearing lined vest and clamped down the straps that crisscrossed his back and looped over his shoulders. Aziz had bought the vest itself on Amazon for thirty-five dollars. It had taken him almost three days to hot glue on the ball bearings. He had made the six bricks of C-4 explosives, tucked into the pockets of the vest, from directions found in *The Anarchist Cookbook,* which he also bought on Amazon. Aziz pulled his black parka on over the vest and zipped it up. As he exited the building, he waved to the new hostess. Callie was her name, he thought, and said "Happy New Year!"

As he opened the door, he heard her reply, in her southern draw, for him to enjoy the party. Aziz pulled the hood of his parka over his head and headed out into the snow-covered street, making his way toward the stage. He wanted to be as close as possible when midnight arrived.

CHAPTER 16
Corpus Christi Army Depot
Corpus Christi, Texas

Sebastian Gray stepped out of the shower and grabbed the towel he had draped over the wall hook beside the shower door. He ran the towel over his buzz cut sandy blond hair and moved to his shoulders, running the towel down his torso and finishing at his feet. He walked into the bedroom, tossing the towel onto the bed as he stepped toward the closet. He was getting used to life on the base. It had been five months since the firefight in Al-Dana and his wounds had healed completely. But Sebastian had spent most of his adult life overseas fighting as a combat MP for his country. Military Police life back home differed greatly from his life as a combat MP. It was a more slowly paced and boring life. One that he was destined to now. His wounds and promotion to Sergeant First Class after Al-Dana assured him of that. Instead of breaking down doors and expecting to find ISIL fighters shooting at him, he now led the humdrum life of pushing papers and filling out duty rosters for the base security forces.

Corpus Christi Army Depot (CCAD) was the Army's premier center for modification, repair and overhaul of rotary wing components and aircraft. The majority of Army Helicopters came to CCAD to be repaired, overhauled, modified, retrofitted, modernized and tested. The Depot also handled repair and maintenance for Navy, Marine Corps and Air Force Seahawk, Super Cobra and UH-1N Huey helicopters. All totaled there were about 5500 personnel employed at the Depot, which consisted of active duty Army, National Guard and civilian contractors who served as teams for analytical crash investigations, field maintenance and those working at the chemical material processing facilities, as well as repair, maintenance and development personnel.

CCAD was located on, and took up almost one-fourth of, the acreage of Naval Air Station Corpus Christi (NASCC). NASCC was the home of the Naval Air Training Command and Naval Training Air Wing Four, which consisted of Navy, Marine Corps and Coast Guard student aviators, flight officers and flight crewmen. The Coast Guard, Border Patrol, U.S. Customs and DEA were also tenants on the base. The base also contained a post office, airfield, cemetery, hospital, barracks and private housing quarters.

Sebastian slipped his button-down shirt over his shoulders and stared into the mirror. His right hand rubbed the circular scar on his muscular chest where the bullet had entered.

"Dumb-ass," he said scolding himself. "You should have seen that coming. Oh well, chicks dig scars." Sebastian lifted the television remote and turned on the television. He flipped through the channels and settled on the ABC network. As he buttoned up his indigo blue shirt, he noticed that the early performer was Jake Owen, a popular country music singer. "Glad to see they actually put some talent on the stage this year. God knows that nobody wants to see Justin Bieber again."

Sebastian rolled up the sleeves on his shirt two times so that they fell halfway up his thick forearms and headed back into the bathroom to finish getting ready for the New Year's Eve Party at Jack Ash's, a local restaurant where his fellow off duty MPs were meeting.

One quarter mile up the base, Sean Ray eyed the pool table as he made his way around it, carefully studying each of the balls left on the table. He took his position at the end of the table and leaned over. He carefully aimed the pool cue and said, "eight ball corner pocket." He nodded toward the leather bound pocket just off his right hip.

The DEA office which the FAST Team occupied on NASCC differed from most DEA offices. It came complete with its own living area, containing a pool table, sleeping quarters, dining room and kitchen, as well as a separate office containing work spaces and an armory for weapons. The layout reminded Sean more of a fire station than the DEA offices he had occupied prior to joining the FAST teams. Since the team spent a large amount of time in the office locating and tracking the bad guys, they had to be ready to move at a moment's notice. They were in fact a lot like firemen, so the living areas in the office made perfect sense and that was the reasoning given to his superiors when he had requested the amenities and extra office space.

Jeff Parker, the team's explosives expert and newest member, stuck out his massive hand with his palm raised at a ninety-degree angle, like a cop trying to stop traffic. "Hey, hold up there, boss. Are you calling that shot clean?"

"Well, yeah," replied Sean with a twinkle in his emerald eyes. "How else would I call it?"

Parker pointed to the bright orange five ball resting against the side rail about six inches above the corner pocket that Sean had just called. "I just wanted to make sure you saw my ball before you called that shot."

"I saw it just fine," said Sean, drawing out the word "just" for effect. His gaze now fixed on the white cue ball, he slowly pulled the pool stick back.

"You do realize that there is no way you can bank the eight ball into this corner without hitting the five."

"Are you kidding me?" replied Sean, turning his head back to face Parker. "Not only can I make it, I'll bet you twenty bucks that it doesn't even come close to the five ball."

"Oh hell, yeah. I'll take that bet," said Parker with a Cheshire cat grin that displayed his deep cheek dimples.

Jace Travers heard Parker and headed over to the pool table from his seat on the large sectional leather sofa. "Oooh, did I hear the word 'bet'?"

"You sure did," commented Swanny, who had been leaning against the bar watching the pool game. He set his beer bottle down on the bar. "And with Sean. On a pool shot."

"On a *shot*? Not a game?" asked Jace.

"Yep, a shot."

"I got a hundred on Sean!" called Jace.

"You haven't even seen the shot yet. You schmuck," called back Parker.

"Dude, I don't have to. It's Sean. There's nothing that the boss can't do with a pool cue or a rifle."

"Okay then, you're on. A hundred bucks says he can't bank the eight ball into this corner without hitting the five ball."

Jace made his way to the table and eyed the shot for a second. "Wanna make it two?"

"You know what, you little smart ass? Since its New Year's Eve and I want to start the New Year with a little cash in my pocket, let's go two hundred. You've got a bet."

Jace walked around the table toward Parker. "Hey, Swanny. You want any of this?"

"No way, man. Parker will kick your ass and mine when he realizes that he just got hustled."

Parker said, "You are a smart man, Swanny. But there's no way that the boss can make this shot clean. Looks like it's just you and me, scrawny." Parker had a habit of calling Travers scrawny because of his tall thin frame. He also knew that Jace hated it.

"Are you guys finished yet?" asked Sean, his eyes still fixed on Parker.

"I think so, boss," replied Parker, raising his beer bottle to his lips and taking a swig. "Whenever you're ready."

Sean slammed the pool stick forward, sending the cue ball into the eight ball, his head and eyes still fixed on Parker. The sheer force of the shot and massé spun the cue ball backwards, sending it speeding at an angle into the five ball. Upon impact both balls rolled hastily to the opposite side of the table as the eight ball slid by and rolled around the edge of the corner pocket before dropping in.

"There is a way, if the five ball isn't there when the eight rolls by," said Dave from the couch, his gaze still on the giant TV where he was playing *Call of Duty* on the XBOX.

"Well, I'll be damned," said Parker, shaking his head. "How did you guys know that he would do that?"

"This ain't our first rodeo, cowboy," said Travers as he walked over to Parker with his hand outstretched, awaiting his payment. "I told you that there wasn't nothing that the boss couldn't do with a rifle or a pool cue."

CHAPTER 17
New York City, New York

Aziz Karimov had spotted the young woman across the stage earlier. She was a petite girl in her mid-twenties, with dark brown hair and high cheek bones. She had been walking throughout the crowd with a clipboard in hand, smiling and talking to the people who had come out for the celebration. It was obvious to Aziz that she was with the network. Occasionally she would stop and point to the area of the stage where Aziz was standing. He noticed that the people she directed toward the stage were going up onto the stage to be interviewed by the hosts of the show. As she made her way toward Aziz and the group of people he had embedded himself with, he maneuvered himself toward the front of the pack, kicking bottles of liquor out of his way in order for him to be spotted by the young lady. Part of the New York City security procedures were to remove all of the trash receptacles on the streets to prevent a bomb from being planted close to the celebration. They also banned vendors on the streets from selling alcohol or food to the massive crowd. This caused the party goers to smuggle in their own refreshments and dispose of their empties onto the street.

The young woman introduced herself as Kristi and told the group that she was with ABC. Kristi asked everyone where they were from and the people around Aziz started shouting out foreign countries. The girl next to Aziz, Claudine he thought she had said that was her name, yelled out France. Her companion cried out Germany in heavily accented English. Aziz took a chance and shouted out Seattle. Kristi walked over to Aziz, smiling as she drew near.

"Is this your first time in Times Square?"

"Yes, it is," lied Aziz.

"You don't sound like you are from Seattle."

"My parents are from Uzbekistan, but I was raised in Seattle."

"Well, what brings you here? I mean, why would you stand out here for six hours in the freezing cold with no food or water, and no bathrooms, just to see the ball drop?" quizzed Kristi.

Aziz pulled back his hood to expose his buzz cut jet black hair. "I am in the Marines and I ship out for my first tour in Syria in three days. I wanted to see the ball drop live in New York City before I go. Just in case I don't get another chance. I also wanted to see if Jenny McCarthy is as pretty in person as she is on TV."

Kristi flashed Aziz a big smile, showing a mouthful of white teeth. "And how has your experience been so far?"

"It has been totally awesome," said Aziz, smiling back. "I guarantee you that this will be the most memorable New Year's Eve ever."

"That's great. What is your name and your rank?" she asked as she pulled out her pen to write down his information on her clipboard.

"Private Aziz Karimov," he lied convincingly.

Kristi flashed him her big smile one more time and said, "Well, Private Aziz Karimov of Seattle, Washington, you are going on stage for an interview with Jenny at eleven fifty-three. You will be up there for the ball drop and, if tradition holds true, you will probably get a kiss at midnight." She reached into her inside coat pocket and pulled out a badge attached to a lanyard. "Put this on around your neck and go on up to that staging area with the other guests."

Kristi pointed to an area about twenty feet in front of Aziz that was blocked off by a four foot high metal fence, the same area next to the stage that Aziz had noticed her pointing to before.

"Awesome! Kristi, I could kiss you right now. My friends will never believe how lucky I am. To be on stage at midnight with Jenny - this will be the most memorable New Years of my life."

"Enjoy it, soldier. You definitely deserve it. Now hurry, you're on in twelve minutes."

Aziz walked to the holding area and showed his badge to the security officer who opened the gate and allowed him to enter. At eleven fifty, Jenny came down the stairs.

"Wow, this snow is bitch, isn't it? Are you Private Karimov?"

"Yes ma'am," he replied. "But you can call me Aziz."

"Well, Aziz, I'm Jenny. Listen, when we get up there, we won't have much time. They have changed the commercial break and we will be running late, so I'll introduce you and ask you where you are from, what you're doing here and if you're having a good time. Then it will be time for the countdown and I want you stay up on stage with me for the whole thing. Is that cool with you?"

"Oh, yes, ma'am! That is way cool with me."

"Great. Listen, I also have this tradition of kissing the person on stage with me at midnight. Is that okay? Do you have a girlfriend or anybody that's gonna get mad at you if you kiss me at midnight?"

"No, ma'am," he said with a big grin. "I mean, yes. I have a girl I'm seeing, but I don't think she will get mad since it is you. As long as your husband doesn't get mad. He looks like a pretty tough guy."

"Well, he is from Boston, but he's a sweetie. He knows how show biz works. Okay. I will head back up and in one minute Larry will show you up to the stage where I will do your interview." Jenny turned and walked up the stairs to the top of the stage.

One minute later, Larry, a heavyset man with giant earphones on his head, walked over to Aziz and told him to start up the stairs and that he was on in twenty seconds. Aziz climbed the stairs and walked up onto the stage. The bright lights, shining down on the stage, blinded him for a few seconds. Once his vision returned, he could see out over the throngs of people packed into Times Square. It looked like a giant ocean made of people, he thought to himself. Jenny took his hand. They faced an enormous camera with a bright light on the top.

"This is Private Aziz Karimov from Seattle, Washington. So Aziz, are you having a good time?"

"I am having an awesome time! This is the greatest place on earth to be tonight!"

Aziz heard Justin Bieber stop singing on the other stage and Ryan Seacrest's voice coming from the speakers on the main stage about fifty feet away. "Justin, help me out here and let's count this thing down. America, grab somebody you love and get ready to count it down with us. Here we go. Ten... nine... eight... seven... six..." Jenny grabbed him by the hand and pulled him in close to her. "Three... two... one... Happy New Year!"

Aziz put his left hand around Jenny's back and dipped her as he kissed her hard on her mouth for at least three seconds. As he pulled her up, he put his right hand into his coat pocket and took hold of the small remote.

As Jenny emerged from the kiss, she had a surprised look on her face. "Wow! That was some kiss. I feel a little flushed." She looked into the camera and said, "Don't worry, baby. I'm coming home to you." She looked over at Aziz, smiled and said, "Well Marine, I know you have one lucky lady at home. If you can kiss like that, there's no telling what else you can do. Aziz, I'm told that you are shipping out for Syria in just a few days. Now that you have all of America watching, is there anything you would like to say to the folks back home?"

"Yes Jenny there is," said Aziz as he stared directly into the camera. "... *Allahu Akbar*!"

CHAPTER 18
Corpus Christi, Texas

Jack Ash's Drinkery was located just across the bridge from the Corpus Christi Army Depot. Being only five miles away from the base, its proximity made it a favorite hangout for the men and women who lived there. With wood-paneled walls adorned with beer signs, two pool tables, shuffleboard and twelve televisions, which always played both the Dallas Cowboys and Houston Texans football games, Jack Ash's was the perfect dive bar and it catered to the soldiers at NASCC.

Sebastian considered the fact that it was not a college bar a bonus. He had seen and done entirely too much in his twenty-six years to have to put up with drunken frat boys trying to prove to their buddies how tough they are by fighting soldiers. The locals who patronized Jack Ash's not only got along with the military men who came there, but they held the soldiers in the highest regard. That's why Jack Ash's always made Sebastian feel comfortable when he came.

Sebastian watched as Dennis Johnson and Malik Faraj played pool and traded comments on the gorgeous bartender, Pilar. Although the two came from different backgrounds and served in two different branches of the military, it was obvious to Sebastian that they had become good friends. In most places Army Grunts and Jarhead Marines spent the majority of their free time fighting with each other, either out of pride or because each branch felt superior to the other. But in Corpus Christi things were different. The base was home to a mixture of branches and these two had done their Military Police training together at Fort Leonard Wood.

Sebastian leaned back on his barstool, resting both elbows on the wooden rail behind him. He took a long pull of his bottle of beer as his eyes scanned the multitude of beer signs adorning the walls. His eyes fixed on the Guinness Stout clock above the shuffleboard table. It was almost midnight.

Sebastian finished his beer and tossed the bottle into the trash can to his left. He headed towards the bar, passing by the life-sized statue of Jack Daniels located a few feet from the front entrance. As he approached the L-shaped wooden bar, the bartender greeted him with a warm smile. Pilar was an attractive, petite young woman with light brown eyes, jet black hair and a smile that could light up the room. She was always quick with a joke and seemed to pay special attention to Sebastian when he came in.

"Hiya, Bash! Can I get you another beer?" she said with a quick wink.

"Sure, Pilar. Make it a Bud Light," he said, as he stole a glance at her pert breasts, which were outlined perfectly by her shirt.

"Here you go," she said, placing the bottle down onto the bar in front of him. "It's almost midnight. You better go find your date for the countdown."

"No date tonight, Pilar. I'm all by myself."

"You know it's bad luck if you don't get a kiss at midnight, right?"

"After this past year, I don't think my luck can get any worse," he replied. "I think I will be okay."

At the back wall of the bar, the second bartender, a large breasted, bra-less girl named Callie clanged the brass bell beside the row of forty beer taps. "Everybody grab your partner or the girl next to you - it's time to count down!" she yelled as she turned the volume up on the three big screen televisions above the taps.

Sebastian could hear Ryan Seacrest talking on the television. "America, grab somebody you love and get ready to count it down with us. Here we go."

Pilar hopped up onto the bar in a single leap. She put her arms over Sebastian's shoulders and with her muscular legs wrapped around his waist, she pulled him close to her. "I heard about what happened to you and your team over in Syria and I don't want you to have any more bad luck. So since you don't have a date and I don't have a date, let's ring in the New Year together."

The bar crowd was counting down in unison. "Three... Two... One... Happy New Year!"

Pilar lifted her head up to Sebastian's and pulled him in even closer with her legs. She kissed him long and deep. He could feel her breasts pressing against his chest and he did not want the kiss to end. The kiss lasted long after the rest of the crowd had finished their embraces and Sebastian could hear his soldiers heckling him. With eyes closed, he could hear the choruses of "Go, Sarge!" and "You big stud." He could hear Jenny McCarthy talking to someone on the TV, followed by the cry "*Allahu Akbar*".

Next he heard the distinct and all too familiar sound of a large explosion. Sebastian cut off the kiss and whipped his head up to see a black screen on the television. He uttered under his breath, "Fuck me."

After a few seconds, the television lit back up. The news anchor, T.J. Holmes, appeared on the screen. "Ladies and gentlemen, it appears that a bomb has gone off in the middle of Times Square. We have lost our live feed and have sustained heavy damages to our studios. But we will continue to bring live coverage of this tragedy. We are going to a live shot from one of our local affiliates, who is covering the scene from a helicopter above Times Square."

The coverage switched to a live aerial shot of Times Square. Windows on the first three floors of the buildings lining Times Square were blown out and portions of the buildings' walls were missing. The stages where Jenny McCarthy and Ryan Seacrest had been standing were no longer there. Only a crater in the street remained of what had been two stages only moments before. Hundreds upon hundreds of dead and wounded Americans lay sprawled and bleeding in the street, with many piled against what was left of the walls of the buildings.

It was a scene of pure horror and carnage. It was not unlike scenes that Sebastian had seen in Syria after a bomb attack. His mind immediately shifted into combat mode as he assessed the situation. He studied the room and could see that all the patrons, including his men, were standing wild eyed and bewildered.

"Everybody pay up and head back to base! We will be on high alert in about one minute and they will need all of us to lock down the base," he said in a calm but resolute voice. He looked down and locked eyes with Pilar, who was still straddling him. Her face was both awestruck by what she had just seen and amazed by how quickly Sebastian had taken it all in and immediately got his men in line.

"Thanks for the kiss," he said, smiling down at her, both because he had enjoyed it and because he wanted to reassure her that everything would be fine. "Do you think we might do that again sometime? You know, like when I don't have to rush back to work."

"You better believe it, soldier," she said with her room-lighting smile. She pulled her legs back, releasing Sebastian from her grip. As he turned toward the front door, she called out to him. "Bash! Be careful."

"Don't worry, Pilar. I got my midnight kiss. I'll be fine." He gave her a quick wink and strolled through the door.

CHAPTER 19
Fort Eustis, Virginia

Santiago Ortiz dressed quickly, putting on his ACU pants and a plain tan T-shirt. He walked out of his room and turned toward the day room positioned in the center of the barracks. Charlie Company's barracks was a three story building which contained a computer lab, laundry room and day rooms on each floor. Santiago walked into the day room and picked up the television remote off the ping-pong table as he passed. Turning on the TV, he immediately changed the channel to the FOX News channel. Everybody else in the company liked CNN, but he preferred FOX, primarily because Ainsley Earhardt was hot.

Santiago could see the early morning heavy snow falling outside of the window. It had been seven weeks since the Times Square attack. He could hear Ainsley talking on the TV and turned his attention towards her voice. She was talking about an attack on the Oscars.

What the fuck? He asked himself. *The Oscars? Was this Khalid? That crazy pendejo did not attack the Oscars just seven weeks after New York. What in the hell was he thinking?*

Santiago had been working the second shift. He was in the hangar from seventeen hundred until zero one hundred and saw none of the Oscars broadcast. Earhardt was saying that the dead gunman was a lone-wolf jihadist named Clifton Nickelberry, a career criminal who had converted to Islam in San Quentin prison. Nickelberry had changed his name to Abdullah Muhammed after his release from prison. Abdullah, armed with three hand grenades and an M249 light machine gun, opened fire on the red carpet, killing ninety three people before being shot and killed by Los Angeles police officers. The names of the people killed by Abdullah were being withheld by the police, however it was known that some of the people who died due to the initial barrage with hand grenades included Matthew McConaughey, Tim Robbins, Susan Sarandon and Melissa Rivers.

Man that sucks, thought Santiago. He liked McConaughey, and the guy was probably going to win his third Best Actor award this year. That crazy son of a bitch, Khalid, could not possibly be behind this. Why would he sneak as many people into the country as he had and then intentionally bring this much attention to himself? This had to be ISIL. The New York attack had all the trademark Al-Qaeda fingerprints. An attack on New York with a bomb was Al-Qaeda's style. The Oscars attack was a lone gunman firing into a crowd, like the Paris attacks by ISIL.

Or was Khalid really this smart? Was his plan to infiltrate the Unites States and then make the government look in the wrong direction? They wouldn't be looking at Mexican immigrants if they were searching high and low for self-radicalized, lone-wolf Muslim jihadists. If it was Khalid, then the man was a lot smarter than Santiago had given him credit for. He wasn't just a terrorist with an impossible plan. He was a strategic mastermind who was more than capable of accomplishing his goal.

Santiago knew that he needed to speak to his uncle, but since the New York attack the base had been on complete lockdown. Nobody was getting passes to go off base and nobody was coming in without clearance. More importantly, all phone calls and text messages were being monitored and internet privileges had been revoked. Santiago knew that he needed to find a way to get the message to his uncle that Khalid was a very dangerous man. Juan Carlos needed to distance himself from Khalid and quickly.

On the television, Steve Doocy and Brian Kilmeade were discussing the attack. Kilmeade was saying that this was the second attack in less than one month perpetrated by radical Islamic terrorists. It was time for the President to stand up for Americans. His policy of not addressing radical Islam for what it truly is, a direct threat to the United States, had led to these attacks. How many more would America have to suffer before the President took a stand? The President's strategy of leading from behind had led to not one, but two attacks on our sovereign ground. It also precipitated the necessity for the US to send their troops into Syria, even though these radical Islamic terrorists could have been dealt with had the President left our troops in Iraq and Afghanistan and not shut down all of his military bases in those two countries. It was time for the United States to start leading the world again and it starts by protecting its citizens at home.

Those guys don't hold anything back, thought Santiago. But Kilmeade was right. One thing Santiago had learned from his short time in the Army was that President Adama was not well liked by the soldiers. Not only had he cut the size of the military in half, but he had handcuffed it at every opportunity. The President did not allow them to do what they were trained to do. Some of the older servicemen had even referred to him as the modern day Lyndon Johnson, as they both had a policy of limited war and, just like Johnson had done in Viet Nam, Adama had no discussions with his Generals on the fundamental issue of how the war should be fought. He had approved hundreds of drone missions in Syria in his supposed war with ISIL, but never allowed the military to have any input on the targets. Just like Johnson, he had personally approved all of the targets. The result was thousands of failed missions, the inability to take out even a single ISIL leader and the eventual deployment of thousands of troops to Syria to fight a two-sided war against not only ISIL but the Assad regime as well. Hell, every person in the United States knew that he should have taken out the Syrian oil fields and cut off ISIL's source of income, but not one mission on the oil fields was ever approved. The President needed to start consulting with someone who knew what they were doing. A war was coming and this was just the beginning.

CHAPTER 20
Panama Beach, Florida

Esan Afridi bounced effortlessly over the waves as he gazed at the horizon ahead of him. The beach was packed with scantily clad partygoers dancing and gyrating to the beat of the music. *The concert has already started,* he thought to himself. Now he would never be able to get up close to the stage.

Esan's family owned a parasailing and watercraft rental company in Panama Beach. His father had insisted on letting one last group rent some of their SeaDoos and of course they were late in returning the watercrafts. Man, he hated those over-privileged Spring Breakers. By the time that Esan had finished loading all of the SeaDoos onto the trailer and returned them to his home, he was running late for the concert. Knowing that the traffic into the Spinnaker Beach Club would be impossible to get through, he had taken his own SeaDoo GTX

Limited iS 260 to the concert. At twenty-two years of age, Esan had attended all the Luke Bryan Spring Break concerts. He had been going since he was sixteen years old and this was the first year that Luke wouldn't be performing. Instead, it was his favorite band, Florida Georgia Line, and he definitely would not miss this one.

Esan had rushed into the house to change clothes, grab his gear and then to the boat house. It had taken him a mere five minutes to get from his home to his current location. He was almost there. Through the salty ocean spray he could see the beach and concert goers about one quarter mile away.

The afternoon sun was setting. Its orange glow in the background made Esan's SeaDoo appear like a black shadow to any of the spring breakers who might have been looking out at the ocean. As he approached the throngs of young people dancing and drinking and living their lives to the fullest, he throttled down his watercraft and beached it. Esan opened the glove box and pulled out the dry bag which easily converted to a backpack. He slipped the backpack over his shoulders, bouncing three times to situate it on his back. Esan could hear Florida Georgia Line playing "Sippin' on Whiskey" from the main stage, the giant towers of speakers flanking the stage blaring out the music.

As Esan stepped off the SeaDoo, a giant of a man walked down the beach toward him. The man was dressed in black shorts and a skin tight, white polo shirt with the word 'security' printed across his massive chest. "Hey, you can't park that here!"

"I'm just here for the concert," said Esan, reaching back into the footwell of the SeaDoo.

The man pushed his way through a crowd of Spring Breakers dancing in the breaking waves of the shoreline. "I don't care! You have to go around to the beach access point over at Club La Vela. You can't park on the beach."

"Okay! Whatever you say, big guy," said Esan as he lifted an AK-47 assault rifle out of the footwell and turned toward the security guard. The first bullet hit the man in the chest, stopping his progress and causing him to step backwards. The second bullet struck just below his nose, sending a spray of blood and brain matter flying onto the Spring Breakers dancing in the water. The sound of the gunfire was stifled by the music blaring out of the speakers. Esan released his right hand from the pistol grip and moved the selector switch up, changing the firing mode from semi-auto to fully automatic.

A busty brunette in an orange bikini top and cut-off shorts, who had been dancing in the water behind the security guard, stopped gyrating. She looked down at her outstretched arms and stared at the blood and gray matter that had sprayed all over them. Looking up into the crowd, she said, "Ewww! Hey, which one of you assholes is throwing jello shots? I'm gonna kick your ass!"

She never saw the bullets that ripped through her body and the bodies of her dancing companions.

After seeing the dozen or so water dancers fall lifelessly onto the beach, Esan turned toward the stage. With a seventy-five round drum magazine attached to his AK-47, the Russian made weapon was churning out deadly projectiles at a rate of 10 rounds per second. Esan kept the stock of the barrel held tight against his right shoulder. He was careful to keep his aim low and toward the waist of his targets in order to keep the recoil from raising it above their heads. Esan knew that he had a limited amount of time and ammunition and he had to make every shot count.

His bullets had no problem finding a home. The free concert had drawn over ten thousand spectators. The sandy path from the beach to the stage was wall to wall people who had nowhere to run. Esan knew that as long as he had bullets, he would be a harbinger of death. Allah was great and merciful, he thought to himself.

"Allahu Akbar!" he exclaimed as he released the drum magazine and loaded another from his backpack. The concert goers had now noticed the bodies falling around them and were screaming while trying to flee. Some fled down the beach, but the majority pressed toward the stage area, packing themselves into the enclosed space like sardines in a can. In the chaos, bodies of young college students fell like bowling pins. The bullets from Esan's weapon tore through their bodies, sending a mist of red up into the warm beach air.

Esan loaded another drum magazine and continued his progress toward the stage. He sensed someone coming up behind him and wheeled around, never taking his finger off the trigger. The arc of bullets shredded through the bodies of the three young would-be heroes who were brave enough to attempt to stop his deadly attack. Esan fired down the beach at more of the fleeing young students. Turning back toward the stage, he continued his deadly assault, stepping over the bodies of his fallen victims while continuing to shoot everything in his path.

Esan smiled as he watched the bodies fall, admiring the results of his attack. Al Rezgui had been careless in his beach attack in Tunisia, he thought to himself. He hadn't chosen a populated enough target. Why kill thirty-eight infidels when you can take out hundreds?

Esan loaded another drum and continued his murderous rampage. "*Allahu Akbar*," he screamed again as he unloaded the drum into the wall of fleeing partygoers. Esan loaded his fifth and last drum and began walking backwards toward the beach. Switching the selector switch to semi-automatic, he was now carefully picking his targets, taking out the strongest looking males who were most likely to rush him. The once white, sandy beach was now red with the blood of his victims. Upon reaching his still running SeaDoo, Esan shoved the machine back into the ocean, turning it toward the open waters of the

Gulf of Mexico. The burning hot barrel of the assault rifle made an evil hiss when he tossed it into the ocean.

Esan climbed onto the watercraft and fired the throttle. The machine burst into life, accelerating to fifty miles per hour. Slicing through the waves, Esan sped through the ocean toward the boat waiting for him. The real mistake that Al Rezgui had made was not having an escape plan. Esan had to hand it to ISIL though. They always learned from their mistakes. His handler had planned this attack to perfection. Since it was a concert, there would be plenty of YouTube and Vine videos published showing the terror attack. Videos which would also be useful in promoting the jihad. He was fifteen minutes from the boat waiting for him in international waters.

Next stop, Syria.

CHAPTER 21
Matamoros, Tamaulipas, Mexico

Sean Ray walked into the debriefing room and set his LAR-15 on the table. He removed his black DEA cap and tossed it next to the rifle. Picking the damp towel up off the table, he wiped the dirt and sweat from his face and head. He and his team were returning from another mission with Inspector Gonzales and the *Policia Federal Division Antidrogas* team. Over the past few months the joint team had intercepted four of the Gulf Cartel's drug shipments and captured their number two and three leaders. Today's raid was also a huge success. They had managed to seize fifty kilos of the Cartel's cocaine.

"Good job, men. We got the bad guys and nobody got hurt."

"Damn straight, boss," said Parker. "Any day that Swanny doesn't accidentally shoot me is a good day."

"Bite me, Parker," chimed in Swanny. "If I didn't cover your macho ass when you ran towards that truck, you would be worm food right now."

"I knew you had my back."

Mexican *Federales* began filing into the room, followed by Jace Travers. The *Federales* were complimenting each other with celebratory slaps on the back and high fives, reliving the excitement of the raid. Jace wondered how the FAST Team always made it back into the debriefing room before the *Federales*. It was *their* building for crying out loud.

Hector Gonzales entered the room with a somber look on his face. A look which belied the cheerfulness of the rest of the men.

"Sean, you and your men should see this," he said, pointing the remote towards the big screen television centered on the wall behind Sean. The television came to life with a reporter from CNN en Español who was standing on the shore of Palm Beach and describing the horrible attack. The bodies of the dead college students still littered the ground behind her.

Sean's jaw dropped and the excitement washed from his face. "What in the hell?" he asked, watching in horror the hundreds of bodies lying covered on the ground.

"Hey, Hector, does this thing get subtitles?" asked Dave Martin. "I don't speak Spanish all that great. I can't keep up with what she's saying."

"Of course," said Hector as he pressed a button, turning on the English subtitles.

The reporter continued, describing how a lone gunman rode up to the crowded concert on a watercraft and opened fire on the unsuspecting college students, who were on Spring Break, and whose only crime was wanting to have a good time and listen to the music at the free concert.

"It is a miracle that more of the estimated ten thousand concertgoers were not injured. The gunman used all of his ammunition and escaped back into the ocean. The local police and Coast Guard are searching for the gunman who is still at large, armed and dangerous."

A picture of the young man responsible was inset next to the reporter's head. The reporter stated that the picture was taken from one of many YouTube videos posted immediately after the attack. CNN would not play the video because of the horrific nature and graphic detail of the young people's deaths which it displayed. No terrorist group had taken credit for the attack, but it was believed that this was another attack by ISIL against the United States. According to the woman, the terror suspect was filmed yelling 'Allahu Akbar' repeatedly as he fired on the defenseless young men and women.

"If this was indeed an attack by the radical Islamic group, then it would be the third such attack in as many months," the reporter concluded.

Every man in the room looked at the screen in complete horror. Although each and every one of them had seen death in combat, none had seen attacks on innocent children to this magnitude. Some of the *Federales*, who had children the same age of the victims, began to tear up. Sean could not believe what he was seeing. An attack on kids. Who the fuck were these guys? Who could be so soulless that they would attack children? There was a special place in hell for people like that and if he ever got face to face with one of those sons of a bitches, he would make sure he sent them there.

CHAPTER 22
Corpus Christi Army Depot
Corpus Christi, Texas

Sebastian watched with disgust as the television displayed the horrific event in Palm Beach. The image of the young Pakistani man responsible was inset in the upper corner of the screen. *How in the hell could that kid do this?* Sebastian asked himself.

He slid around Maryam Saleh, moving closer to the television to get a better view of the carnage. Sebastian had seen the savage and horrific things that ISIL had done in Syria first hand. Beheadings, crucifixions, cutting off hands, rape and human trafficking were just a few of the horrors he had witnessed. He thought he had seen the worst that they could do. But he was wrong. Sebastian had never seen an attack like this one and the others that had occurred so far this year in the United States. The Tunisia beach attack had nothing on this one. How is it that a lone gunman can kill hundreds of young men and women on American soil and then just slip away?

The reporter was asking the same question on the television. She was pleading with the public to contact their congressmen and force the government to protect its citizens.

"Yeah, right," Sebastian said out loud.

"You don't think that the government can do something about these attacks, Sarge?" asked Maryam.

Sebastian turned toward her. "No, Maryam, I don't. Tomorrow the President will come out and give another speech about how we need stronger gun control laws. He'll blame the gun and not the evil person who used it. The Democrats will try to pass some stupid gun control law and the Republicans will block it. In the end, they will all say they tried to do something good for the country and nothing will actually get done. It'll be business as usual." His eyes moved to the television and then back to Maryam. "And all of those kids will still be dead."

"I take it you aren't in favor of gun control. That is how we keep guns out of the hands of crazy people like that guy," she said, nodding towards the television.

"I am a realist, Maryam. You can never keep guns out of the hands of people who want to kill people. They will always find a way to get one. That kid was shooting a fully automatic AK-47 with a seventy round drum mag on it. There are somewhere around eighty to a hundred million AK-47s in circulation around the world and they don't sell them at Wal-mart or Cabela's. So no, I don't think stronger gun control laws are going to help. And you can't just get rid of every gun in America."

"Why not?"

"First off, it's a Constitutional right of all Americans to own guns. Secondly, gun laws only punish the people who break them. They don't prevent crazy motherfuckers like that from getting them. Third, you could never find every gun out there. Even if you could track down and destroy every single gun owned by every single American today, you would never keep guns from coming into the country after that. Americans are real good at getting what they want. Look at Prohibition. Congress outlawed booze and the Kennedys become millionaires running rum up from Cuba. And Prohibition only dropped alcohol consumption by like twenty-five percent. So how could you possibly expect more gun control to be effective? The Cartels down in Mexico would be chomping at the bit to sell guns in the States."

"So what is your solution?" asked Maryam. "Arm everybody?"

"Everybody who wants to be armed. And get more cops. And give them the freedom to do their jobs without fear of being fired because they are enforcing the law." Sebastian turned and held his left arm toward the television. "If any of those kids had a weapon, or if there was a cop with a gun at the concert, then *that* would not look like it does. That kid knew that he would be shooting fish in a barrel, because he knew that the only one there with a gun would be him. And he didn't give a rat's ass about being charged with possession of an automatic weapon. Because if he was caught by the cops, he was either gonna be dead or charged with about three hundred counts of murder."

"Or they could have just had cops for security, instead of the bouncers or whatever they were using."

"Yeah, but the way that people hate cops right now, and how everybody posts every little incident on YouTube, what cop in their right mind would want to work security at a concert with thousands of drunk college kids and their cellphones? That's just asking to be fired. But we do need more cops. More cops, Feds and special Anti-terrorist cops or something like that. We need the ability to track down kids like that," he said nodding towards the television, "and those crazy sons of a bitches in New York and LA. We've been attacked by terrorists on American soil three times this year and the President still thinks the way to defeat ISIL is drone strikes. I've been there and seen how they are. They're tough, pretty damn smart and not afraid to die. The only way to defeat them is to search them out and kill them. And not with a drone. It's a boots on the ground job. And now that we have them over here, we need to track them down and kill 'em just like in Syria."

"How do you plan on getting more cops when you just said that everybody hates cops these days?"

"America has thousands of soldiers who came back from Iraq and Afghanistan and who are well trained and perfect for the job. We tracked down those assholes back when they were AQI and ran their ass right out of Iraq. We can do it here too, if the government would just let us. But we can't hunt down these savages *and* be worried about political correctness. The government and the people have to be willing to catch them and not be worried about their feelings. They're sociopaths. They don't have any fucking feelings."

Maryam could see the contempt that Sebastian had for the terrorists etched on his face. Whenever he talked about them, his jaw tightened and his eyes turned from blue to gray. "You really hate them, don't you, Sarge?"

"After everything I have seen in Syria, Afghanistan and Iraq and now this, the killing of innocent kids for no reason, you bet I do. Those kids weren't soldiers. They were just a bunch of kids having fun and they were slaughtered for no reason except for where they lived. ISIL kills women and children because they serve no purpose to them. They murder fathers in front of their families and then sell the families into slavery. They are nothing but low life thugs hiding behind a religion. You're damn right I hate them." He nodded toward the television again. "I wish they would try some of that shit here. I would unleash some serious hate on 'em and put them down without any hesitation or remorse."

CHAPTER 23
Corpus Christi, Texas

Khalid removed the screeching teapot from the stove and carried it toward the table in the kitchen of his small one-bedroom apartment. He had rented the apartment under his new name, Enrique Martinez. He liked living in Corpus Christi more than he had Houston. It was a much smaller city than Houston, with only about three hundred thousand people, but it was still populated enough for him to hide from the prying eyes of the United States government. Khalid found it ironic that the name of the city, when translated from Latin, meant the Body of Christ. Such an appropriate name for what he had planned. Just as Christ had sacrificed himself for his beliefs, this city would sacrifice itself for the infidel ways of its occupants.

He liked the city most of all because here he was free of the godless heathens employed by Juan Carlos. Khalid liked Juan Carlos.

He reminded Khalid of himself. Juan Carlos was intelligent, educated and religious, even if it was in the wrong faith. He had a sense of morality, although he would not hesitate for a second to kill anyone who opposed him. When Khalid had discussed the benefits of beheading one's enemies in order to strike fear in those who would oppose him, Juan Carlos immediately put the tactic to use, striking fear into the police and other Cartels who sought to harm his business. Juan Carlos was a just man who could turn savage at a moment's notice and just as easily revert back.

Khalid was sure that the Coahuilans that Juan Carlos had sent across the border were also good people, just as Juan Carlos had described them. But the men he employed in Houston were not the same. They were filthy, uneducated men who bathed sparsely, constantly listened to that horrible rap music and drank alcohol to excess daily. They did not possess a moral code, had no honor, and they were savages for the sole purpose of being savage. If Juan Carlos did not care so much for his men, Khalid would have ended the infidels' lives months ago on Allah's behalf.

From the table, he had a clear view of the television in the living room. The reporter was talking about the latest attacks. He was describing the awful events that had taken place in Louisville, Kentucky. A lone gunman, most likely an ISIL terrorist, had opened fire at the Kentucky Derby, killing one-hundred and thirty-two people and three of the race horses before being gunned down by local police. This was the latest in a succession of attacks against the United States by ISIL. The President was expected to address this latest attack later on today. The reporter added that the public outcry after the Spring Break Massacre and the attack at the Chicago Cubs spring training baseball game had caused the President and Congress to spring into action by ordering the development of a special police force operating through the Department of Homeland Security. The special police force's purpose was to track down terrorists and stop lone wolf attacks on American soil.

The reporter's words caused a smile to form on Khalid's lips. How easy it was to manipulate the infidel politicians in America, he thought to himself as he poured the hot water into his teacup and added the tea. Their predictability was uncanny. After only a few attacks, they had scrambled through their sacred opinion polls and immediately passed laws to protect the citizens. The Democrats had called for stricter gun laws while the Republicans vied for more freedom to spy on their citizens via cell phones and internet use. This was why Khalid knew that the jihad would succeed: Sharia law needed no amendments. It was strict, concise and not subject to public opinion. It was certainly not subject to the opinion of the American public, who were unwilling to sacrifice and changed their position on most topics almost daily. Today they wanted to destroy the Islamic State. Tomorrow they would protest in the streets about the tactics used to accomplish the task. Americans had a short attention span and no fortitude for violence, which was evidenced by their politicians.

Khalid focused again on the television. The reporter reiterated that the President had promised to reinforce local police and the FBI to put an end to these attacks. The camera panned behind the reporter to show the bodies of the victims lying on the ground and the survivors, still wearing their oversized hats and brightly colored party clothes, huddled together and weeping over the tragedy they had witnessed. The reporter opined that it was time that the President focused on protecting Americans from Islamic extremists and stopped focusing on the war in Syria. Khalid sipped his tea and his smile grew wide. Almost all of his people were in place and his plan was working just as he had expected. Just as he had told Abdul it would. He had only a few more steps left to complete before Muhammad's Sword would come to full fruition.

CHAPTER 24
Naval Air Station Corpus Christi
Corpus Christi, Texas

Sean Ray focused intently on the reporter who was speaking on the television. He could not believe what he was hearing. It was another attack on America's sovereign ground. This was the fifth attack in as many months. Something had to be done. It wasn't that long ago that every country in the world feared the United States, but the President's policy of leading from behind had weakened that view. ISIL no longer feared the United States. Instead, they believed that America had become old, tired and weak. And just as they had done in the Middle East, when a dictator became weak, ISIL was now on the attack. Strike when you believe that your enemy is the weakest.

The lack of a significant response after New York and the Spring Break Massacre had prompted them to strike again, first at the

Chicago Cubs spring training and now at the Kentucky Derby. Each time ISIL struck, the President did nothing except give speeches about how ISIL was weak and how America would prevail. And with each strike and lack of response, Sean knew that ISIL was growing stronger and braver.

"Do you believe this?" asked Swanny, motioning toward the television with his left palm upstretched. "Last month they hit Spring Training. Baseball is America's game, for crying out loud. And now the Kentucky Derby. There is nothing more American than baseball and horse racing. These jackasses think that they can just come in and shoot up Spring Training and the Derby. I mean, they even shot the damn horses. What kind of sick fuck shoots horses? And whatever happened to that joint terrorism taskforce that President Adama promised? You mean to tell me that nobody could figure out what this dude was going to do? I mean, the dude drove all the way from Maine to Kentucky and even got pulled over for speeding. Hell, if I was a cop and I pulled over a Somali in Ohio, who had Maine license plates, I would question something about the dude. Or better yet, apparently this asshole was a Somali Muslim refugee just like the dude who shot up my beloved Cubs. Why wasn't he on a terror watch list in the first place?"

"Well, I'm pretty sure that we expect refugees to be thankful enough for the refuge that they receive from us that they won't go shooting up the Kentucky Derby or a damn Cubs baseball game, Swanny," said Jace Travers from behind his tree of computer screens.

"Maybe that's the problem. We *expect* people to act right. Don't forget that we fought a war in Somalia. Remember *Blackhawk Down*? The whole damn town came after our guys. The Somali's were savages, just like those assholes over in Afghanistan that we had to deal with. Why should we expect them to love us when they hated us before they got here? Just because we give 'em a new home?

Besides, there are always some bad guys that sneak through with the good ones. Remember *Scarface*? Pacino was a refugee. He was also one bad Mofo that didn't deserve to be in the country. So therefore we should expect that the refugees *will* do harm to us and our country and put 'em all on a list just as a precaution."

"So you want to register every immigrant and what? Have 'em report to a probation officer so that we can keep track of them?" asked Travers.

"Damn straight. When a country welcomes you in, you should be grateful enough to submit to a little supervision. Besides that, they already register when they get their visas. A little supervision could have prevented this attack, the one in Boston, Times Square and most, importantly, the attack on my beloved Cubs. They had a real shot at winning the World Series this year. Do you remember what Hector said about Mexico? They hardly let anybody in. If anyone who does get in breaks the law, then they don't get a trial or nothing. They get sent straight back to where they came from. A little supervision would be a lot more desirable to refugees than Mexico's policy."

"Hey, you're preaching to choir, brother. I just don't think that the President or Congress will ever do that."

"Amen to that. But you can't tell me that if this dude had been on a watch list or had gone missing from his whatever you want to call it, Immigration Case Officer, that we couldn't have tracked him down and stopped this from happening. I mean, it was the Kentucky Derby for Christ's sake. Just a bunch of folks drinking mint juleps and wearing hats and goofy looking clothes. And he shot *American Dreamer*. They say that horse had a shot at the Triple Crown this year."

The phone on Sean's desk rang, interrupting the men's conversation. "DEA Special Agent in Charge Sean Ray speaking," he said after pushing the speaker button to answer the phone.

A woman's voice came through the speaker. "SAIC Ray, please hold for Deputy Director Collins."

"Well, since you asked so nicely, Sheila," he said as he reached across his desk for a notepad and pen. Sean knew that if Warren Collins had his personal assistant, Sheila, place the call that this was going to be official business and definitely not a personal call. So he might as well get ready.

"Good morning, Sean," said the Director, his voice clear over the phone's speaker.

Sean lifted the receiver from the cradle, turning off the speaker. "Good morning, sir. To what do I owe the pleasure of your call?"

Sean and Deputy Director Warren Collins were old friends. They had worked together at the DEA ever since Sean had joined the Agency. Collins had been the SAIC running Sean's first assignment. They had been stationed in Miami and tasked with stopping the influx of cocaine from Bolivia to the United States. Sean's career had led him to the FAST teams and Collins' had taken him to the Deputy Director's chair.

"I suppose that you have seen this latest ISIL strike."

"Yes, Warren, we've been watching it all morning. Swanny is particularly upset about this one."

"I know how he feels. The terrorist even shot the damn horses. What kind of asshole shoots horses? Swanny isn't the only one upset about it. The President called the Director personally and asked for our help with this ISIL problem."

"Why? Is his approval rating down? I don't know why he would think that radical Islamic terror attacks on our sovereign ground would negatively affect his legacy."

"That's enough of that, Sean. The last thing that I need is for the Secret Service to come knocking on your door and have a conversation with you about criticizing the President."

"Why? Do you think our phones are tapped?"

"I'm the Deputy Director of the DEA and you're a federal agent located on a U.S. military base. I *know* that the phones are tapped. Yours more so than mine. So cut the negative crap about the President."

"Yes, sir, Deputy Director. How can we be of service to the President?" Sean began twirling his pen between his fingers, sending a signal to his team who were watching him intently. His team knew that when he started running his pen through his fingers, he was either concentrating, worried or pissed off.

"Do you remember the task force that the President was going to commission after the Spring Break Massacre? Well, Congress has finally given it the green light and he wants us, or more specifically, your team to head up the training."

"My team? What the hell do we know about tracking down terrorists? We track down drug dealers and stop drug shipments. Shouldn't this be handled by the FBI, Homeland Security or somebody whose actual job is tracking terrorists?"

"The FAST teams are the best in the world in tracking down drugs. Drugs that nobody else in the world is capable of locating. And your team is the best one that we have. Hell, you guys tracked a submarine last month. Besides, the Cartels are just like terrorists except they attack us with drugs, not bombs and guns. And you guys have a great track record in taking down the high level members of the Gulf Cartel. The President wants that kind of skill to lead this new domestic terrorism unit. And he wants *you* to train the task force so that we can go after these homegrown lone wolf ISIL recruits."

"But Warren, we don't know jack shit about tracking down terrorists. Our Intel comes from local sources who lead us to the shipments. Once we have even just a little Intel, then we can go to work. Last time I checked, nobody is doling out Intel on these lone wolf terrorists. They work alone so that there is nobody to rat them out."

"You would be surprised at the Intel the FBI and Homeland have. What they aren't good at is weeding out what they don't need and tracking down these terrorists. That's where we come in."

"So they get us the Intel and we just do what we do best? Track 'em down and take 'em down?"

"That's right. But first you have to train the teams on the task force. The President is tasking the military and National Guard to send their best men to be trained. He is even calling for anybody in the military with combat experience and the recently discharged to apply."

"That sounds great, Warren, but by time we get all of these people organized and trained it may be too late. ISIL is attacking us at the rate of once a month."

"That's why the President wants people with combat training. We can eliminate that portion of training and focus on tracking these guys down and stopping the next attack."

"You're the boss, Warren. You just tell us where to go and when to be there."

"I'm glad you agree. Your team leaves first thing in the morning. There is a transport plane leaving at 07:30 from the base airfield and they need to be on it. You will stay behind and shut down the office and then meet your team at Fort Bragg in five days. I expect that will be enough time for you to close the office."

"Five days? No problem."

"Then I look forward to seeing you at Bragg in five days. Goodbye, Sean."

"Goodbye, Warren."

Sean hung up the phone and stopped twirling his pen. "Well, Swanny, you got your wish."

CHAPTER 25
Corpus Christi, Texas

Khalid, dressed in a pair of khaki cargo shorts and a navy blue Houston Texans T-shirt, walked down the long wooden pier, taking in the names of each of the boats docked in their berths. Saad and Kassim, who now went by the names of their new identities Mateo and Ignacio, followed behind Khalid. The pair also wore Khaki cargo shorts like Khalid, but each wore a U.S. Marine Corp T-shirt, Mateo in orange and Ignacio in black.

Khalid was amazed at the names that the infidels chose for their boats. The vessels ranged in size from smaller thirty-one foot vessels up to luxurious sixty-seven foot yachts with names like *Mamma's Honey, Caliente, Cowboy Heaven, Breaking Wind,* and *Sea Serpent.* Upon reaching slip number twenty-three, Khalid saw the name of the ship he was looking for, *Lottie Dottie*. The *Lottie Dottie* was a sixty-seven foot, custom-built Carolina convertible sportfish boat. The boat had three large fighting chairs lining the rear deck, allowing multiple fisherman to fish at the same time. The solid white seats contrasted nicely with the dark wood that trimmed the boat and deck. Khalid took notice of the immaculate condition of the boat. He could tell that the captain took pride in his vessel.

Khalid had chosen this particular charter from its description on the fishing guide website. The Captain, who went by the name Captain Steve, had served in the Marine Riverboat Patrol and traveled the world, accumulating over twenty years of fishing experience. The website said that Captain Steve's love of the ocean and desire to help others bring fish into the boat had established him as one of the top guides in Corpus Christi. The *Lottie Dottie* was a luxury Sport fisherman vessel that could cruise at a speed of forty-eight miles an hour, allowing for more fishing time and less travel time. It was also the pride of Captain Steve's fleet.

A voice came booming from the cockpit above Khalid and his two friends. "Ahoy there. You must be Enrique."

"*Jes*, I am Enrique Martinez," Khalid said, using his well-developed Mexican accent, "and these are my friends, Mateo and Ignacio."

Khalid took in the middle aged man with slightly graying temples and the slight beginnings of a pot-belly. The Captain was also dressed in khaki shorts and wore a blue tank-top.

"Nice to meet you, boys. Y'all climb over and welcome aboard the *Lottie Dottie*. I'm Captain Steve and that young buck climbing down to you there is Billy, my first mate."

Khalid and his companions stepped off the pier and over the boat wall onto the wooden deck of the *Lottie Dottie*. "Thank you, Captain."

"Hey Enrique, anybody ever tell you that you look a lot like Enrique Iglesias?"

"*Si*, I get that a lot."

"I bet you do." Captain Steve noticed the shirts worn by Mateo and Ignacio. "So you fellas are Marines?"

Khalid nodded back toward his two companions. "They are. I am not."

"That's okay, Enrique. I won't hold that against you. Are you boys stationed here at the Naval Air Station?"

"Yes, Captain," said Mateo. "We are in the Security Forces on base."

"MPs, huh? Billy was in the Army, a Ranger Scout, and I was a Riverine myself, SBU-26. Joined straight out of high school. We patrolled the rivers down in South America mostly. Places like Bolivia, El Salvador, Columbia and Ecuador. I was in Operation Just Cause down in Panama right after I joined up. We took down that bastard Manuel Noriega. Damn drug cartels back then were almost as bad as those ragheads that are shooting up everything today. Tell you what, if those ISIL guys show up here, you boys take 'em out for me. Semper Fi!"

"Semper Fi! Capitan Steve," replied Ignacio and Mateo.

"Billy will get you fellas squared away and show you how the fighting chairs and rods and reels work. He'll teach you how to bait your hooks and stuff while I get us out to sea. We are going about five miles out today and it should be a good day for catching Sailfish, Mahi, Tuna and Wahoo. We might reel in some Snapper, but they don't really come into season until next month. There are soft drinks, water and some grub in the fridge in the salon. The coolers on the deck and up in the cabin are stocked with cold cervezas for you boys. I also have some Dramamine and Pepto in the cabinet by the fridge, just in case you boys don't take to well to the open sea."

"Thank you, Captain," replied Khalid as he motioned to Mateo and Ignacio, signaling to them to retrieve two beers from the cooler. They each opened their beer and took a long drink. Khalid looked at Billy and motioned toward the salon door with his left hand. "The *aqua* is *ahi*?"

"Yes, sir," said Billy, opening the door for Khalid. "Straight back to the galley and it's the big stainless refrigerator. Water is on the top two shelves."

"*Gracias, amigo.*"

"What's up, Enrique? You don't partake in the cervezas? I ain't met many of you boys that would refuse a cold beer."

"Unfortunately I had to give up the drinking, Captain. Alcohol turns me into a bad person."

Captain Steve reached into his pocket and pulled out a large gold coin about the size of a silver dollar. He held it up with his right index and middle fingers to show to the group. "Ten years sober myself. Do you have a group here in town?"

"Not yet. I moved to Corpus Christi two weeks ago and haven't found one yet."

"Well if you need to talk to someone, or a sponsor, I will be glad to hook you up." Captain Steve pulled a business card out of his pocket and wrote on the back of the card. "That's my home address and cell phone number. If you need anybody to talk to, day or night, you just call or come by and I will be there for you."

Khalid took the card from the captain and placed it into his wallet. "*Gracias,* Captain. Your wife does not mind people coming over at all hours?"

"I'm not married. I was once. Alcoholism has its price and mine was the love of a really good woman." Captain Steve turned and began climbing the ladder to the cabin. "Well, it's time to get this show on the road and catch us some fish. You boys settle in while Billy casts us off."

Upon reaching the top of the ladder, he looked down toward the men. A large smile creased his face as he said, "*Lottie Dottie*, it's time to Pahty!"

.

CHAPTER 26
Jack Ash's Drinkery
Corpus Christi, Texas

Sebastian Gray walked through the doorway to Jack Ash's. He laughed as he walked past the life-size statue of the legendary Jack Daniels. Years ago someone had put a sombrero on the statue and it had never been taken off. It always made him laugh when he saw it. He saw the usual crowd of guys doing their best to hit on the bartenders, including Pilar. He wondered if they would stop hitting on her if they knew that they had no chance.

Sebastian strolled closer to the bar and could hear one of the men talking to Pilar. He was a short man in his mid-twenties. Not very muscular, but reasonably good looking.

"Come on, Pilar. You know you want to give me your number. So why are you playing so hard to get?"

"I don't date the customers, Johnnie. It's bad for business. After I break your heart, you will stop coming in."

Sebastian pulled up a bar stool and sat down right next to the man. "I would really like a Bud Light, ma'am, and if it's not too much trouble, do you think I could get your number? I have never seen anyone as beautiful as you."

The man next to him looked at him and shook his head. "Man, you're going to have to do better than that. She don't date patrons. It's like a hard rule and she don't ever break it."

Sebastian saw the beer bottle sliding down the bar and stopped it by holding out his left hand. He took a long draw from the bottle. As he set it back down on the bar, Pilar's face was directly in front of his. She had climbed up onto the bar and was straddling him with her legs draped over the edge and her arms around his neck.

"I can do better than just my number, soldier," she said, giving him a long deep kiss. The men sitting around the bar started cat calling as they watched in amazement. "I get off at eleven. If you're lucky, you'll be getting off by eleven-thirty," she said with a devilish smile.

Sebastian smiled and played along with her. "Sounds good to me. Your place is probably closer?"

Pilar slapped him lightly across the face. Her eyes glowed with mischievousness. "It's always my place. Why can't we go to yours?"

The men around the bar nodded in affirmation to each other as they realized that Sebastian was Pilar's boyfriend and not just some random guy who had broken her of the no-dating policy. Even though he was the one man who had.

"You know why, baby. I live on base and we have been on lock down since New Year's Day. Nobody gets on base without a base ID or clearance."

"Nobody? You're in charge of the MPs. You could sneak me on if you *really* wanted to."

"That would be treason and I would be shot. Okay, maybe not shot, but at least put in prison. You don't want me to go to jail, do you?"

She gave him a crooked, naughty grin. "No, baby. I would miss you too much. Besides, I hear they only let you have two conjugal visits a month. I would have to find someone else to take care of me the rest of the month." Pilar glanced at the patrons and the hand of every man along the bar was raised to volunteer for the job.

Sebastian gave her a playful smile, revealing his dimples. "I'm sorry, Pilar. I just can't bear the thought of you and all of these guys. We'll just have to go to your place. The only way you can get on base without clearance or ID is if you go to a funeral. All funeral traffic is automatically sent straight through."

Pilar cocked her head as if a light bulb had gone off. "So all we have to do is kill one of these jokers and then I get to come over to your place?"

"They would have to be military and have already requested to be buried on base, but yeah. However, we can't just go around killing people so you can get laid." Sebastian paused for a brief second, smirked and then looked around the bar at the men who had raised their hands. "On second thought, are any of you guys in the military?"

CHAPTER 27
Corpus Christi, Texas

Khalid walked down the sidewalk towards the front door of the large two story brick house. He noticed the immaculate manicured lawn and thought to himself that fishing boat captains must do well for themselves in Corpus Christi. But one would expect as much from a man who piloted a one-million-dollar boat. He strode to the large wooden door and rang the doorbell. He was greeted by Captain Steve, who was wearing a chef's apron over his polo and cargo shorts. His sunglasses had been replaced by a pair of Ralph Lauren glasses.

"Hey, *mi amigo*! What's shaking? I was just cooking us up some dinner. Hope you like it. I made my specialty, fresh sautéed asparagus, zucchini, Brussel sprouts, carrots, green beans, jalapenos, onions and garlic topped with poached tilapia." Captain Steve shook

Khalid's hand and then turned toward the kitchen. "I don't mean to be rude, but I've got to stir the veggies or we'll be eating pizza."

Khalid entered the house, following Captain Steve through the home. "Don't worry, Captain Steve, cooking is a passion of mine also."

They walked down the white marble hallway, lined with photographs of Captain Steve and his crew on the many boats he had owned through the years, and turned into the living room. Khalid noticed the seventy-two-inch television and leather sofa, which reminded him of his home in Al-Dana. They continued into the majestic kitchen. "You have a very nice home, Captain Steve."

"Thanks, Enrique. But it's just plain Steve here at the house. I'm only Captain on the boat. I'm glad you called. I know it's hard moving to a new town. The strangeness of it all and not knowing many people. A lot of us fall into temptation and start drinking again. It's good to have friends in your situation. Friends that don't drink, I mean. So I'm really glad you called me."

"I am pleased that you offered. Ignacio and Mateo are dear friends, but they do not understand why I do not drink," lied Khalid. "I mean, they know what will happen if I drink, but since they do not have the same problem with drinking, they do not understand my situation." Khalid moved to the bar, taking a seat on one of the brown leather barstools where he had a good view of Captain Steve working at the stove. "Is there anything I can do to help you prepare dinner?"

"Just sit there and look pretty," said Captain Steve with a wry grin. "I'm just messing with you, man. You can make us something to drink. I've got sweet tea made in the fridge, or there's water and diet cokes in there too."

Khalid rose and rounded the bar toward the stainless steel refrigerator. "Sweet tea sounds delicious," he lied. The one thing that he found most irritating about having to live amongst the infidels was their love for iced tea. Tea was meant to be served piping hot, not over ice. But in order to legitimately pass himself as a Mexican immigrant, he had taught himself to stomach the beverage. He found two glasses in the cabinet next to the refrigerator and filled them with ice. As he poured the tea, he asked, "So you were in the Navy?"

"Marines," said Steve as he spooned the vegetables onto their plates. "Technically it's a branch of the Navy, but we don't really associate with the squids. Marines fight for a living."

"I am sorry. I did not mean to offend you," said Khalid as he set the glasses down on the table.

"No apologies necessary, my friend. People get us confused all the time with swab jockeys." Steve pulled the fish out of the oven and placed them over the vegetables. "Dinner is served."

He picked up a plate in each hand and carried them over to the table, placing one in front of Khalid and the other at his spot at the table.

Khalid looked at the delicious plate of food and could smell the aroma of the fish and vegetables blend together.

"This smells wonderful." He took a bite of the fish and said, "So is it true that all military men are buried on the bases or in Arlington National Cemetery?"

Steve let out a chuckle. "No, not all of us. Most servicemen are buried on their family lots in private cemeteries. You can request to be buried on base. As a matter of fact, I've got me a nice spot picked out over at the base. But I don't plan on using it anytime soon."

"I thought you said that Marines did not like to associate with the Navy."

"That's true, but there aren't any Marine bases in the great state of Texas and I refuse to have my bones rest anywhere but here. After God made Texas, he should just have stopped right there." Steve's teeth shone bright as he raised his glass toward Khalid in a symbolic toast.

Khalid raised his glass to Steve and they finished their tea. "Let me get you some more tea."

Steve handed his glass over to Khalid. "Why, thank you very much, sir."

Khalid took the glasses and placed them on the kitchen counter. He removed the vial from his pocket and poured the deadly puffer fish toxin into Steve's glass. Khalid knew that the effects of the toxin would take at least four to eight hours to cause death. The poison would first cause the Captain's face and extremities to go numb and then total paralysis would set in, ending with the failure of his respiratory muscles. His death would look like a heart attack to the local authorities when his body was found and the toxin would be untraceable to the medical examiner's toxicology screen. It would be a frightening and painful death, for which Khalid felt sorry. Hopefully the Captain would be asleep when the poison took effect. For an infidel, Captain Steve was a genuinely kind person. A man worthy of *dhimmī* status in the Caliphate. A *dhimmī* was a non-Muslim person who was allowed to live in the Islamic state as a second-class citizen. The word literally meant protected person. Very few *dhimmī* would be allowed in the Caliphate, however Captain Steve would have been one of those chosen few. Unfortunately, his death was necessary for the completion of Muhammad's Sword.

CHAPTER 28
Naval Air Station Corpus Christi
Corpus Christi, Texas

Sebastian, dressed in his favorite pair of blue jeans, black T-shirt and cowboy boots, stared down at the headstone of the Unknown Soldier. Today was the anniversary of the deaths of his team. He had taken a one month leave when he had arrived back in the States one year ago, going to the families of each member of his team who had fallen in Al-Dana. Sebastian had recounted the events of that day in Al-Dana, telling each of the families how brave the men were and going into great detail of the heroic acts they had performed. He had told the families how the men were more than just soldiers under his command. They were more than friends. They were his brothers. He told the families how he was responsible for the deaths of the men and if he could go back and change anything that he did on that day to save them, he would gladly do so. He told them that they deserved more than a form letter from the President and a flag from a military representative who did not know his men. In the end, all the families had thanked him for letting them know how their loved ones had died and each and every one had told him that he did not need their forgiveness for that day. War was war, and they were happy that at least he was still alive so that he could be the one to tell them of the bravery of their loved ones.

But today was the day that he owed it to his brothers to remember and honor them and so he had come to the grave of the Unknown Soldier to pay his respects to his brothers.

Sebastian placed a six-pack of beer next to the headstone. One beer for each of his fallen friends. "Sorry, guys. I wish I had done better. I miss y'all every day. I promise you that I will never lose another man. I owe y'all that."

He opened a beer, taking a long drink, and then placed the bottle at the foot of the grave in a symbolic toast to honor his brothers.

He turned and walked back down the path to his motorcycle. A he approached it, he could see a funeral procession pulling down the drive. He had seen the memo come across his desk. The soldier was also a fallen hero. He had been a Riverine, a Marine patrol boat captain down in Central and South America who had retired as a fishing boat Captain in Corpus Christi. The poor soul had died of a heart attack at only forty-three years old.

As the hearse pulled passed him, he raised his right hand to his head and saluted the fallen soldier. He held his salute as the cars passed. As the last vehicle passed by him, Sebastian took notice of the driver. He looked exactly like Enrique Iglesias. With his medium cut black hair brushed to the side and wearing a black suit and tie, he looked like Enrique Iglesias in the Dirty Dancer video.

"It couldn't be. That guy was in Syria. There's no freaking way he could be here on the base. And today of all days," he said aloud. He chalked it up to his mind playing tricks on him. The driver was probably one of the captain's deckhands.

Sebastian hiked his right leg over his Harley Davidson and straddled the bike. He fired up the V-twin engine as he raised the kickstand. The tailpipes roared as he sped down the road. One more stop by the post office and he was off to see Pilar. They had planned to spend the day together to remove the somberness of the day from his mind.

CHAPTER 29

Dennis Johnson opened the patrol car door and stepped outside. He reached in to grab his M4 carbine rifle and hurried to catch up with his partner, PFC Nathan "Trey" Jessup, III. Trey always joked that he was glad he wasn't a fourth because then his family would have called him Quad.

Dennis caught up with Trey and they strode to the guardhouse at the entrance to the base. The guardhouse sat in the middle of the road between the two lanes entering the base and the one lane exiting it. The incoming lanes were divided by concrete barriers and had to pass under the reinforced brick carport located adjacent to the guard house. Both sides of the road contained electronic barrier arms, which raised up and down by a control in the guardhouse, and tire spikes to prevent vehicles from entering or exiting the wrong way. If a driver drove over the spikes the correct way, the spikes would recess into the ground and allow safe passage. If a driver entered from the wrong direction, the spikes would puncture any tire they came into contact with. In case of an emergency, the spikes could be locked in the up position, preventing any vehicle from entering or leaving the base.

Upon entering the guardhouse, Dennis greeted Privates Malik Faraj and Scott Patillo, the two MPs that he and Jessup were relieving. "What's going on? You guys have an easy night?"

"A lot easier than I would have at home," replied Patillo.

"How's that new baby coming along?" quizzed Jessup.

"She's beautiful, man," said Patillo as he reached into his front pocket. He pulled out a photo and held it out toward Jessup. "But I have to tell you, I get more sleep up here at night than I do at home. She's got her days and nights all mixed up. Sleeps during the day and stays up all night."

Malik reached in and snatched the photo out of Patillo's hand before Jessup could take it. "Man, don't let him show you baby pictures. The next thing you know, he'll have his phone out and we won't ever get out of here."

Dennis seized the picture from Malik. "What's wrong? You tired? God knows you need some beauty sleep, because yo face is killing me."

Jessup noticed the bright orange Fitbit Surge activity tracker on Malik's left wrist. "Jesus Christ! Is that thing big enough?"

Malik held up his left arm and proudly displayed the device. "Man, this thing is the bomb. It'll track your heart rate and pulse all day long, even while you're sleeping. Plus, it's got GPS and it'll even get your text messages and email from your phone. Not to mention it'll play your music through your Bluetooth while you're running."

"No shit? Really?" asked Jessup, reaching over to look at the wrist device. "Well, I knew that you and Dennis were tight, but I didn't realize that you were so close that you had to go out and buy matching wristbands." Jessup reached over and grabbed Dennis's left arm, holding it up to expose the matching Fitbit.

"Holy shit," said Patillo. "You guys even bought matching colors. Well, you know what they say, don't ask, don't tell."

"This is the new, President Adama's military, Patillo," chimed Jessup. "You can be anything you want to be. If these two want to be butt bandits, it's perfectly all right."

Dennis laughed at the good natured ribbing. "You two better step off. We ain't like that."

"You got that right," said Malik, jerking his arm away from Jessup's grasp. "Come on, Patillo, let's bounce. It's almost nine."

"You got it, buddy. It's time for me to go home and see my girls. You guys should have an easy morning. Most of the civilian contractors have already made it in."

"Thanks," said Dennis. As Patillo and Malik grabbed their M4s and walked out the door of the guardhouse, Dennis reached over and silently flipped a switch, locking the gates and spikes. Jessup had his back turned to Dennis as he watched Malik and Patillo cross the road toward their parked police vehicle. Dennis pulled the Beretta M9 pistol from his holster and fired into the back of Jessup's head, sending a spray of fine red mist flying out into the street.

Patillo heard the shot and spun around, raising his M4 as he turned. Expecting to see an intruder, Patillo stared in shock when he realized that it was Dennis who had pulled the trigger.

"What the fuck, Dennis? Put the gun down now, or I will end you!" He watched as Dennis held out the pistol and placed it on the control panel. Scott Patillo looked down at the body of Jessup, now lying slumped in the street. "Tell me you didn't shoot him over the gay comments about your wristband."

"It wasn't about the comments, Patillo. But it has everything to do with the wristband. And you don't got one."

Patillo looked at Dennis, dumbfounded. By the time Dennis's statement finally sunk in, it was too late. He spun his head back toward Malik and saw the muzzle of the M4 inches from his face. The bright flash was the last thing he saw before the bullet entered his brain.

CHAPTER 30

Sebastian exited the Post Office and turned left down the sidewalk towards his motorcycle. He glanced to his right and noticed the patrolman, Ignacio Munoz, exiting his vehicle and carrying his M4. It wasn't normal practice for the Security Forces to walk around with their M4 rifles. Sebastian wondered if there was a threat on the base. His thought was interrupted by the soft laughter and he turned his head forward to see two very attractive women walking in his direction. They were Navy nurses, lieutenants according to the shoulder badges on their uniforms. He could see them staring at his defined muscles showing through his tight black T-shirt and it gave him a good feeling, knowing that their giggles were aimed at him. Since it was his day off and he was out of uniform, he was under no obligation to salute the two officers, but he gave them a warm "Ma'ams" with a wink as they passed.

Sebastian heard the sound of an M4 firing behind him and instinctively dove for cover between two parked cars. He rolled over and put his back against the front wheel of the pickup truck giving him cover. He heard the clanking sound of bullets pelleting the truck and ducked his head as a wash of flying metal sailed over. Who in the hell was shooting on the base? That must be why Munoz had the M4. There *was* a threat on the base.

He maneuvered himself to get a better look at who was firing at him. Sebastian jerked the side mirror from the truck and held it around the bumper to get a clear view of who was shooting. He saw Munoz with his weapon raised and firing. It took a moment for him to process what he was seeing. Ignacio Munoz was firing at everyone. *He* was the shooter.

The circle drive on which the Post Office was located also accommodated the Officer and NCO mess, as well as an administration building which housed the various offices necessary to make the base operate. It was the most populated section of the base at this time of the morning and this asshole was taking full advantage of it. Sebastian crouched next to the pickup and readied himself. His left hand braced against the fender while his right dug into his pocket. His hand came out holding a four-inch lock blade pocket knife. He knew that it wasn't much of a weapon, but it was all he had, so he would have to make it work.

Munoz stopped firing and released his magazine. Sebastian seized the opportunity. Leaping into action, like a cheetah hunting gazelle, he ran full tilt towards Munoz, leaping over the bodies of the two nurses he had spoken to just moments before. Upon reaching Munoz, Sebastian reached around with his left hand, covering the man's mouth and nose, and plunged the knife into the base of the man's skull. Once the knife reached the hilt, he gave it a vicious twist, severing the man's spinal cord from the brain, killing him instantly.

Sebastian allowed the man slump to the ground at his feet. As he bent down to remove the M4 from Ignacio's dead body, he noticed the bright orange Fitbit.

"Freeze right where you are, asshole! Put down your weapon and raise your hands above your head," a voice screamed.

Sebastian heard the man behind him and spun to face the voice, raising his rifle as he turned. He was staring face to face with an athletic-looking bald man, in his mid-thirties, pointing a LAR-15 at him. The man was dressed in khaki cargo pants and black T-shirt with a tactical vest that read DEA in bright yellow capitalized letters across the top.

The man trained his rifle at Sebastian and flashed him a menacing look. "I'm not going to tell you again. Lower your weapon and raise your hands."

"Who the hell are you?"

"Special Agent Sean Ray. I'm DEA. Who the hell are you and why the hell are you shooting these people?"

"Sergeant First Class Sebastian Gray. I'm with the base Security Forces and *I* didn't shoot anybody. This guy did," he said, nodding at the body lying on the ground behind him.

"You don't look like military police to me. But he does," Sean nodded his head toward the body of the slain MP, "and he's dead."

Sebastian cocked his head. "It's my day off." Realizing that he needed to use more tact to convince the man, Sebastian raised his eyebrows and locked eyes with Sean's. "Look, dude, I came out of the Post Office and this guy starts shooting everybody. I stopped him, that's all." Sebastian moved the rifle out in front of him with his fingers raised and holding it with his thumbs. "You seem like a rational guy, so I'm gonna put down the rifle and we can discuss our situation. But we need to do it quickly, because there are a lot of soldiers over there that need medical attention."

He knelt down and began to place the rifle gently on the ground in front of him. Sebastian heard the initial blast come from behind him.

"Oh shit. Incoming!" He dove for cover between the cars, grabbing Sean by the arm as he flew by and pulling him to safety.

The two men lay on the ground, covering their heads with their arms, as the shock-wave from the explosion sent a hailstorm of shrapnel screaming through the surrounding air. Jagged bits of brick and glass embedded themselves into the vehicles, trees and people exposed in the circle.

Sean faced Sebastian with a confused look. "What in the hell was that?"

Sebastian heard the clinking sound of ball bearings bouncing along the sidewalk and both men turned to watch the blood-stained metal spheres roll by. "IED, judging by the ball bearings."

"IED? You mean a bomb?" Sean raised his rifle and pointed it at Sebastian. "How'd you know about the IED?"

"First off, you *really* need to stop pointing that thing at me. Secondly, I didn't know about it. I heard it. And third, I just saved your ass, so you should be thanking me, not pointing a fucking gun at my head."

"Second, not secondly," remarked Sean.

"What?"

Sean lowered his rifle. "You said secondly. You can't say first and third with secondly in the middle. You should say second, or second of all. But not secondly. And what do you mean you heard it?"

Sebastian rose from the ground and walked over to the dead security officer. "What is this, English class? I spent five tours in the Middle East. You get used to the sound of IEDs over there. When I hear the first sound of an IED, I hit the ground." Sebastian grabbed the dead soldier by the left wrist and rolled him over. He couldn't help but notice the bright orange Fitbit fitted around the outside of the MPs sleeve. He removed the man's tactical vest, which was fully stocked with two more magazines for the M4 and a Beretta 9M in the holster with three magazines.

Sean eyed the gaping hole in the second floor of the Officers' and NCO mess halls. Black smoke was billowing out of the ten-foot hole that had replaced the brick and glass that had been there minutes before.

"Holy crap! Do you see that?" he asked, pointing toward the smoking building. Looking back at Sebastian he asked, "What are you doing? We need to be helping those people, not taking a dead guy's gear."

Sebastian zipped up the vest and fastened the clips to secure it. "First off, he doesn't need it any more. Secondly... I mean second," he looked at Sean and received an approving nod. "There is no way that this guy could have set off the IED in the Mess Hall, because he was dead at the time. Meaning that third and most importantly, we are under attack by more than one unknown persons and I want to be fully armed in order to defend this base and stop whoever is behind this." He pointed to the building with the smoke still pouring from its wounded shell. "Whoever is doing this is smart and they've done their homework."

"Why do you say that?"

"Because of that hole right there," said Sebastian, pointing again at the smoldering building, "is where all three base COs, Army, Navy and Coast Guard have breakfast every morning at nine o'clock sharp. Along with their highest ranking officers. Whoever is attacking us has successfully taken out all the Commanders on base. Second, this guy is a real MP, not some imposter that snuck onto the base. That means that whoever is doing this has infiltrated the base personnel. They are organized and I don't think this is the end of it. I think it's just the beginning."

CHAPTER 31

The break room was filled with forty-two MPs, who were getting off duty or working in the office. Maryam Saleh let a smile spread across her face. All forty-two were singing happy birthday as her CO, Lieutenant Commander John Sinclair, walked through the doorway holding a birthday cake with nineteen lit candles adorning the top. Sinclair placed the cake in front of Maryam as the MPs chanted for her to make a wish.

"Thank you all so much. How did you know it was my birthday?"

Sinclair gave her a boisterous glance. "This is my station, Maryam. I know everything about everybody. Now make a wish and blow out those candles before we burn down the building."

Maryam closed her eyes and took a deep breath. As she blew out the candles, she pressed the send button on the cell phone in her pocket. The call connected to the cell phone attached to the C4 bomb, which was located underneath the table the MPs were crowding around.

"Allahu Akbar," she breathed, not bothering to open her eyes.

Sean heard the explosion from two blocks away. "What was that?"

Sebastian checked the ammunition in the magazine and reloaded his M4. "Sounded like it came from the police station."

"What do you mean, the police station?"

"Judging by the direction of the explosion, it would have to be the Security Forces Headquarters, I.E. the police station. I told you that whoever is doing this has it well planned out. Whoever it is, they've just taken out all three of the Base Commanders and the security forces. Basically, anybody and everybody who is equipped to stop them and coordinate a counter attack. Except for us and the few MPs who are on duty. We need to track them down and organize a plan of attack."

A white patrol cruiser screamed into the circle, flashing its red and blue lights and with its siren blaring. As it skidded sideways to a stop, Sebastian gave Sean a quick smile and a wink.

"Here comes the cavalry." He watched as Malik and Dennis exited the vehicle with their weapons drawn. Sebastian instantly noticed the bright orange Fitbit fastened around Dennis and Malik's left wrists and his mind went back to the orange wristband on the MP that he had killed. His smile faded to an angry scowl as he realized what the orange wristbands were. The Fitbits were not some random jewelry. It was an identifier to let the attackers know who was on their side. It was their uniform.

Sebastian raised his rifle and raced toward the patrol car. "No fucking way!"

Seeing Sebastian take off running, Sean sprinted behind him. "No fucking way, what?"

"They're not the cavalry!"

Malik and Dennis opened fire on the soldiers who were helping the wounded in front of the administration building. Firing in three-round bursts, the pair eliminated the twelve soldiers closest to them in a matter of seconds. Sebastian took aim while in a dead sprint and fired his M4, striking Malik in the shoulder.

The force of the bullet knocked him Malik to the ground. "I'm hit!"

Dennis rotated to see Sebastian and a stranger wearing a DEA vest heading straight for them. He squeezed off a three-round burst, causing the two men to dive for cover behind a group of parked cars. Dennis rushed to Malik, pulling him to safety behind the patrol car.

"What the hell is Sarge doing here? He's supposed to be off base today."

"It don't matter. He's here now, so we gotta take care of him. Who's that other guy?"

"Beats me. He's wearing a DEA vest. I thought the DEA guys left the base for Washington or something." Dennis cringed as the window of the cruiser exploded, showering him in thousands of tiny glass thorns. "Damn! Those muthas can shoot."

Using the hood of the car to brace his arm, Dennis fired his weapon, striking the open door of a pickup that Sean was using for cover.

Malik aimed his rifle down the street and continued to cold heartedly gun down the innocent men and women running for cover. "You take care of them. I will keep us on task."

Dennis fired again, this time pinning Sebastian as he tried to maneuver around a gold Toyota Camry. "Roger that."

He dropped down behind the fender well and replaced his magazine. Returning to the hood of the car, Dennis let loose three more volleys before the bullet from Sean's LAR-15 struck him in the head. His limp and lifeless body reeled backwards and dropped onto the black asphalt with a sounding thud.

Sebastian locked eyes with Sean. He pointed to Sean and then to the front of the patrol car, signaling for Sean to approach the gunman from the front. He pointed to himself and then to the rear of the car, letting Sean knew that he was moving around behind the remaining gunman, who continued to fire at the unarmed navy personnel who frantically sought shelter from his assault.

Sean nodded, acknowledging that he understood the plan.

Sebastian locked eyes with Sean. "Don't forget, we need to take him alive. We have to interrogate him and find out how many people they have."

"Roger that," said Sean as he darted toward the front of the patrol car.

As Sebastian rounded the rear of the patrol car, he could see Malik sitting on the ground with his legs extended and ankles crossed. He was shooting left handed due to the bullet in his shoulder. His right elbow was resting on his knee to support the rifle and steady his aim. Malik continued to assassinate the navy men and women scampering to find cover. Sebastian heard the familiar click of Malik's now empty magazine. "You're outta ammo, Malik. Put down the rifle and slowly turn towards me."

The rifle made a metallic clank as it landed on the asphalt road.

"Okay. Don't shoot. You got me, Sarge," said Malik, raising his hands above his head.

"Damn right. Now why don't you tell me what the fuck is going on?"

Malik drew the M9 pistol from the holster in his vest and, with lightning speed, rolled to his right. Lying prone on the hot black asphalt, he aimed the M9 at Sebastian's chest. As his finger began to squeeze the trigger, his body suddenly convulsed as two rounds from

Sean's LAR-15 struck his neck and head. The pistol clanked to the ground as Malik's lifeless body collapsed onto the road, the thick red blood oozing out from under him like an oil spill.

Sebastian lowered his rifle and shook his head in disbelief. He looked toward Sean, giving him a slack-mouthed stare. "Dude! What the hell? I said we needed him alive."

Sean walked over to Malik's dead body and kicked the pistol away. "What the hell? Really? He was about to shoot you. How about a thank you? 'You saved my life, Sean. I owe you one'."

"I could see what he was doing. But we needed him alive. That's why I didn't shoot him. You could have shot him in the leg or something."

"I wasn't trained to shoot people in the leg. This is real life, not the movies." Sean walked over to Sebastian and flashed him a cocky smile. "You're alive. Right?"

Sebastian shook his head, dismissing the older man's cockiness. "That's beside the point. We needed him alive, Ray-Ray."

Sean's eyes narrowed. "You call me that again and I'll shoot you myself."

"Okay then, how about Stingray? You're bald and deadly."

"I kinda like that."

"Well, Stingray, now we have to find us another bad guy to interrogate. Any ideas as to where we go next?"

CHAPTER 32

Khalid, dressed in his black suit and tie, stood at the back of the funeral tent behind the mourners, who had come to honor Captain Steve. He listened to the Methodist Minister talk about how Steve had spent his life helping others. How Steve had fought his battle with alcohol and won. How Steve had devoted himself to helping others win their battle addiction by becoming their sponsor and giving them the strength to keep fighting, even when they did not think that they could. Listening to the man speak, Khalid knew that Captain Steve was the honorable man he had thought him to be. It was a shame that Captain Steve had had to die. Even more so, that he had to die an infidel. Never getting to know the words of the Prophet. Never entering Paradise. Never getting to taste of the many rivers and gardens there.

Khalid turned his mind back to the mission. The reason that he was here in the land of the Great Satan. The reason Captain Steve had to die. This would be the day the Great Satan felt the Muhammad's Sword. The day where Al-Qaeda would take its revenge on the United States for its decades of tyranny and interference in the Levant.

Khalid heard the first explosion and knew that the assault had begun. The Preacher stopped the eulogy as everyone looked beyond Khalid toward the explosion. Khalid looked toward the noise and back to the crowd. In his perfect Spanish accent, he attempted to calm the crowd. "I am sure that everything is fine. The army is probably detonating ordinance."

He was acknowledged with a sea of nodding heads from the twenty mourners in front of him. As the Minister spoke again, Khalid heard the second explosion, followed by gunfire. Knowing that he could not explain the second round of explosions as a normal base activity, he pulled the B&T MP9 machine pistol from the holster under his suit jacket and began firing.

CHAPTER 33
Naval Air Station Corpus Christi

Sean whipped his head toward the explosion. "What in the hell was that?"

Turning to see the area from which the explosion came, Sebastian nonchalantly said, "Claymore. Sounded like it came from the pilots' barracks."

Sean heard the next two explosions in quick succession. "Claymores? Is that standard issue on the base? I don't think that Navy pilots, Army helicopter mechanics, or the Coast Guard use claymores."

Sebastian began running toward the explosions. Without looking back, he said, "They're not standard issue. They're kept in the bunkers for use if the base comes under attack."

"So do you think that we have help?"

Sebastian led the way through the grassy alley between the red brick buildings. "Doubtful, since the three hostiles so far have been MPs. My guess would be that they took the claymores out of the bunkers to use on the pilots' barracks. The air jockeys are the only guys on base that stay in the barracks. Everybody else either stays in base housing or lives off base. But they could use claymores at the barracks."

Stopping at the corner of the Post Office, Sebastian placed his back against the wall. He peered around the corner and nodded to Sean that the alley was clear. Sebastian followed around the corner as Sean took the lead. "The barracks are T-shaped with three entrances. Claymores will kill most of the pilots when they bottleneck at the doors. That's what I would do," he said, sprinting down the alley between the red-bricked buildings.

As they approached the hospital, Sean could hear automatic gunfire coming from the inside the building. Dozens of people, dressed in blue surgical scrubs, streamed out of the doors and dashed around the giant white columns decorating the front of the building. Sean slowed as he approached and stopped one of the frightened doctors by grabbing the man by his arm and jerking backwards. "What's going on in there?"

The doctor looked at him with his eyes wide. He glanced at Sean's rifle and then at his tactical vest, his eyes stopping at the large yellow letters on the front. Recognizing that Sean was not a threat, he began spitting out the words as fast as he could. "Two MPs came into the ER and started shooting everybody. Doctors, nurses, patients... everybody. And then they started down the halls, stopping at each room."

Sebastian leaned into the man and stared him in the eyes. "Are they still on the first floor?"

"Yes. I think so."

"You and the rest of these folks find cover. But don't go too far. The base is under attack and we will need all of you here at the hospital working."

The fear in man's eyes was obvious. "What about those two MPs?"

"You let us handle them. You just make sure you come back to take care of the wounded." Sebastian looked at Sean and motioned toward the front doors of the hospital. "What do you think, Stingray, shall we dance?"

Sean shot Sebastian a quick wink. "I thought you'd never ask."

Sebastian took the lead and moved to the doorway. After verifying that it was clear to enter, he started down the left side of the long, wide hallway with his rifle aimed straight ahead. The central hallway was the main corridor through the hospital. Doctors' offices lined the hallway on both sides. Two more hallways intersected the corridor, leading to more wings. The ER where the MPs had entered the building was located at the far end of the corridor.

Sebastian looked to Sean, who was paralleling him on the right. "Remember to keep your head on a swivel. These guys could be in any room."

"Roger that."

"And try not to kill them this time."

Sean flashed Sebastian a quick wink and a half smile. "I'll do my best," he said and continued down the corridor.

Sean saw a young brunette dressed in blue scrubs come racing around the corner of the first hallway and turn in their direction. She shrieked when she noticed him walking down the hallway with his rifle up and ready. He could see the fear in her eyes, the realization she had escaped only to be gunned down before making it to the final exit.

Sean gave her a calming smile as he motioned for the woman to come toward him. "C'mon, c'mon, c'mon. Hurry this way," he said in a loud whisper. As the busty young lady neared him he asked in a hushed voice, "Where are they?"

The woman pointed toward the hallway. "Down there, at the end of the hallway. They are going room by room, executing people. I hid in a closet and watched them murder Dr. Billings. I was so scared."

Sean looked at her with reassuring eyes. "Don't worry, it's gonna be all right. Go outside and find cover. We're gonna go down there and take care of those two."

He watched her run for the exit, still trembling. He glanced over at Sebastian. "You catch that?"

"Yep. Two bogeys to our right. Should be as easy as a turkey shoot."

"Yeah. I bet that's what they thought when they started shooting unarmed victims." Sean reached the corner and peered down the corridor. The hallway was lined with offices. A gurney was parked on the right side about halfway down. There was no sign of the shooters, except for the echo of gunfire rumbling down the hall. Sean looked toward Sebastian. "Clear."

Sebastian walked briskly down the hallway with his rifle raised and ready. Out of the corner of his eye, he could see Sean.

Suddenly a rifle barrel protruded from an office at the far end of the hallway. An Army MP exited the doorway and Sebastian could see the bright orange Fitbit attached to his left wrist.

PFC Derek Vinson turned toward Sebastian as he exited the room. Vinson's eyebrows raised and he recoiled at the sight of Sebastian, shocked that his Sergeant was standing before him. His eyes narrowed when he noticed Sebastian's unadorned left wrist. Before Vinson could react, his head jerked sideways from the impact of the two bullets from Sean's rifle. Vinson's body slumped to the ground, leaving a fine red mist painted on the wall beside him.

Sebastian clenched his jaw and gave Sean an icy stare. "Do you even know what 'take them alive' means?"

"I didn't have a shot at his leg because of the gurney. Besides, there's two of 'em. You can shoot the next one in the leg." Sean noticed the black steel barrel of an M4 swing around the corner of a doorway at the end of the hall. He shouted, "Gun!" as he dove to the floor.

Sebastian dropped to one knee, narrowly avoiding a flurry of steel that fractured the concrete wall above his head. He fired three rounds at the doorway and inched closer toward the cover of the gurney. "Drop that weapon, soldier, and come on out with your hands raised."

A figure dashed out of the room and across the hallway. Sebastian let loose two rapid shots, striking the man in the thigh and sending him sliding face first through an open doorway. Sebastian flashed his eyebrows and shot Sean a jaw-dropping smile.

"Did you see that? I shot him in the leg. Not in the head or heart. But the leg." He dropped low to the ground as the terrorist peppered the corridor with another swarm of bullets, causing the hallway to fill with a dense fog of dust. "See... I didn't kill him."

Sean fired four rounds at the doorway. "Not yet anyway." He raised his hand to his mouth, cupping it like a megaphone. "Throw your weapon out and come out with your hands up." There was a long pause. Sean looked to Sebastian, who just raised his shoulders. "Did you hear me? I said, throw out your weapon!"

Sean stood and walked cautiously down the corridor with his rifle ready.

Sebastian pressed his back against the wall, aiming his M4 at the doorway. "Throw out your weapon asshole!"

No sound came from inside the room. He looked to Sean who was across the hall and had a clear view of the doorway. He watched as Sean crossed over and peered into the room. Sean looked back at him, shaking his head with a lopsided smile on his face. Sebastian round the corner and entered the room. He saw the MP sitting against the side wall with his rifle lying in his lap and his chin resting on his chest.

"Aww, fuck me! Why did you have to kill this one too, Stingray?"

Sean nodded toward the body. "You better look again, Hoss. He only has two bullets in him and they are both in the leg. You must have hit the femoral artery."

Sebastian eyed the two wounds in the man's upper thigh. "I guess you're right. My bad."

He heard the faint but distinguishable sound of multiple weapons firing coming from outside of the building. "You hear that?"

Sean raised and lowered his head in affirmation. "Sounds like it's coming from that way down the street," he said, pointing toward the back of the building. "Let's move."

Sebastian dropped the magazine from his M4 and loaded another. He bent over the body of the dead MP and removed two magazines from the dead man's tactical vest, inserting them into the empty mag pouches of his own vest. "Right behind you, Stingray."

CHAPTER 34
Naval Air Station Corpus Christi

The sounds of automatic gunfire emanated in the distance as Sean stepped through the sliding exit doors of the ER and out into the ambulance drive. After checking for any would be assailants, he turned to Sebastian and asked, "Which way?"

Sebastian pointed straight down the perfectly manicured grass alleyway. "We'll go this way. Two buildings down and then turn right. It will lead us straight to the barracks and provide us with cover."

"Roger that," said Sean, sprinting after Sebastian, who was moving at a dead run ahead of him. "How'd you know that those two guys back there weren't the cavalry?"

"They were wearing orange Fitbits."

"Orange whats?"

"Their wristbands were bright orange Fitbits. People use them for jogging and crap like that. The first shooter I killed was wearing one also."

"You determined that they were terrorists because of an orange wristband? That's pretty thin evidence, don't you think? Damn near anorexic."

"Three guys with the same ugly ass orange Fitbits, that's no coincidence. Out of all the colors to choose from, three MPs picked bright-ass orange. No way that's a coincidence. That's a signal to let them know who's on their team. Besides, it's against Army regulations to wear anything that fucking ugly."

Sean had no time to react as a figure come streaking from between the buildings. The young sailor slammed into Sebastian at full speed, sending both men tumbling to the turf. Sebastian hit the ground and rolled onto his back in one fluid motion. With his knees up, he lifted his body into a crunch position and trained his M4 on the sailor. Sean closed in on the young man with his rifle trained on him. The sailor shook his head trying to regain his composure. Realizing that he was staring at the barrel of not one, but two automatic rifles, he raised his hands above his head and said, "Don't shoot!"

Noticing that the sailor wasn't wearing an orange Fitbit, Sebastian lowered his rifle. He gave Sean a look to let him know to keep his weapon trained. The sailor was a young, thin Hispanic man with dark eyes and black hair. He was no more than eighteen or nineteen years old, but the insignia pins on his lapel indicated that he was an ISPO2, an Intelligence Specialist Second Class Petty Officer. The sailor's rank caused Sebastian more than a little concern. It was a high rank for someone as young as he was. "What's your name, kid?"

"Jaime. Jaime Gomez."

"Hyman?"

"No, it's pronounced *High-Me*."

"Whatever. Where are you heading in such a hurry, Jaime?"

"Like, I was walking down Lexington Boulevard and then there were these explosions, so I hit the ground. The next thing, I know the MPs started shooting people, so I hightailed it out of there and then you tackled me. And now you dudes are trying to shoot me."

"I didn't tackle you. You ran into me. How old are you kid?"

"Eighteen."

"How long you been in the navy?"

"Just over a year."

Sebastian's eyes narrowed until they became small slits. He raised his rifle and aimed it at Jaime's left eye. "There is no way you made PO2 in a year. Where's your Fitbit, you little fuck?"

Jaime's eyes grew wide and his voice cracked from fear. "What Fitbit? I don't even wear a watch! I was recruited out of high school and they made me a PO2 as soon as I finished advanced training at C School."

Sean moved closer, keeping his rifle trained on the young man. "What do you mean, you were recruited? Recruited by ISIL?"

"ISIL? No way, Dude! I was recruited by the FBI. They told me to join the Navy, so I did what they said. The Navy made me Petty Officer."

Sean lowered his rifle. "The FBI recruited you to join the Navy?"

"Yeah. I swear."

"What did you do?"

Sebastian looked at Sean, confused by his question. "What do you mean, what did he do?"

"You don't get recruited by the FBI to join the Navy. You get recruited by the FBI to join the FBI. Unless you did something to make the FBI come knocking on your door. Look, this is how it works. The FBI catches some high school kid who has hacked into a bank, or airline, or something like that. Then they build up a file on the kid.

When they need something done that they don't have enough evidence to get a warrant for, they knock on the kid's door and threaten him with jail time unless he helps them out by secretly hacking into whatever they need access to, like cell phone records or some pedophile's hotel room. Usually they will let the kid go and recruit him into the FBI after college. But the Feds told Jaime here to join the Navy and then made him a high ranking NCO straight out of boot camp. He must have done something pretty special for them not to wait until after college to get him into service."

Sebastian turned his gaze to Jaime. "Okay, Jimmy, what was it you did to warrant the FBI sending you to the Navy and giving you a PO2 rank?"

Jaime's voice trembled as he spoke. "I hacked into American Airlines and the Setai Hotel in Miami for them. They needed to know if some drug dealer was coming into the States."

Sean's eyes grew wide. "Are you talking about Jose Linares?"

"Yeah, that was the guy."

"I wondered how the hell the Feds got that collar. Linares was the largest drug kingpin in Colombia. He's shipped tons of cocaine into the U.S. over the last decade. But he was protected by FARC, the Revolutionary Armed Forces of Colombia. That made him impossible to track. I mean the guy was like a ghost. And then one day the Feds pop him in the penthouse of the Setai. That was because of you kid?"

Jaime let an impish smile spread across his face. "Yes, sir."

A smirk formed on Sean's face. "We *really* wanted that guy. Good job, kid. So what do you do here on the base?"

"Cyber Intelligence. I'm with the U.S. Fleet Cyber Command."

Sebastian raised himself off the ground and extended his hand toward Jaime. "Well, Jamey, I'm Sebastian and the old guy is Stingray."

"My name is Sean."

Jaime took Sebastian's hand and pulled himself off the ground. "Nice to meet you. But it's Jaime."

Sebastian removed the Beretta M9 pistol from the holster in his tactical vest and handed it to Jaime. "Isn't that what I said? You know how to shoot, sailor?"

"Not really. I'm a computer guy, not a marine."

Sebastian rolled the pistol over, showing it to Jaime, and flipped the safety upward. "This is the safety. It should always be up. The real safety is right here." Sebastian rolled the pistol back to its upright position and tapped his index finger against the barrel of the gun. "Do not put it on the trigger until you are ready to shoot. Then aim and squeeze the trigger. Don't pull it. Squeeze it." He pulled the hammer back on the weapon and handed it to Jaime.

Sean moved next to the wall of the building and stepped toward the second row of buildings. "Do you hear that?"

Sebastian cocked his head as if he was listening for something far off in the distance. "I don't hear anything."

Sean picked up his pace with his rifle trained ahead. "Exactly. They stopped shooting."

Sebastian and Jaime hurried to catch Sean, who was almost to the end of the second building. A Marine MP, dressed in a camouflaged Marine Corps Combat Utility Uniform and carrying an M4 carbine, stepped out in front of Sean. Sean spotted the bright orange Fitbit attached to the MP's left wrist and fired two rounds into the man's chest, which were followed by two rounds from Sebastian's M4. The impact of the bullets caused the MP to take two steps backwards as he stared in amazement at his chest. Before the man could react, two more bullets buzzed through the air, skirting Sean's head and striking the man in the nose and left eye. The terrorist came to rest slumping into a seated position against the red brick wall.

Sebastian turned back to Jaime, beaming like a proud parent who had just taught his son to throw a ball. "Hell, yeah! Good shooting, Jimbo!" He moved toward Jaime with his fist straight out, ready to give his protégé a fist bump.

Sean turned just in time to see Sebastian's broad smile fade into a wide open gape. His focus shifted to Jaime, who was holding the pistol with both hands, his eyes clamped shut.

"Ho-ly shit! Tell me you didn't just shoot two bullets by my head with your eyes closed! Didn't you hear what Sebastian told you? You aim and then you fire. Aim... Fire. You *never* close your eyes! Especially if you're aiming right by my damn head!"

Jaime peeked out at Sean with one eye. "Sorry, Dude. I *did* aim. It's just that the noise made me close my eyes."

Sean's eyes closed to a squint and his jaw tightened. He pointed his left index finger at Jaime. "Next time, you keep your eyes open or I'm gonna..." His sentence was cut short by blaring sirens coming from three white Security Forces cruisers screaming down Ocean Drive.

Sebastian's face became washed with trepidation. "They're heading toward the Army Depot. They're going after the civilian contractors. We need to move."

CHAPTER 35
Corpus Christ Army Depot

Smoke billowed up from the rubble that was once the Security Forces Headquarters. As the trio raced up Ocean Drive, Sebastian's thoughts shifted to his friends who had perished in the building when the explosion occurred. Who had the terrorists gotten to set off the bomb? He had trusted every one of the MPs with his life, but now no one was beyond suspicion.

His thoughts turned to Dennis and Malik. Both men were well liked and at the top of their classes. They were natural leaders. They didn't fit into the ISIL profile. Sebastian could understand how ISIL recruited lonely, socially awkward kids who didn't fit in to do their suicidal lone wolf attacks. But somehow they had recruited those two guys and probably half of the base security forces as well. People who did not fit the profile of your typical radical jihadist. Hell, the first guy he killed was a Mexican, and so was the one that Jaime shot. They definitely weren't Muslim. Maybe this wasn't an ISIL attack. But who else would be crazy enough to attack a U.S. Military base? No country in the world would be bold enough to attack America on their sovereign ground. It had to be terrorists. And only crazy, well-funded terrorists like ISIL, who had billions of dollars from black market oil sales, would have the resources necessary to carry out this attack.

Sebastian's face turned flush and he could feel his blood boil as his rage took over. *Don't do that*, he thought. *This was battle and emotions will get you killed in battle*. There would be time to mourn his friends later. He took a deep breath to calm himself, exhaled, and then looked back at Jaime who was bringing up the rear. "So tell me, James, what did you do to get busted by the FBI?"

Jaime shook his head and said, "Its Jaime."

"Yeah, that's what I said, isn't it?"

"I hacked into BlackRock Advisors. You know, the hedge fund group. I set myself up a portfolio funded by using money that I borrowed from the portfolios of the board of directors. I had a program set up to piggy back the trades on my portfolio with theirs."

"No shit? Didn't they notice that their money was missing? No wonder you got caught."

"Nah, they didn't even know that their money was missing. I put a worm in their system that took out five hundred thousand dollars at a time from half of the board members accounts and placed it in mine. Then it would take five hundred from the other accounts and replace it. The money was never out of any one person's account for more than fifty seconds. I got caught because BlackRock was hired by the Treasury department to manage the toxic mortgage assets owned by Bear Sterns, AIG, Freddie Mac and all of those guys who crashed the economy back in 2008. Treasury did an audit on BlackRock and came across my closed out portfolio, but no one could tell them who had managed it."

There was a twinkle in Sean's emerald eyes. "So how much did you get, kid?"

"Two point eight three million. I had it in a Cayman bank set up under a Panamanian shell corporation."

"Holy shit!" Sean said, shaking his head in amazement. "What happened to the cash?"

"The government seized the two point eight three million in my account."

Sean laughed at the thought of the government keeping millions of dollars that technically belonged to BlackRock. He had to hand it to the Adama Administration, they took money from everybody. "So you didn't get to keep any of the money? Even after you helped the Feds catch Linares? They should have at least paid you the reward that the government had on old Jose."

Jaime's jaw dropped. "There was a reward?"

"A million bucks. The Feds probably kept that too. Those guys made out like bandits off of you, Jaime."

"Well, I don't feel so bad then."

"What do you mean?" asked Sebastian with a confused tone in his voice.

"My portfolio had been closed for two years when they discovered it and it took the FBI another year before they used it against me."

"Yeah, so what?"

Jaime beamed from ear to ear. "I said took the money in the account. I never said anything about the interest it made. That was in a different account. In Switzerland."

Sean continued moving down the left side of the street with Sebastian making his way down the middle. Jaime had taken his position between the two, bringing up the rear. The trio noticed the three patrol cars, parked in an arrow formation blocking the street, with their lights still flashing. The doors were wide open, giving Sean the impression that the terrorists had exited in a hurry. Sean glanced at Sebastian and motioned for him to check out the vehicles while he moved closer to the massive building on his left that was at least a city block wide. "Jaime, you're with me."

Sebastian approached the three cruisers, his eyes scanning the area for any sign of the six men who had exited the vehicles. On the right side of the road were two large, semicircular, aluminum hangars with glass fronts. The hangars were separated from the road by concrete planters and a single row parking lot located in front of each. On the left was a large manufacturing facility made of concrete with the words Building Eight above the front door.

His eyes darted from building to building, looking for clues as to where the attackers could be. He had heard gunfire as they raced up the street, but now it had stopped. Where in the hell could they be? Sebastian knew that he was easy pickings standing out in the middle of the street. He tightened his hand around the pistol grip of the M4 and pulled it tight to his shoulder as he leaned in to examine the first car. The keys had been removed to keep the vehicles in place. "They aren't coming back for these, Stingray. They took the keys with 'em."

Sean rested his back against the front wall of Building Eight and motioned for Jaime to fall in behind him. "Roger that. We need to clear these buildings until we get eyes on them."

Suddenly the concrete wall erupted from a barrage of automatic gunfire, sending dust and debris flying in all directions.

"Shit!" exclaimed Sean as he dropped to his stomach and searched for the source of the gunfire. "Jaime, get to the side of the building! Stay low and use it for cover!"

Sebastian dove inside the patrol car as the exploding windows showered him with thousands of minute glass fragments. Lying flat across the seat and holding his rifle close to his chest, he could hear the all too familiar cry of *Allahu Akbar* coming from the hangar.

"Fuck me!" he said, wincing from the glass shards raining down on his face. "Stingray, do you got eyes on that asshole?"

Sean fired his rifle at the hangar across the street. "Front door of the hangar across the street." He rolled to his right as the concrete sidewalk erupted from a maelstrom of bullets. "Contact north," he exclaimed as he continued to roll, barely staying ahead of the deadly salvo hurling concrete fragments flying into his face and torso. Sean heard a swarm of bullets from Jaime's M4 fly over his head, temporarily stopping the barrage. He pushed himself up and dove toward the corner of the building, taking up a position next to Jaime. "Thanks for the covering fire. That was close."

"No problem. Are you hit? Your head is bleeding."

"Nah. It's just a few scratches. You kept your eyes open this time, right?"

Jaime grinned. "Yes, sir." Over the noise of the gunfire, he heard a loud ringing coming from the patrol car that Sebastian had taken refuge in. Jaime watched as Sebastian took a cell phone from his pocket and put it up to his ear. "Is he taking a phone call?"

"Hey baby. What's up?" Sebastian spoke into the phone.

Pilar's voice come from the other end of the line. "You were supposed to be here thirty minutes ago. What's keeping you?"

"I ran into a little trouble here at the base, so I'm gonna be a little late. We may have to reschedule for after lunch." Sebastian winced as bullets impacted the vehicle from the rear this time, sending more glass and metal falling down on his face.

"Is that gunfire? What is happening?"

"Yeah baby, its gunfire. A coupla terrorists thought it would be cool to attack the base. But it's no big deal. Me and a coupla guys got it all under control."

Pilar could hear the automatic gunfire coming through the phone. "It doesn't sound like you've got it under control."

Bullets struck the rear of the vehicle and Sebastian could tell that a third gunman had joined in the fight. "Look, baby. I'm gonna have to call you back."

"Sebastian Gray, you better not die on me!"

Sebastian's face grew pained. She called him by his full name. That was something that Pilar did only when she was very angry, or she wanted his full attention. "Don't worry, baby. I got this. I'll call you in a little bit." He heard her tell him to be careful as he ended the call and slipped the phone back into his pocket. Sebastian looked down beyond his feet toward Sean, who was firing at the front door of building eight. "Where is the third asshole?"

"South corner of the hangar." Sean continued to fire at the terrorists. "Were you just talking on the phone?"

"Yeah. That was my girl, Pilar. I'm late for our date."

"Don't you think that you've got more important things to worry about?"

"Hell, no! She's a little spitfire. I don't want to make her mad. She might just kill me."

"What do you think these guys are trying to do?"

"Yeah, but they're just tryin'. She would actually do it."

Sean chuckled at the thought that the soldier was more afraid of his girlfriend than the men trying to kill him. "What in the hell are those guys screaming?"

"*Allahu Akbar*. It's what the Muji's scream when they are in a firefight."

"Why do they scream it continuously? Don't they ever take a breath?"

"It means God is the greatest. In Afghanistan and Syria, we figured that they yelled it because they were such bad shots. You know, hedging their bets. They figure they're gonna die so they scream *Allahu Akbar* hoping Allah will hear them and take 'em up to Paradise."

"Well, how do you get them to shut up?" asked Sean, wiping the blood and sweat from his eyes. "They're giving me a freakin' headache."

"That's easy... Shoot 'em," said Sebastian with a grin. "Y'all give me some covering fire. I've got a plan."

Jaime aimed his rifle at the front of the hangar and fired his M4. The glass front of the hangar shattered, causing the terrorist to halt his fire. He watched as Sebastian slithered out of the passenger door of the patrol car and disappeared from sight. The terrorist, still shouting *Allahu Akbar*, stopped firing and covered his head to shield himself from the falling glass. In a blink of an eye, Jaime observed Sebastian leap onto the hood of the third patrol car and, with one step, dive toward the hangar. The sunlight hit the glass shards falling from Sebastian, causing them to sparkle. The entire scene reminded Jaime of Superman flying through the air.

With his body parallel to the ground, Sebastian fired two rounds at the terrorist. He missed with first, but the second found its mark, striking the man in the shoulder. Jaime watched in admiration as Sebastian landed with a diving roll and rose to one knee, firing three rounds into the corner of the hangar. The bullets pierced the thin aluminum, striking the second terrorist in his right elbow. The wound caused the terrorist to step away from the cover of building and into the open. The man's body shuddered as it was ripped apart by five well placed bullets from Sean's rifle.

Jaime watched in disbelief as Sebastian stood up amidst the barrage of bullets flying around him. The terrorists hiding from inside the safety of the doorway of Building Eight had Sebastian in their sights and were firing on full automatic. He watched as Sebastian fired three rapid shots. Two struck a slender, Hispanic-looking terrorist in the throat, nearly severing his head from his body, while the third flew high and shattered the glass door. The terrorist fell backward holding his throat, drowning in his own blood.

Another terrorist entered the fray, firing from the north side of the hangar. His first salvo flew by Sebastian harmlessly. Jaime watched as a bullet sped so close to Sebastian that it ripped the denim on his right thigh. Unfazed by the surrounding chaos, Sebastian squeezed off six more rounds at the front door of Building Eight, striking the terrorist in the forehead and sending him backwards to the ground with such force that the thud could be heard over the thunder of the gunfire.

Sean watched as the last terrorist, who was still hiding behind the hangar, dropped his magazine to reload. Seizing the opportunity, Sean fired six shots into the corner of the hangar, hitting the man in the chest and sending him spinning around in a circle. Not missing a beat, Sebastian spun around on one foot and fired two more rounds into the man's head, causing the terrorist to step backwards and fall down, coming to rest in a sitting position.

The firefight was over in less than four minutes, but it seemed to Jaime that it had been half an hour. With his hands still trembling from the adrenaline coursing through his body, Jaime followed Sean to the front of the hangar where Sebastian was standing. "That was crazy Sebastian! Who do you think you are, Superman?"

Sebastian shot Jaime a quick smile. "Superman? No way. Superman wore a cape. I wanna be somebody cool... like Captain America. He rode a Harley."

Sean looked Sebastian in the eyes and winked. "He also wore tights."

Sebastian looked flustered. "Naw, man," he said, shaking his head. "Not in the beginning. He wore jeans and a T-shirt. That's it. I wanna be the cool, blue jean and T-shirt wearing, Harley riding Cap'n Fuckin' America."

From the somewhere in the dark heart of the hangar, Sebastian heard the familiar cry of *Allahu Akbar* as a bullet grazed his right bicep. He casually raised his weapon and fired two bullets into the terrorist's head.

Sean locked eyes with Sebastian. "So I guess we aren't trying to shoot them in the leg anymore?"

"Nope. Now that we know they're terrorists, we kill 'em all. This isn't just an attack on the base. It's an attack on America. I don't want 'em to get sent to some prison for a few years and then get let back out to do this shit all over again. We're gonna hunt these bastards down and kill every last one."

"Now you're talking," said Sean with a twinkle in his eye.

CHAPTER 36
Corpus Christ Army Depot

Sean Ray could still smell the pungent odor of gunpowder which filled the hangar. He spied the bodies of the eight dead servicemen killed by the terrorists. He bent down over the body of a dead terrorist and removed the remaining M4 clips from the man's tactical vest. Sean relieved the man of his M4 carbine and dropped his LAR-15 to the ground. The look of sadness and confusion in Sebastian's eyes said everything. "Did you know him?"

Without looking up Sebastian said, "Yeah. His name was Mateo Vasquez. Or so I thought."

"What do you mean by that?" asked Jaime.

"He was a new guy. Only been here two or three weeks and until five minutes ago he spoke with a heavy Mexican accent. Even heavier than yours, Haiku."

"Dude! It's Jaime. And I don't have an accent. I'm from Oceanside, California, not Mexico."

Sebastian flashed Jaime an engaging smile. "Like I said, he had a thicker accent than you. But five minutes ago he developed a very Syrian accent."

Sean eyed Sebastian. "How do you know he had a Syrian accent?"

"If y'all had been through as many firefights as I have over there, you would be able to tell too. We used to place bets on where the Muji's were from just by the way that they yelled *Allahu Akbar*. You see, Al-Qaeda, the Taliban and ISIL all recruit their *mujahedeen* from all over the Middle East. Whether they're from Afghanistan, Syria, Turkey, Yemen or Saudi Arabia, it don't matter to ISIL. They'll take people from anywhere, even France and England. After a while you learn the accents. This guy was definitely from Syria. Those two over at Building Eight were Paki and Libyan."

Jamie stared in disbelief at Sebastian and nodded at the south corner of the hangar. "What about that guy?"

"I'm not sure. Jersey, I think."

"Jersey?" asked Sean.

Sebastian shrugged. "I didn't say they were all Mid-eastern. The two MPs back at the circle, Dennis and Malik, they definitely weren't."

Jaime had a look of devastation on his face. "Man, this sucks."

"What do you mean by that?" asked Sean.

"We're up against an unknown number of bad guys from the Mid-East and the U.S. who are heavily armed. That makes me the unnamed guy in red."

Sebastian turned Sean with a confused look on his face. "The who?"

"Really?" asked Sean. "You know, from Star Trek. The guy in red that beams down with Kirk and always gets popped in the first five seconds."

"I'm drawing crickets, dude. But don't you worry, Jaime, I've seen you in action. You'll be just fine."

"Yeah, right. You're just saying that. I'm not like you two. I'm a hacker, not a soldier. I belong behind a computer. I can't just stand out in the middle of the road with bullets flying all around me and not be scared."

Sean winked at Jaime. "Don't lump me in with his craziness. I take cover when the bullets start to fly. By the way Sebastian, what was that? Didn't you say that you had a plan?"

"I did. The plan was for me to get out of that car. After that, I just played it by ear," said Sebastian. "And we all get scared, Jaime. The trick is to use your fear and not let it control you. It's a simple fight, flight or freeze response. It's not until you have bullets flying around you that you know what kind of person you really are. Some guys run for the hills. Some guys let the fear take hold of them and they freeze up and do nothing. Those guys die. Fighters use that fear and fight back. I've seen you in action. You're a fighter. Don't get me wrong, you ain't no Cap'n fuckin' America. But you're at least a Bucky."

"A who?" asked Jaime.

"Bucky. He was Captain America's sidekick," answered Sean.

"By the way, Stingray, where in the hell did you learn to shoot like that?" asked Sebastian. "That ain't normal government agent shooting."

"Fort Bragg."

"No shit. You Delta?"

"Nah. All the FAST Teams train at Bragg for our Advanced Urban Training."

"FAST Team, huh? That explains it. You guys are bad ass. I worked with Nate Reardon and FAST Team Two over in Afghanistan. You guys are no joke... tough SOBs for civilians. And training at Bragg makes you a grunt by association." From the back of the building,

Sebastian heard the echo of metal on concrete and a cry of *Allahu Akbar*. Before he could turn to inspect the source of the noise, the man was silenced by five rounds from Sean's M4. Sebastian looked over to Jaime with a smile. "Like I said, Bucky, Sean's a bad ass."

In the distance Sebastian heard the whirl of a helicopter warming up its engines.

Sean looked at Sebastian with wide eyes and nodded toward the noise. "What kind of choppers do they have over there?"

Sebastian's forehead wrinkled as his mind raced through helicopter inventory. "There's a Huey, a Sea Hawk and a Pave Hawk. Whatcha thinking? That's their exfil? Grab a chopper and head to Mexico." His eyes grew wide and his jaw dropped. "Fuck me. That's not their exfil. That's an Apache."

CHAPTER 37
Corpus Christ Army Depot

Santiago Ortiz looked on in anger as Husain Al-Wadhi, who now went by the name Javier Carrasco, continued to gun down the helpless helicopter repairmen. From the cockpit of the Boeing AH-64 Apache helicopter, he could see the men fall one by one as they scrambled for cover. Santiago had heard the massive explosions and the continuous automatic gunfire in the distance. This was not the plan that Khalid had told Santiago and his uncle, Juan Carlos Real, the plan they had agreed to help him with. He had assumed that when the AH-5X unmanned Little Bird helicopter drone came into the Depot, it was their target. Khalid had told them that his plan was to infiltrate the base and steal a drone. Since Santiago was asked to train as a helicopter repairman, stealing the AH-5X made sense. But with the explosions and the senseless killing of the men in the hangar, Santiago knew that this was something far worse.

Santiago cursed himself for not being more forceful in his attempts to dissuade his uncle from helping that radical Muslim infiltrate the United States. He had known from the first time that Khalid had spoken of a worldwide Caliphate that the man was not their ally. Khalid was an evil man who worked for an organization whose solitary goal was to rule the world. The Al-Yad were businessmen. Businessmen who had used La Familia for their own purposes and would now discard him and his uncle because they served no further purpose. Or worse, they would blame La Familia for this attack and the Americans would wage their war on La Familia and put an end to his uncle and the cartel. Santiago watched as Specialist Fernando Perez fell to the ground a mere five feet from the Apache. The gravel being tossed into the air from the helicopter's four giant propellers pelted Perez's face and torso as he made one final attempt to crawl to safety before succumbing to his wounds.

Santiago climbed down from the cockpit and stood over the body of Perez. With a single pull, he unfastened the bright orange Fitbit from his own wrist. Santiago knelt down over the body of Perez and fastened the Fitbit over the left sleeve of the Specialist's ACUs. Above the whirring of the powerful propellers, Santiago heard Husain's voice.

"Santiago, what are you doing? You need the Fitbit for the mission. How will the others know that you are on our side?"

Santiago rose and faced the terrorist. "Yeah, about that Husain," he said, reaching behind his back and removing the Beretta M9 pistol from his waist. "I don't want anybody knowing that I was a part of this."

He fired three bullets into the terrorist's chest. A smile crept onto his face as he watched as the man's lifeless body fall to the ground.

Sean Ray rounded the corner of the hangar and spotted the young man pull the trigger three times, each bullet striking a soldier holding an M4 carbine in the chest. Sean could see that the young man was not wearing an orange Fitbit, while the man with the M4 was. *Good job, kid*, he thought to himself.

Sean let his thoughts drift to the events of the day. This attack had caused soldiers to kill their friends. The terrorists knew who their targets were, but the real soldiers, soldiers like this kid and Sebastian, were being forced to kill people they had thought were their friends. People they worked with. People they drank with. ISIL was not only attacking the base, it was messing with people's minds. Sean was brought back into the moment by the sound of Sebastian's voice.

"Show me your hands, Specialist," shouted Sebastian so as to be heard over the roar of the Apache's twin turbines.

Santiago turned to his left and faced the oncoming trio. He trained the pistol on Sebastian and barked, "Show me yours!" He doubted that the Caucasians were part of Khalid's plan, but he was not sure about the third man, who was Hispanic, although he could not see a Fitbit on the man's wrist.

Sean aimed his M4 at Santiago and moved closer. "Look, kid, we're the good guys. Those two guys you shot, they're the bad guys. Do you see those bright orange Fitbits? That's how you can tell. So do me a favor and lower that weapon, so that my friend here doesn't shoot you."

Santiago lifted his chin. How did these guys know about the Fitbits? Were they part of the Khalid's plan or merely observant? How was it that they were all carrying M4s and wearing tactical vests? Why did one of the vests say DEA in bright yellow letters? Santiago had too many questions and not enough time to process them. The man in the blue jeans and cowboy boots looked like he was ready to pull the trigger. Santiago did not want to tempt him, just in case his motto was to kill them all and let God sort it out.

He bent over, placing the Beretta on the ground, and raised his hands above his head with palms out. "I'm one of the good guys. I promise."

Sean motioned for Sebastian to keep his weapon trained on Santiago as he lowered his M4 and moved closer to the young man. He cupped his hands to his mouth and shouted, "Do you know how to turn this thing off?"

"Yes," replied Santiago, climbing into the cockpit and flipping the switches to power down the turbines. As the Apache's powerful blades started to slow, he turned to climb out of the cockpit and noticed that Sebastian was still pointing his M4 at him. "I'm one of the good guys," he said with his hands raised.

Sebastian studied at the name on Santiago's ACUs. "I'm still trying to figure that out, Specialist Ortiz. So far today, we haven't run into any good guys other than Petty Officer Bucky back there."

Jaime looked at Santiago and raised his chin. "It's Jaime. He has this thing about names."

"Good to meet you. I'm Santiago Ortiz."

Sean offered Santiago his hand. "I'm Sean. Can you tell us what happened here?"

Santiago shook Sean's hand and pointed toward the glass door located between the two giant bay doors. "I was standing over there by the door, having a smoke. I heard some really loud explosions come from down that way," he said, pointing toward the police station and barracks. "Then there was screaming and gunfire coming from inside. I looked into the hangar and saw Javier and Fernando shooting everybody. So I dropped my smoke and took cover behind those barrels. That's when Fernando," Santiago motioned to the body at his feet, "came out and started the Apache. Once he got it going, he climbed out and went back inside the hangar. I could hear more gunfire but I couldn't see anything. Fernando came back out, but before he could get into the Apache, he got shot. I saw the pistol and ran for it. Javier walked out of the hanger and was yelling something at me that I couldn't understand. He had an M4 and I didn't want to die, so I shot him before he shot me."

Sean put his hand on Santiago's shoulder. "You did good, kid."

"What was the MOS for these two?" asked Sebastian. "They weren't MPs."

"No. They were helicopter repairmen like me. Why?"

"All the other terrorists we have come into contact with have been MPs. That these guys were repairmen means the terrorists have infiltrated the base even more than I thought. They could be anywhere and the only way to identify them is that stupid orange Fitbit."

"Terrorists? That would explain the explosions. Do you mean that Fernando and Javier weren't alone? How do you know that they all wear orange Fitbits?" Santiago asked, thankful that he had managed to put his own Fitbit on Fernando's dead body.

Sean locked eyes with Santiago. "Your two guys were definitely not working alone. We have run into about six or seven of these guys."

"Closer to a dozen," chimed in Sebastian.

"A dozen or so of these terrorists," corrected Sean, looking at Sebastian and getting an approving nod, "and they have all been wearing one of those Fitbits. There is no way it's a coincidence."

Sebastian stepped in toward Santiago and pointed at the Apache. "Can you disable that thing? Pull the wires or something?"

"It's not that simple, Sergeant, but yeah, I can take it out of commission."

"Weapons systems too?"

"Yes. It will take a few minutes, but I can get it done."

"That's your mission, Specialist. Field strip this Apache so that those Muji's can't come back and use it against us. The last thing we need is an Apache firing a 30mm chain gun at us." Sebastian turned his gaze to Sean and Jaime. "You two on me," he said, darting down the dirt road toward the airfield.

Santiago watched as the three men moved down the road toward the airstrip. He waited until they were out of sight and walked into the hangar. He strolled over to the lifeless body of SPC Hector Ramirez and removed the man's tunic. Santiago then swapped his own dog tags with those of the dead soldier. He climbed up into the truck containing the AH-5X drone and fired it up. It was time for him to leave.

CHAPTER 38
Naval Air Station Corpus Christi

Sebastian pulled at his sweat-soaked shirt as he moved hastily down the center of the L-shaped tarmac. He could hear the now all too familiar sound of gunfire coming from the hangars up ahead. How many terrorists had infiltrated the base? He and his makeshift team had killed over a dozen terrorists so far and they just kept coming. He understood that no matter how quickly he put an end to this attack, the death toll would be horrendous. One lone gunman, armed with a single 9mm pistol, had killed and wounded over forty people at Fort Hood. And that guy was only a Psychiatrist. This attack was being led by MPs. Soldiers who had been trained to shoot and keep their heads in situations like this. Dennis and Malik had doubled the Fort Hood body count by themselves. Add in the IEDs, the hospital and everywhere else that they hadn't discovered yet and this could be the worst attack ever on American soil. At the very least, it would be the worst attack that didn't involve airplanes. The body count would be in the hundreds, but most likely over a thousand American soldiers would end up giving their lives today.

And for what? What could ISIL possibly gain from an attack on America? What was their endgame? ISIL attacks were normally more like a high school shooting. They were random, uncoordinated and messy; suicidal Mujis who were looking to die and take their virgins in heaven. ISIL wanted the notoriety and the press coverage and the terrorists' lives were inconsequential. But this time seemed different. It was coordinated. It wasn't a lone gunman, like Kentucky or Arizona. It was multiple terrorists acting in synchronization. This time they used Fitbits to identify themselves. There was no way that the President could call the events of today workplace violence. The enemy was wearing uniforms as defined by the Geneva Convention.

That was it. ISIL believed that its Caliphate made it a legitimate country. This was not a random terrorist attack. It was an act of war. One sovereign nation versus another and they wanted the whole world to know.

The right side of the tarmac was lined with orange and white Beechcraft T-6 Texan trainer planes. Sebastian noted that the single engine turboprop planes were perfect for training pilots, but with their high center and small three-wheeled landing gear, the aircraft would not provide much cover if the terrorists were to spot them coming down the tarmac. On the left side of the tarmac was a large metal hangar used for the maintenance and repair of the planes. Sebastian could see seven bodies sprawled on the ground in front of the hangar. The crimson blood poured onto the tarmac, staining the white concrete.

He motioned to Sean and Jaime to keep moving to the far corner of the hangar as he looked on at the bodies littering the ground inside. This was quickly becoming a massacre. If only military personnel were allowed to carry firearms on base, maybe this wouldn't have happened. It had always baffled him why the only people in America who were actually trained to use firearms could not carry them. Never mind the fact that it was in their job description as soldiers to use firearms. He wondered what politician had gotten the no gun on base rule passed. He would like to personally show that asshole how he felt about it. Dumb-ass politicians always let their opinion polls get in the way of good old-fashioned common sense.

Sebastian noticed Sean peering around the corner of the hangar with his right arm up, signaling all stop. Jaime was kneeling behind him.

"Whatcha got?" asked Sebastian as he approached from the rear.

"Six guys in NWUs and Fitbits doing something with the planes," he whispered loudly without turning his head. "They're taking something out of their knapsacks and attaching it underneath each plane, but I can't make out what it is."

Sebastian moved up between Jaime and Sean. He observed two men, forty feet away, and said, "Well, there's only one way to find out."

Jaime tapped Sebastian on the shoulder. "Only one way?"

Sebastian's blue-gray eyes lit up as he flashed Jaime a sheepish grin. "Yeah. Let's go ask 'em."

Jaime moved backward. "I don't think that's a good idea, dude. Did you notice they had machine guns?"

Sebastian gave Jaime a playful slap on the back. "Don't worry, Bucky. We got this. Besides those are M4s, not machine guns. Machine guns would be bad."

Sean shook his head. "Do you ever take anything serious?"

Sebastian showed him a mouthful of teeth. "I take everything serious, Stingray. However, I've found that in times of great stress, it's best to keep your sense of humor."

Jaime nodded in affirmation. "Really? I've found that when people are shooting at me, I want to crap my pants."

"I wouldn't tell that to anybody else, Bucky. You might lose your man card," said Sebastian, rising to his feet. He noticed the airmen moving toward two planes farther down the runway and decided that it was time to move. He tapped Sean on the shoulder and signaled for him to provide cover. "Just remember to hold that in when they start shooting, Bucky," he said, strolling down the tarmac toward the two men.

Sebastian closed the distance between the first man and himself. As he neared the man, he whistled and said, "Hey, buddy. Whatcha doin' there?"

The airman, a black man in his mid-twenties, stopped what he was doing and looked up from behind the fuselage of the airplane. "Excuse me?" he asked. The airman's eyes widened when he noticed Sebastian's M4 and the absence of a Fitbit.

Sebastian trained his rifle on the man's head. "I asked what you were doing with these planes."

The airman pulled the canvas bag over his shoulder and moved out into the open. "Look, Sergeant, I don't want any trouble," he said, placing his left hand inside the bag. "It's Standard Operating Procedure to disable all planes when the pilots have been terminated during an attack on the base."

"How do you know that there aren't any pilots?"

"Huh?"

Gunfire erupted from the hangar to the south, causing Sebastian to turn his gaze towards the sound. The airman seized the opportunity, pulling a Beretta M9 pistol from inside of the canvas bag.

"Oh shit!" growled Sebastian, diving for whatever cover the Beechcraft could provide. Rolling under the wing, Sebastian popped up in a crouched defensive posture with only the thin aluminum wing between him and the terrorist. The airman let loose four shots which raked the aluminum wing inches from Sebastian's face and showered him with metal shards. Sebastian recoiled as the flying debris pelleted his face. "Fuck me," he said, wiping his face to remove the sweat and debris. Raising his M4 above his head, Sebastian fired off a wild three-round burst, causing the airman to take cover behind the propeller.

Sean fired two shots into the back of the man's head, sending a spray of bright red onto the clear canopy. Sean noticed the remaining five terrorists scurrying up the tarmac toward Sebastian with their weapons raised. He watched two of the men move to the rear of the planes in an attempt to flank Sebastian. The remaining three men moved up the tarmac, using the planes for cover.

Sean looked at Jaime. "Kid, you've gotta get to that plane over there," he said, pointing to the plane closest to them. "I'll cover you. When you get there, shoot those two assholes coming up behind Sebastian."

"Okay."

"You ready?"

"As ready as I'll ever be."

Sean took aim at the terrorists and began firing, causing the airmen to seek cover behind the airplanes. He fired two rounds at a baby-faced terrorist who had ducked under the propeller of a T-34. The bullets found their mark, striking the young airman center mass and sending him backwards on to the asphalt.

Jaime slid beside the plane on the far side of the tarmac, narrowly escaping the flurry of bullets crackling the air above his head. He made his way to the tail of the plane and, with a heavy breath, he raised himself up on the tip of his toes in order peer over the fuselage of the plane. Jaime watched as Sebastian crawled to the rear of the T-34, using the fuselage and tail as cover. Jaime took notice of the two terrorists making their way to the tail of the plane closest to Sebastian. The terrorists rushed around the tail of the plane, advancing menacingly toward Sebastian. Jaime saw Sebastian let loose with a flurry of rounds from his M4, striking the first terrorist in the ankle and sending him to the ground.

Jaime seized his opportunity and swung around the tail end of the T-34. He squeezed off five rounds at the remaining terrorist, who was still standing. Three of the rounds flew wild and ripped through the tail of the plane. Two of the rounds found their mark, sending the terrorist to the ground with a resounding thud. Jaime adjusted his aim to the terrorist writhing in pain on the tarmac who was holding his right ankle. He squeezed the trigger and the man's head exploded.

Sebastian brought himself up off the ground, looked back at Jaime and gave him a thumbs up. "Now that's how you shoot, Bucky!"

He moved around the tail and advanced. Sebastian spied a terrorist hiding behind the bullet-ridden canopy of a T-34. He leveled his sight and fired three rounds in quick succession. The bullets sliced through the glass canopy, snapping the man's head backwards and silencing his cries of *Allahu Akbar*.

Sean saw the terrorist closest to him go down and readjusted his aim to the last remaining terrorist, a short muscular man with dark hair. He maintained his fire, pinning the terrorist behind the T-34. Sean watched through his scope as Sebastian made his way around the rear of the plane. To his surprise, Sebastian didn't shoot the terrorist. Instead he slung his M4 over his back and charged.

The force of the tackle brought both men out onto the tarmac. Sebastian climbed on top of the terrorist, braced himself with his left arm, and let loose with four violent punches to the terrorist's face, shattering the man's nose. The terrorist slammed down hard on Sebastian's elbow and pushed Sebastian off with his legs.

Both men rolled to opposite sides and immediately sprang to their feet. The terrorist moved toward Sebastian with both fists raised in front of his face, like a boxer. Sebastian advanced with his hands open. The terrorist threw a hard right at Sebastian. Sebastian ducked, allowing the punch to fly harmlessly over his head. Sebastian hammered the man with four thunderous blows to the kidney, grabbing the man's wrist as he stumbled forward. Not wasting a second, Sebastian twisted the man's arm backward, pinning it behind his back. Grabbing a handful of the man's jet black hair, Sebastian pushed the man toward the T-34, slamming his head into the plane with such force that it caused the terrorist to fall to one knee.

Sebastian, still holding a tight grip on the terrorist's wrist, twisted the man's arm until his elbow locked and his palm faced the clear blue sky. Sebastian forced the man onto the ground with his boot, causing the terrorist to cry out in pain.

"How many people do you have?"

"Fuck you."

Sebastian twisted the man's arm further while pushing harder with his boot. "Wrong answer. What's your mission?"

"Fuck you."

Jaime rounded the rear of the pane and walked up behind Sebastian. He noticed a small black disc attached to the side of the plane. It reminded him of the charging dock for his Apple watch. "What's this thing on the plane?"

Sebastian looked back at the disc. "It doesn't look good, whatever it is." He looked down at the terrorist. "Okay, asshole. Let's try an easy question. What's the black thing on the plane?"

Sebastian didn't notice that the terrorist had worked his left hand into his pocket. The man removed his hand from his pocket, revealing a thin black device with a red light on the bottom. The terrorist pressed a button on the top of the device.

"*Allahu Akbar*!" exclaimed the man in an unmistakable Syrian accent.

Sean was walking at a rapid pace down the tarmac when he heard the first explosion. The noise was close behind him, causing him to turn his head. A second explosion followed an instant behind the first and then a third and a fourth, each one coming closer than the one before. Sean could see the smoke rising from behind the hangar and realization set in.

His walk turned into a jog and then into a full run. "It's the planes!" he exclaimed, cupping his left hand to his mouth as he sprinted for the hangar opposite of Sebastian. "They're blowing the planes. Get to cover!"

Sebastian heard the explosions and saw the smoke billowing up from behind the hangars. "Aww, now. Why did you have to go and do that, asshole?" he asked, looking down at the terrorist with hatred in his eyes.

"Paradise is for those who kill and are killed," growled the terrorist.

Sebastian pulled the Beretta from his vest and fired a round into the terrorist's thigh.

"Enjoy Paradise, asshole." Sebastian turned to Jaime. "Bucky, get to that hangar before we get blown to bits."

Jaime raced past Sebastian. "You don't have to tell me twice. What about you?"

"Right behind you," said Sebastian as he dashed toward the hangar, carefully dodging the debris raining down from the sky. He sensed the blasts getting closer as the planes on the tarmac detonated in rapid succession. Sean and Sebastian reached the hangar simultaneously, both diving through the bay door to avoid the flying debris. Sebastian rolled to a stop and turned back in time to see the wounded terrorist being ripped apart by the explosion.

CHAPTER 39
Naval Air Station Corpus Christi

Shrapnel from the exploding planes pierced the air around Sean. As the dangerous projectiles ripped through the hangar, Sean took refuge behind a fifty-gallon drum. He cursed as the blade of a propeller sliced through the air four inches above his head. He could hear the clanking of metal on metal as plane fragments bombarded the roof of the aluminum hangar.

"That was close," he said aloud. If Sebastian was correct and this was an ISIL attack, then the President had been completely wrong. ISIL wasn't the Junior Varsity. They had infiltrated an American military base and, through a coordinated attack, set the U.S. Navy's pilot training program back by years. Not only had they eliminated an entire training class, but they had now destroyed the entire fleet of training planes. They were not the J.V. team at all. He supposed, however, that the President was right when he called them killers with good social media. How else would ISIL have been able to recruit U.S. citizens and convince them to join the military? How else could ISIL carry out an attack on the sovereign ground? ISIL was not the uneducated barbarians that the press made them out to be. An attack like this took planning and patience. The type of strategic planning that barbaric savages were simply incapable of.

A bullet zipped by Sean's head, interrupting his thoughts. He dove to his right as eight more bullets bombarded the barrel in front of him, causing its gray-green contents to spill forth from the holes. Sean rolled onto his side and eyed a terrorist, dressed in blue and gray digital patterned NWUs, readjusting his aim in an attempt to follow Sean's path. Without hesitation, Sean squeezed the trigger, striking the man first in the chest and then rupturing the man's head, sending the terrorist violently to the concrete floor.

Sean canvassed the hangar and, seeing no more threats, he asked, "Do you see any more?"

Sebastian surveyed the hangar. There were over thirty dead bodies littering the hangar floor. It appeared that each one had been shot as they scampered for what little cover the hangar provided. "Negative," he replied. "Looks like he was alone. That was impressive. You move pretty quick for an old man."

The sound of gunfire erupted again and a hailstorm of bullets buzzed through the entryway of the hangar. Sean dropped to the ground and crawled closer to the entryway. He spotted five more terrorists, dressed in NWUs, advancing on their position.

"I count five tangos in NWUs, all wearing Fitbits." He surveyed the hangar and realized the same thing that the dead soldiers strewn about the hangar had come to realize: the barren hangar provided little cover. Definitely not enough cover for a gunfight with six well trained sailors. "We need to move, or they're gonna pin us in here."

Sebastian peered around the corner at the approaching terrorists. "Roger that." He moved outside of the hangar and took cover behind four large crates. "Sean, you and Bucky move up to the next hangar. I'll cover you."

Jaime moved up beside Sebastian, his face showing his insecurity. "Are you sure you can cover five guys?"

"Do you want to stay here and take your chances?"

"That's a big negative."

Sebastian flashed him a confident grin. "Don't worry. I got this. When I start firing, you run like hell. It's only twenty yards."

"Roger that," replied Jaime.

Sebastian glanced at Sean, who had joined them. "You ready?"

"Ready."

Sebastian rose and placed his M4 on the top of the crate to steady his aim. He carefully aimed at the terrorist closest to him, who was hurrying up the center of the tarmac one-hundred yards away, and fired three rapid shots, hitting the man center mass. The bullets ripped through the man's chest, casting out a spray of blood which showered the terrorist following two feet behind. Sebastian put two bullets into the second terrorist's chest as he tried in vain to wipe the blood from his eyes.

The gunfire caused the three remaining terrorists to move behind four large wooden crates at the far end of the next hangar. Sebastian fired another salvo into the crates, pinning the men down. Sean and Jaime ran for the side of the hangar and took refuge behind the crates, just as a volley of bullets riddled the front of the barricades. The terrorists, in a synchronized manner, leapt out from behind the crates one at a time, each man firing a quick salvo and then leaping back again. The constant barrage was enough to keep Sean and Jaime pinned behind the quickly eroding crates.

Seeing the tactical disadvantage that he had led them into, Sebastian decided on a new course of action. As bullets snapped away at the wooden crates, Sebastian darted out onto the tarmac and raced for the cover of the burning wreckage, narrowly escaping the bullets ripping through the air around him. As he neared the burning planes, Sebastian executed a baseball slide, coming to rest between the fiery husks that were once T-34s. He popped up on one knee and squeezed the trigger. Sebastian could feel the heat against his face and the smoke burned his eyes, causing his aim to be off. His bullets missed their target and splintered the wooden crate above the terrorists' heads.

Sean locked eyes with Jaime. "What in the hell is he doing?"

"Playing Captain America again," replied Jaime nonchalantly.

Sebastian eyed the three terrorists who were racing toward Jaime and Sean. Realizing that Sebastian had flanked them, the terrorists broke off their attack and quickly retreated. Sebastian squeezed off three more rounds. This time each one reached its mark, killing the young terrorist leading the retreat and sending him tumbling onto the tarmac. The remaining two terrorists leapt over the dead man's body, never bothering to look back or return fire. Seeing an open window for advancement, Sebastian streaked toward the cover of the crates that the men had vacated. He was halfway across the tarmac when he felt a thud against his shoulder. The force of the impact caused Sebastian to twist and stumble. Pivoting on his right foot, Sebastian spun to his left, completing a full turn before he dashed toward the crates. Bullets filled the air around him as he dove with his arms outstretched, holding his M4 like a running back trying to extend the football over the goal line.

Sebastian sat up with his back pressed against the wooden crates. Feeling the white hot pain in his shoulder and the warm ooze running down his chest, he observed the damage.

Sean reached Sebastian just as he was inspecting the wound. "Are you okay?"

Sebastian looked over his shoulder and eyed the exit wound. "Yeah, I think so. Looks like it went all the way through. Who the fuck shot me? Those two running off had their backs to me."

Jaime moved his head around the corner of the crate and spied the flatbed semi-trailer in front of the next hangar. "Looks like they have friends. There's a flatbed HEMMT in front of the hangar with two more bad guys hiding behind it. One of them is dressed in ACUs, but the other one is wearing a black suit. And both are wearing bright orange Fitbits."

Sebastian's eyes grew wide. "Did you say black suit?"

"Yeah. Black suit."

Sebastian's blue eyes turned dark. "Is he a pretty motherfucker that looks like Enrique Iglesias?"

"Yeah. How did you know?"

"Okay, now I'm really pissed. That asshole's shot me twice."

Sean looked quizzically at Sebastian. "Twice?"

Sebastian rose and faced Sean. "Yep, twice. Once in Al-Dana and now here. I'm definitely gonna kill that asshole." Sebastian looked to Jaime. "Did you say that there was a flatbed in front of the hangar?"

"Yes."

"What's on it?" asked Sebastian.

"I can't tell. It looks like a long, tan container of some sort with a bright orange cover on the top. About thirty feet long and maybe ten feet tall. It's not very wide though."

"Holy shit!" exclaimed Sebastian. "They're stealing a predator drone."

Sean looked at Sebastian with anger in his eyes. "You mean to tell me that all of this was to steal a stupid drone?"

Sebastian stared Sean in the eyes. "No. I don't think so. I think their purpose was to declare war on the United States. Stealing a drone is more like icing on the cake."

"I don't know why they would even want one," said Sean. "We used those things fifteen times a day in Syria for two years and never hit anything of importance."

Sebastian shook his head and chuckled. "That was user error. The President handpicked the targets instead of letting the professionals do their jobs. But you put one of those bad boys in the hands of someone who knows where he *wants* to strike and they are one of the most lethal weapons in the world."

"But wouldn't ISIL have to arm them?" asked Jaime.

"ISIL's making somewhere around one million dollars a day selling their oil on the black market. They can buy all the arms they want. The former Soviet Union is chock full of arms dealers willing to sell anything to anybody with enough cash," said Sebastian.

"We've got to stop them!" said Jaime excitedly.

"Now you're speaking my language, Bucky," replied Sebastian.

CHAPTER 40
Naval Air Station Corpus Christi

Sebastian surveyed the battlefield, knowing they were at a tactical disadvantage. The four terrorists had taken up positions at the hangar and had a clear view of any advancement that Sebastian and his team could attempt. Two men hid inside the hangar, another took cover on the rear of the flatbed behind the drone container, and Enrique was positioned at the front of the truck. Sebastian knew that advancing would not be an easy task. He leaned back against the wooden crate, holding his M4 close to his chest. The searing pain in his shoulder reminded him of his wound.

"It don't look good, Stingray. They're dug in and have good cover. If we move straight ahead, it's gonna be like shooting fish in a barrel and we're the fish."

Sean looked down the asphalt corridor between the two hangars. "How about that way?" he asked, nodding down the alley.

"We could make it around the hangar. But we would be sitting ducks coming back down the other side. We'd be pinned in between two hangars with zero cover. We're good, but we ain't that good," said Sebastian. He moved his eyes to the burning planes across the tarmac. Their fiery remains were sending up a thick black wall of smoke. "I think our best bet is to move forward just like last time. I'll head for the planes and y'all cover me. When I get behind the smoke, I'll move forward and cover your advance."

"That sounds dangerous," said Jaime. "Last time you got shot."

"Then this time y'all do a better job covering me," replied Sebastian. "When I take off, Bucky, you lay into that hangar with everything you've got. Sean, you take the truck. There's one tango on the flatbed about six feet back. He's using the drone carrier for cover. Enrique is at the front of the truck. Make sure you make him move, or I'm toast."

"Roger that."

Sebastian moved out from the crates, allowing Sean and Jaime to take their positions.

"Ready? On my mark. Three... two... one. Go!" Sebastian took off across the tarmac, running at full speed with a swarm of bullets flying around him like angry bees. He heard the rapport of his teammates' M4s which halted the onslaught of projectiles. As he reached the downed aircraft, he shielded his face from the white hot flames emanating from the molten debris and spilled fuel. The thick black wall of smoke burned his eyes and lungs. Sebastian raced through the smoke, dropping to one knee upon reaching the clean air on the other side. His heart pounded from the increased adrenaline and was working overtime from the loss of blood from his wound.

He took a moment to slow his heart rate and then proceeded forward. He scurried around the next three aircraft, careful to stay low and avoid the random bullets penetrating the smoke wall. He knew that these terrorists were trained by the military, but he had one advantage over all of them. They had never seen any actual combat. He had spent his entire adult life in war zones, honing his combat skills. That was his advantage. There was a huge difference between being trained to shoot accurately and accurately shooting when someone was shooting back.

From his vantage point, Sean watched as Sebastian emerged from the flames like a wraith, squeezing off rounds at the terrorists. Sebastian's first salvo struck the grill of the truck, inches from the suit's head. The impact of bullet on metal sent up a flurry of flashes like a sparkler on the fourth of July. The deluge caused Enrique to retreat, taking cover behind the truck.

Sebastian's next volley blasted the hangar, causing one terrorist to retreat deep inside. Sebastian adjusted his aim and fired off three more rounds, striking the second terrorist in the stomach and sending him to the ground writhing in agony. Sean tapped Jaime on the shoulder and said, "Let's move."

Sebastian noted the forward movement of his teammates and turned his fire toward the terrorist maneuvering along the flatbed. His bullets missed their mark, striking the container and showering the man with aluminum shards. Sebastian continued forward, replacing his magazine with one of the two remaining in his tactical vest. As he pressed the bolt release to load the first round, he watched helplessly as Sean took two rounds in the chest, sending him flying backwards onto the tarmac. The rounds were from the suit, who was lying prone one the ground under the flatbed. Sebastian squeezed off five rounds, which missed their mark and flattened two of the tires on the flatbed.

Holding his M4 out beside him using the pistol grip, Sebastian fired wildly at the suit as he raced toward his fallen comrade. Ignoring the pain, Sebastian grabbed Sean's tactical vest with his left hand, dragging his lifeless body to safety behind the crates. Sebastian studied Sean's chest.

"No blood," he said, unzipping the tactical vest to get a closer look. "Thank God you have a chest plate."

Sean sat up straight, gasping for air and startling Sebastian. "Damn! That hurt like a motherfucker," exclaimed Sean rubbing his chest.

Sebastian's face showed his gratitude that Sean was alive. "Good thing you were wearing a chest plate, or else you would've been toast."

Sean rubbed his chest where the projectiles had struck. "Aww... You were worried about me."

Sebastian cocked his head in mock disbelief. "You've got one hell of an imagination. What happened? I thought you were fast."

"I am fast. You were supposed to cover me. What happened to you?"

"I had to reload."

"Next time do it faster. Who shot me?"

"Enrlque."

"Well, now he's *definitely* gotta to die. He shot both of us in the last five minutes." Sean turned to Jaime and flashed his white teeth. "You know that you're next. Right?"

Jaime smiled back. "I'm going to pass on that. If that's all right with you guys. I don't need a purple heart." Jaime heard the sound of the flatbed's diesel engine starting. "Besides, it sounds like your guy is trying to run for it."

Sebastian locked eyes with Sean. "Are you okay to shoot?"

"Hell, yeah," said Sean, lifting himself off the tarmac.

"Good. You take out the tango in the hangar," said Sebastian as he bolted for the flatbed.

"Screw that," said Sean, racing down the tarmac behind Sebastian. "Jaime, you take out the guy in the hangar. I'm not gonna let Cap'n have all the fun."

Jaime moved toward the opening of the hangar and two shots rang out from inside. The terrorist was firing at Sebastian and Sean. Jaime pressed his back against the wall and controlled his breathing. He swung through the opening and spied the terrorist standing behind two fifty-gallon drums. Jaime aimed carefully through the sights and squeezed the trigger three times. The bullets struck the terrorist's chest, sending him crumbling the ground.

"Epic," he said, excited that he had made the shot. In the distance, Jaime heard a muffled boom, followed instantly by a much larger explosion.

Sean reached the rear of the slow moving flatbed as Sebastian finished his ascent to the trailer. He tossed Sebastian his M4 and leapt up onto the trailer.

"What was that?" he asked, referring to the explosions.

"Sounds like Ortiz blew the Apache," replied Sebastian, tossing back Sean's M4.

Sean moved toward the front of the truck along the left side of the container. "That would be the easy way, I guess."

The truck bounced hard, sending Sean tumbling toward the edge of the flatbed. Sean felt his pulse race as the asphalt tarmac raced toward his face. Grasping desperately, he latched onto a nylon tie-down fastening the container to the flatbed and halted his descent.

Sebastian stretched his neck over the container, his cheek dimples on full display. "Watch that first step, old man. It's a doozy."

"Gee, thanks," growled Sean with his eyebrows raised. "What the hell is wrong with this truck, anyway?" He asked, pulling himself up. "It's bouncing more than a cheerleader on prom night."

Sebastian gave him a close-lipped smile. "It has two flat tires on your side."

"How'd that happen?"

"I might have shot 'em when I was trying to take out Enrique."

"Were you aiming at them?"

"Not really."

"And I thought you were a good shot. Let's move." Sean turned his gaze to the cab of the truck and noticed that terrorist had not noticed them yet. "Keep low. I don't think he knows that we're back here."

Khalid shifted the truck into fourth gear as he struggled with the steering wheel. The soldier must have shot the tires, he thought to himself. But no matter, all he had to do was make it across the bridge and then he could navigate safely through the city to the warehouse he had arranged. Today was a good day for the Caliphate. Today would go down in history as the day that the Great Satan was struck down by Muhammad's Sword. His people had fought well and sacrificed themselves for the jihad. Their sacrifice would not be in vain.

He would deliver the Predator Drone, just as he had promised, and begin planning the Al-Yad's next assault on the Great Satan. An undetectable drone could inflict great damage in a large city such as Houston. Khalid turned the steering wheel hard, narrowly missing the wreckage of the planes as he made the sharp L-turn.

The erratic turn caused Sebastian to lose his balance and slam hard into the carrier. He cursed under his breath as his wounded shoulder impacted the container, sending a searing, electric pain coursing throughout his entire body. Using the container as a brace, Sebastian reset his feet and regained his balance. His eyes moved down the tarmac.

"You better hold on to something, Stingray. It looks like we have a hard left coming up."

Sean observed the upcoming turn and snaked his arm through the black tie-down. The look on Sebastian's face told him everything he needed to know about the man. Sebastian was in obvious pain from his gunshot wound, but he was determined to stop this terrorist from delivering his payload. Sebastian was one tough kid.

The truck made a hard left, slamming Sean into the container as the vehicle swung wide onto Ocean Drive and raced towards the causeway leading into Corpus Christi. After regaining his footing, Sean released the tie-down and moved forward toward the cabin.

Khalid battled with the erratic steering of the truck, struggling to keep the vehicle on the road. He straightened the giant truck and begin the final leg of his mission. The bridge to the city was just ahead. Once he was into the city, his mission would be a success. The Americans would be too consumed with treating their wounded and searching for more *mujahedeen* than they would be concerned about looking for missing drones.

A tap on the rear window of the cabin disrupted Khalid's train of thought. The handsome, bald man staring at him through the rear-view mirror, with his chiseled jaw and a bulging vein on his forehead, was pointing an M4 at Khalid's head. It was one of the men from the hangar, but how had he climbed aboard the truck without Khalid noticing?

Khalid's eyes moved to the road ahead. The causeway was only a few meters away. The infidel would not fire once they reached the bridge. He would not risk sending the truck into the ocean below. One thing Khalid had learned from fighting the Americans was that they valued their own lives above the sanctity of anything else. They always retreated when facing sure death. The infidel would not risk killing himself over one predator drone. That is why the Great Satan would fall. True *Mujahedeen*, such as himself, were willing to sacrifice themselves for the jihad.

The American tapped the window again with the muzzle of the M4. "Stop this truck, asshole!"

Khalid turned his gaze back to the rear-view mirror. The American was staring at him with squinting eyes and a tight, unsmiling mouth. Without hesitation, Khalid pressed down hard on the gas pedal, sending the truck speeding down the causeway. Suddenly, the passenger door swung open and another American appeared. This one looked strikingly familiar.

"Hi-ya Enrique!" he said, gripping the handle on the side of the Hemmitt with his left hand and pointing his M4 at Khalid with his right. "Remember me?"

Khalid studied the man for a moment. "You are the soldier from my home in Al-Dana. I thought you were dead."

"Yeah, well, I'm not that easy to kill. Now why don't you pull this truck over like my buddy asked you to?"

Khalid stared into the man's steely blue eyes and then moved his gaze to the man in the mirror. A calmness enveloped Khalid as he realized he was now destined to be a martyr for the jihad. His eyes darted to the Kel-Tec 9mm resting on the seat beside him.

Sebastian could see the look in the terrorist's eyes and knew that the man would rather martyr himself than be captured. He could sense that Enrique was about to make a move for the pistol.

"I wouldn't do that if I were you, Enrique. I owe you a coupla bullets and going for that pistol will give me the perfect opportunity to pay up."

"I am not afraid to die, infidel. Are you?"

"Just try me, asshole."

Khalid studied the man's rugged face and cold eyes. He knew that this soldier was prepared to die. Finally, an American with a resolve which matched his own. A man worthy of sending him to Paradise. Allah would welcome him with open arms for dying at the hands of such a warrior.

Khalid pulled hard on the steering wheel, sending the truck speeding toward the thin guardrail separating the road from the deep, watery grave below.

"*Allahu Akbar*," he said, and reached for the pistol.

CHAPTER 41
Naval Air Station Corpus Christi

Sean pulled the blanket tight around his wet shoulders as he sloshed toward the triage area set up outside of the Naval Health Clinic.

The military had moved quickly in response to the attack. Less than twenty minutes after he and Sebastian had cleared the hospital, the Navy doctors and nurses had already been performing surgery on the wounded. Within thirty minutes, they had set up the triage area and a second surgical unit in the neighboring building for minor surgeries. The entire attack had lasted less than forty-five minutes and the doctors and staff had been rescuing fallen soldiers before the bloody battle was halfway over.

Sean walked over to Sebastian, who was seated on the bed of a pickup truck parked outside of the triage area with water still dripping from the bottom of his blue jeans. Seeing Sebastian wince as the medic sewed up his shoulder gave Sean a sense of amusement and he allowed himself a little smile. "Don't be such a sissy, Cap'n."

Sebastian looked up from the medic stitching his wound and glared at Sean. "Who?"

Arriving at the scene, Jaime said, "Cap'n. You know, like Cap'n fucking America."

The remark made Sebastian laugh. After all these years of giving everyone else nicknames, somebody had finally tagged him. "I can live with that."

"All done, Sarge," said the medic as he packed up his surgical kit and moved away toward his next patient.

"Captain America, huh? You look more like a drowned rat than a superhero. And where are your tights?" came a voice from behind.

"Well, you know how it is Colonel," replied Sebastian without turning to face the voice. "After a hard day of fighting terrorists, we like to take a dip in the bay... with predator drones... just to cool off. And no tights for me. I'm the cool, blue jean and T-shirt wearing, Harley riding Cap'n America."

Colonel Black circled around to face the men. "Of course you are. You men did a good job today. You saved a lot of soldiers and kept a Predator drone out of the hands of terrorists. Even if you did put it in the bottom of the bay."

Sean eyed the dark haired man wearing ACUs. "We didn't save enough. A whole lot of people died here today."

"Four hundred and ninety-one."

"What?"

"Four hundred and ninety-one dead and wounded soldiers. At least so far, Special Agent Ray. The casualty rate could have been a lot higher. While you weren't able to stop the IEDs, you were very expedient in taking out the armed terrorists. You did better than the rest."

"What the hell does that mean, Colonel," asked Sebastian. "As near as I can tell, we were the only guys on base hunting these assholes down. Except for that kid at the Apache. What was his name?"

"Ortiz," replied Jaime.

"Yeah, Ortiz. Anybody seen him around? We owe him a beer for taking out the Apache."

"There was a Specialist Ortiz found by the wreckage of the Apache. He was shot and his body was burned from the wreckage. He was identified by his dog-tags," said Black.

"Man, that sucks," said Sean. "We should have checked the bodies of those terrorists to make sure they were dead before we took off. He seemed like a good kid. A real fighter. So who else was hunting these guys that we don't know about?"

"You were the only ones on *this* base, Sean."

"You mean to tell me ISIL attacked another base?" asked Sean. "And how do you know my name?"

"So far, there have been eighty-three military installations attacked today, all of them in the continental United States. ISIL has destroyed or crippled the 1st Fighter Wing at Fort Langley, the 9th Recon wing at Fort Beale and the 2nd Bomber Wing at Barksdale. They used tanks at Forts Benning, Bragg, Bliss, Lewis and Knox. They utilized Apaches and other attack aircraft at Forts Campbell, Lewis-McChord, Pendleton and Air Station New River. The death tolls there were massive. The latest count was just over eighty-three thousand dead and one hundred forty-three thousand wounded. Due to the pull back of troops from the Mid-East, all of our bases were at full capacity and we were easy targets. Gentlemen, the United States has just witnessed the single greatest attack against it in American History and it occurred on our sovereign ground."

"Whoa," said Jaime.

"Exactly, Petty Officer Gomez," stated Black.

"Hey! How did you know my name too?"

Sebastian slid off of the tailgate. "That's kinda his thing. You guys don't think that he's an actual colonel, do you?"

Black alternated his gaze between the three men. "Gentlemen, I know everything there is to know about each of you. Special Agent Ray, over the last year, you and your FAST Team have hunted and brought down the Gulf Cartel. Petty Officer Gomez, your creation of the STUXNET virus was sheer genius."

Jaime looked flabbergasted. "Um... uh," he stammered. "I don't know what you're talking about, Colonel. And if I did, I would say that information is so far above Top Secret that just mentioning it in front of anybody without eyes-only clearance would be grounds for treason."

Sebastian beamed at Jaime, flashing his dimples. "Holy shit, Bucky. You've been holding out on us. What's a STUXNET?"

"I couldn't tell you," said Jaime, shaking his head.

"STUXNET was the world's first digital weapon," interjected Black. "It was a computer virus."

"Worm," corrected Jaime.

"A *worm,*" continued Black, "that infected every computer on the planet. How it worked is complicated, but the simple version is that it sought out and manipulated the computers that controlled the Iranian nuclear centrifuges. The ones used to enrich their Uranium for nuclear weapons. It manipulated the centrifuges to spin at different speeds, making their Uranium useless and setting their nuclear program back decades. It was sheer genius."

Sean looked at Jaime with a twinkle in his eye. "*You* did that, Jaime?"

"I don't know what you're talking about," said Jaime, nodding his head. "And neither should you, Colonel."

"Gentlemen," said Colonel Black, addressing the trio again. "What you did today was spectacular. The three of you circumvented an attack on this base. Other than Fort Hood, no other installation came close to having your level of success. This was a coordinated attack on the United States and it wasn't committed by ISIL alone. They have neither the resources nor the talent to accomplish an attack of this magnitude. I believe that this was the work of Al-Yad."

Sebastian shook his head warily. "Here we go again. I told you, Colonel, the Al-Yad is a myth."

"Who is the Al-Yad?" asked Sean.

"The Al-Yad is a group of extremely wealthy and intelligent men who were loyal to Bin Laden and who secretly control Al-Qaeda and their affiliates. The Taliban, ISIL, AQAP and the others in the Mid-East, as well as Al Shabaab and AQIM in Africa and the IEC in Chechnya. They are all controlled by the Al-Yad. Only the Al-Yad has the resources to pull off this attack and we know absolutely nothing about them. We don't know who their members are, where they are located, or how they communicate. However, I believe that Sebastian came across one in Syria and I have been looking for him ever since. I would like for the three of you to join me and help me hunt down every member of the Al-Yad and kill them."

Sean eyed the colonel. "And by join you, you mean what, exactly?"

"I run a company whose sole purpose is to hunt down terrorists."

"That sounds intriguing," said Sean. "But I'm not in the military."

"And in case you don't remember, Colonel," said Sebastian. "I lost part of a lung and the Army doesn't consider me fit for combat duty anymore."

"Well, Sebastian, I believe that you proved them wrong today. Didn't you?" replied Black. "You don't need to worry about any of those things, because I don't work for the military. We are more like DHS consultants. Consultants with access to all governmental information and facilities, but none of the oversight."

"So we would work for the CIA?" asked Jaime.

"No. The CIA is a government agency that specializes in spying. My company is private, better funded, and not under the scrutiny of Congress."

Sebastian eyed Black. "So Private Military Company, like Blackwater? No thanks. I'm a soldier not a mercenary. Plus most of those guys are tools that either couldn't hack it in the military or were kicked out for being psychos."

"Not a PMC either, Sebastian," replied Black. "We do the work that our Government can't do for political reasons. And I only pick the best people to work for me. Men like the three of you. Men who are exceptional at hunting down and taking out the enemy. Men who do it because it's the right thing to do. Men who don't do it for the glory because there will be none. You will have the privilege of protecting the United States from its enemies but you will never get any credit for it. There will be no medals or awards. Only the satisfaction of knowing what you have done to keep America safe."

"Count me in," said Sean.

"Do I have to go into the field?" asked Jaime. "I don't like getting shot at."

"No," replied Black. "Your skills will be better utilized behind a computer."

"Then I'm in too."

Sebastian stared into Black's eyes. "So you're tellin' me that I get to go into the field and *kill* the people who did this? Not capture 'em and send 'em to Guantanamo just so some dumbass President can release them to do it all over again?"

"That's right. You get to kill them and make sure they never hurt anyone again."

Sebastian walked to the side of the pickup truck. "Well then, count me in. And I have a little bonus for you, Colonel." Sebastian reached down beside the pickup truck and lifted a figure to his feet. "Colonel, I would like for you to meet Enrique."

CHAPTER 42
Del Rio, Texas

Santiago Ortiz was singing along to the music as he turned the corner and steered the eighteen-wheeler through the front gates of the Rancho Villa community development. Santiago was ecstatic that his plan had gone so well. America had been dealt a serious blow. A blow that would satisfy his uncle's desire for revenge. That madman Khalid and the Al-Yad had poked the bear and he, his uncle and La Familia would not be implicated.

His escape from the United States had been simple. After exchanging his dog-tags with Perez and blowing up the Apache to burn the body, all he had had to do was drive the AH-5X helicopter drone off the base and into the warehouse in Robbstown in the western section of Corpus Christi. After moving the drone from the

Army transport into the semi-trailer truck, getting from Corpus Christi to Del Rio had been a snap.

Santiago carefully backed the rig onto the driveway and into the garage, which was actually an elevator leading down to the tunnel and back into Mexico. This had been a great score. A helicopter drone would be very useful to La Familia's drug operations.

He wondered what had become of those three heroes. Hopefully they had made it.